LOVE at FIRST Ink

A NEW BEGINNINGS ROMANCE NOVEL

ANASTASIA DEAN

ISBN:

E-book: 978-1-968095-01-7

Paperback: 978-1-968095-00-0

Edited By: On the Same Page Editing and Mountains Wanted

Cover Designer: Ebook Launch

For older sisters. You're enough. You've always been enough.

Author's Note

This book contains elements of:

- Childhood trauma
- Fatphobic comments toward a side character
- Struggles multiracial people face (specifically identity)
- Panic / anxiety attack
- Explicit sexual scenes

Please make sure you are protecting your mental health. If you need more information, send me a message on any of my socials. Otherwise, happy reading!

CHAPTER 1
Marisol

Marisol Roberts contemplated pulling out of the parking lot and driving to the nearest bakery. She would buy her own damn birthday cake and eat it in peace and quiet. After all, it wasn't every day a person turned thirty, and that felt like a milestone worth celebrating. But a friendless, husbandless woman like herself didn't want to be reminded of the years swiftly ticking by.

Marisol could hear her mother now, droning on about how much cardio Marisol would have to do if she so much as looked at her birthday cake. She was certain her mom would have a heart attack if she ever saw Marisol eating a slice of the sugary pastry. Even at thirty, she couldn't seem to get her mother out of her head.

Which is why she turned off the engine, grabbed her Michael Kors bag and emotional support water bottle, and got out of the car. The gust of wind that greeted her was a welcome reprieve from the unusually hot day. The last remains of summer clung to the California air, and she couldn't wait until sweater weather officially began.

Her therapist's office was located in downtown Berkeley, nestled between two other office buildings. Her beige heels tapped loudly against the porcelain tiles as she made her way through the building and up to the second floor where her therapist resided. Using her hip, Marisol opened the door to a small but cozy waiting room.

The walls were painted a light gray color with inspirational photos adorning them. A bookshelf full of self-help books was nestled between two upholstered chairs. They looked stiff, but Marisol had never sat in them because her therapist, Alice, was always waiting to greet her. Today was no different.

Marisol was not a stranger to therapy. For a year, her sister Lola had convinced her to see a therapist. Dr. Edmon was a nice enough man, helped the sisters learn how to communicate better with one another, but Lola stopped going once she became a mom of two. There was still much Marisol had to work on, but she didn't feel comfortable seeing Dr. Edmon by herself. He was too intense. Far too serious. She needed someone more nurturing.

After four failed therapy visits with different therapists, Alice was the one Marisol clicked with the most. Perhaps she made Marisol comfortable because she was an older woman who gave off grandmother vibes. Or the fact that she would smile when Marisol walked into the room, making her feel like Alice was genuinely happy to see her. Not many people were, and, honestly, she couldn't blame them.

"Good morning, Marisol, and happy birthday." Alice smiled, making the wrinkles near her eyes more prominent. She was dressed in her usual attire and color scheme: beige slacks and a lavender button-down shirt with minimal jewelry on.

Marisol did her best not to cringe at the mention of her birthday. Just another reminder she was getting older with nothing to show for it. No friends, no fulfilling career, and no husband.

Technically, she did have a husband—one she desperately wanted to be free of. Like most things in her life, that was still a work in progress.

Alice motioned for Marisol to follow her back to the office she was very familiar with. Alice's leather chair sat at one side of the room, while the small, matching couch sat at the other. Only a coffee table separated them, but it still felt like a safety barrier. Like if things got too intense, Marisol could retreat into herself without Alice probing her mind.

It was delusional, of course, because Alice read her like a gossip magazine.

"So, how are you doing today? Do you have anything planned for your thirtieth?" Alice asked just as Marisol plopped on the couch, putting her bag and water bottle on the coffee table.

Marisol shrugged, something her mother hated. *Use your words, Marisol; don't make people guess what you have to say,* was what her mother always lectured. "I'll call my lawyer and ask him if Archie has signed the divorce papers yet." Which would be the greatest gift of all.

Her almost ex-husband, a man she regretted marrying, was taking his sweet time addressing their divorce papers. Marisol could have pushed her lawyer to take action, but...she hadn't yet. The longer she dragged her feet, the more time she had to prepare for her mother's inevitable nuclear fallout from her divorce.

It was her mother who got her into this predicament in the first place. She had hand-chosen Archie for her. The only problem was that Archie wasn't single at the time. No, Archie had been dating Lola, but her sister never fit her mother's beauty standard. Was never her puppet. That was Marisol's job, and like an obedient sheep, she went along with it. She always went along with it, which only chipped away at her relationship with Lola until it nearly shattered completely.

"It is important to check up on the divorce, but that isn't a proper way to celebrate your birthday. Thirty is a big milestone. Maybe we should take this time and think of ways you could celebrate," Alice suggested.

As if Marisol's life couldn't be more pathetic, now she needed her therapist to help her celebrate her birthday.

"How have you celebrated your birthdays in the past?" Alice asked.

"My mom always threw me parties."

"Did you enjoy them?"

"I mean, I'm not really a birthday person, but I guess." Marisol hadn't been a birthday person ever since she hit double digits, and her birthdays changed from celebrating her into more of a networking event.

Alice didn't say anything. She did this when she wanted Marisol to continue talking. She learned the hard way that her therapist had the patience of a saint and would sit in her chair all day if she had to. But bottom line, Marisol had to speak.

"I guess they could have been better," she offered, hoping this was enough to satisfy her.

"What could have been better?"

What couldn't have been better? The guest list, the decorations, and even the menu had all been planned by her mother. She had no say in the themes of the parties. She remembered being thirteen and begging her mother to let her have a pool party because it was the one perk of having a summer birthday. Her mother had scoffed at her, stating pool parties were for little children and were tacky.

Because Marisol strived for her mother's approval, she had nodded in agreement and let her mom plan her birthday party like she wanted. She never did this for her sister, though. Lola got to have any type of birthday party she wanted. They were never as grand as Marisol's, but that didn't matter because Lola got to celebrate with her friends. Real friends who actually liked her sister and weren't forced to be there by their parents.

Everything in her sister's life had been real, while Marisol obediently lived in the fabricated, and often distorted, reality her mother so carefully crafted for her. That was the start of her resentment toward her younger sister.

"I would have liked to at least invite a few of my classmates. It was always the children of potential investors or well-known names in my parents' social circle. They were okay, but I didn't know them. Not really," Marisol said.

"Was that a common thing? Where you didn't know people your age at social events?"

"Yes, but eventually I started seeing these people at many social events my family and I hosted or was invited to. None of us really developed friendships, but we still had an image to uphold."

The image was being perfect, beautiful daughters of rich business owners. In reality, she hardly knew the girls she was instructed to talk to. They were expected to be friends, so they played that part. They showed up to each other's events. Hell, these women had been Marisol's bridesmaids, but she didn't know basic facts about these women, even though they had known one another since they were teenagers. It was all about proximity and making sure their parents received perfect staged photos.

"Did that make your mother proud?"

And there was the question she hated. The question she

asked herself every day. One that she could never quite live up to. There was always one small flaw. One small thing she needed to fix. She was never good enough.

Thinking about her mother and her expectations made Marisol fidgety. She played with a stray thread on her otherwise pristine jeans, avoiding Alice's gaze like the plague. The room felt like it would close in on her. Like if she admitted she hadn't —and probably never—made her mother proud, all of her failures would slowly unravel until she was nothing but a shell for disappointment and lost dreams.

"Can we talk about something else?" Marisol didn't recognize her voice. It was a far cry from the normal haughty tone she had adopted over the last few years, never able to completely hide her bitterness.

"We'll talk about that at another session," Alice said. Marisol let out a sigh of relief. Then Alice said, "Let's get back to our original topic. Your birthday. What are your plans?"

Marisol wanted to gesture around and say "this," but that made her sound too pathetic. "I don't know, I'll probably go home. Maybe call for takeout."

It would be the first birthday she didn't have a party. Her mother and father had taken a vacation together. She was supposed to go with them, along with Archie, but clearly plans changed. She supposed she could call Lola, but her sister was too busy being a mother to Camilia and her one-year-old son, Fabian. He was a cutie but a damn handful—and the perfect reminder as to why Marisol didn't want kids.

They were always sticky, smelled strange, and got into everything. She loved her niece and nephew—they were everything to her—but she was better suited to be an aunt. She liked the freedom of being able to give them back to their parents.

"No, that's something you can do any day. Think hard,

Marisol. There has to be one thing you've always wanted to give yourself but have never gone through with out of fear of what others think." Alice smiled in what Marisol took as encouragement.

What did she want? She never allowed herself to think about things she couldn't or shouldn't have. But maybe Alice was right. Thirty *was* a major birthday, and her mother wasn't here to plan a party she didn't want. For the first time in her life, her birthday was entirely hers.

That was both terrifying and exhilarating.

So, how would she maximize this situation? She could go shopping and try out stores she actually wanted to go into. Or try out the new sushi restaurant she'd been dying to visit but never had the courage to go to alone. Or maybe she could do something truly reckless. Something that would make her mother spontaneously explode.

She had the answer immediately. But was she brave enough? Could she do it? She'd definitely need some liquid courage.

"Well, I've always wanted to get a tattoo. My mom—"

"I don't care what your mother thinks. I only care what Marisol thinks," Alice cut her off. "This is your day. You're an adult who is capable of making decisions about herself, especially when it comes to your body. I think getting a tattoo would be a marvelous thing. Doesn't have to be too big. It's the principle of the matter."

She guessed Alice had a point. She didn't have to get a tattoo that would take up half her arm or cover her face. She could make it dainty, in a place that could easily be hidden. The thought of doing something she knew her mother would hate made her stomach churn. It was almost enough for her to kill the idea before it fully took form, but a small, rebellious part of Marisol wanted to do something a little reckless.

The rest of her session, Alice made her talk about her day and goals she had set for herself. Marisol's mind was occupied, though, still debating if she would actually go through with the whole tattoo thing.

She hadn't even realized her hour session was up until Alice stood from her chair. "Our time is done today. Maybe next week I'll see you with a tattoo?" Her kind smile gave Marisol confidence she didn't know she needed.

Grabbing her things, Marisol nodded. "Thank you. I'll see you next week." She followed Alice out of her office and back toward the lobby. Usually, her therapist didn't walk her back, but she didn't question it. Alice may have forgotten something in her car that she needed to get, or maybe she needed to run to the bathroom.

When Marisol opened the door to the lobby, she was surprised to see it wasn't empty like it normally was. Their session must have run over. A man, roughly in his early to mid-thirties, occupied one of the seats in the lobby. His broad shoulders and tight black shirt hinted at the muscles under-neath. His jet-black hair was slicked back, giving him a *I just stepped out of the shower, and I look this damn good* look. If that was even a thing. Surely it had to be.

And he smelled good. Like really good. Even from the opposite side of the room, Marisol got hints of mint and cedarwood. She couldn't help but notice the man's biceps and the artwork all over both arms. Tattoos of mermaids, sugar skulls, various flowers, and other beautiful pieces that all fit together to create a gorgeous canvas.

The man could easily be a model for some alternative magazine.

The stranger looked up from his phone and gave Marisol a once-over. She was used to having men stare at her, but his attention quickly moved on to Alice. Something akin to disappointment colored her features.

"See you next week," Alice whispered from behind her, a gentle push to get Marisol walking again.

Right. She had been here staring like a creep. Before she could further make a fool of herself, she hiked her bag up her shoulder and headed to the door. Just before the door closed behind her, Marisol heard Alice say, "It's good to see you, Cisco."

CHAPTER 2

Marisol

The luxury condo Marisol bought after working up the courage to leave Archie was located just ten minutes from downtown Berkeley. Her condo was on the top floor, which made her feel safe from any robbers and intruders. That and the twenty-four-hour security team also helped ease her worries. There had never been a break-in at her complex, and from everything she extensively researched, her building was ranked one of the safest in the city. However, what really put her on edge was living alone for the first time ever.

Her home had three bedrooms, far bigger than any one person needed. She liked having an extra room for visitors when they came by and wanted to sleep over. So far that had only been her sister and her sister's husband, Javi, after helping her move into her new place. They didn't live far, but they had worked well into the night to unload her things. The third bedroom was reserved for her closet, since the small walk-in one in the primary bedroom only held her extensive shoe collection.

Javi was a contractor and all-around handyman. He was able to create shelving units in the room for her, hung a beautiful glass chandelier, and installed lighting in all the storage areas. It was over the top and excessive, but she absolutely loved it. Sometimes she would go in there when she was overwhelmed and just sit on the fluffy pink chaise and admire all of her beautiful clothes.

If that made her vain, then so be it. She couldn't change entirely, and even if she could, fashion had always been a statement for her. She liked expressing herself through her clothes, even if she was the only one who understood what vibe she was going for.

Using her keycard, Marisol unlocked the door to her home. It had not looked like this when she left for therapy, but the cleaning service her dad paid for stopped by just as she was on the way out. Mrs. Baker had been employed by her family for a long time, so she trusted the woman in her home. She used her signature lemon cleaning supplies, making Marisol's condo smell of summer.

The stash of unwashed clothes by the laundry room had disappeared. Mrs. Baker knew Marisol's closet organization and probably put it all away for her, which Marisol appreciated. The kitchen was also in pristine condition. She didn't know how that room always got so messy when Marisol didn't cook. She was lousy at it and had tried multiple times to learn basic recipes but stopped attempting after the one time she undercooked chicken. She had never been so sick in her life.

She vowed never to cook again afterwards.

Setting her bag and water bottle on the counter, Marisol's gaze landed on a neatly wrapped gift box adorned with a large, elegant pink bow. Beside it sat a small envelope with her name scrawled across the front in a cursive script. Her brows knitted together as she reached for the card, fingers trembling slightly as she tore it open.

The message inside was brief—just two simple words. *Happy birthday.* At the bottom, Mrs. Baker had drawn a small heart, and a lump formed in Marisol's throat as her eyes welled with tears.

Blinking them away, she carefully set the card down and reached for the package, tugging at the silky bow until it unraveled. The moment of hesitation that followed—almost guilt for ruining such a beautifully wrapped gift—vanished as she peeled away the delicate paper. Her breath hitched when she lifted the lid and uncovered a pair of stunning pink earrings, their soft shimmer catching the light.

Her first birthday gift, and it was absolutely perfect. She placed earrings back on the counter, already excited to add them to her jewelry box later, but right now her stomach demanded a snack. She walked to her pantry, which was perfectly stocked, also thanks to Mrs. Baker, and grabbed a bag of vegetable chips to tide her over until she figured out what she would have for her birthday dinner. Would she spring for dessert? She supposed she could spare the calories for her birthday. Probably.

Marisol took her snack and her water bottle to the living room and sank down on her white couch. She was just about to turn on the TV when her phone started to vibrate. Fishing through her skirt pocket, she pulled out her phone to see she was getting a video call from her sister. She bet it was her niece and nephew, and she answered without a second thought.

Two zoomed-in faces greeted her as soon as she answered. Camilia grinned widely, while Fabian drooled on the phone. Camilia made a noise of dissatisfaction and snatched the phone away from her brother. "Daddy, Fabian drooled on Mamá Lola's phone and my hand!"

Fabian's tiny giggle told Marisol all she needed to know. Her nephew didn't care in the least. Oh, to be a one-year-old with no responsibilities.

"See, preciosa? He's Niagara Falls. The amount of drool that comes out of this boy is not natural," she heard Javi say.

Her sister's voice then boomed into the phone, "It is natural if he's teething."

"Anyway!" Camilia said loudly over her parents. Marisol watched the screen as Camilia moved, showing the ceiling. Once her niece found a new location—her bedroom—she appeared on the screen again. "Hi, Tía! Happy birthday!"

Camilia was the sweetest little girl in the world. The eight-, almost nine-year-old, had taken to Marisol quickly, and not just for what Marisol could provide her. Camilia thought Marisol was pretty, smart, and funny. Her niece looked up to her. No one in her life had ever looked up to her. It was both a beautiful and terrifying feeling. She imagined this was what Lola would have done if Marisol had been a good big sister.

"Thank you, Bug." She smiled warmly.

"Did you get presents? Oh! Did you get the card I made you? Mamá Lola said it should have gotten to you today."

That morning, Marisol had checked the mail to find a letter from Camilia. It was a drawing of the two of them with a sweet note that said she loved her and finished with Camilia hoping they could go shopping soon. It was one of the only cards Marisol received, and that made it the most important letter.

"I hung it up on my fridge. I loved it so much. You're a talented artist."

"I know," she said with all the confidence a young girl could have. "Daddy says I'm a natural."

"You are. You should make him get you more art supplies."

"Oh, Abuelo already did. He bought me an easel! And paints! But I'm not allowed to paint on the carpet because I could make a mess. So I have to paint in the kitchen, but Fabian tries to take my paints and eat them," she pouted.

"Well, he's a—"

"Baby, I know," she sighed, like she had heard that line a million times before. "So, now Mamá Lola makes him fake paint that's actually pudding for him to do art and eat. Isn't that so funny?"

"It is very funny, Bug. And your Mamá Lola is smart to think of something like that." Lola wasn't Camilia's biological mother. Camilia's mom died when she was a baby, and Camilia had only known Lola since her father and Lola started to date three years ago. It was amazing how quickly Lola fell into the role of mother. She was a natural, and for some reason, that made Marisol jealous.

Not about the mother part, but how Lola could be so nurturing and loving. Nothing at all like their own mother. She envied Lola's ability to separate herself from that and not carry on the trauma from their childhood.

The rest of the video call was Camilia catching Marisol up on every single part of her life. Which meant Camilia spoke animatedly about school. What she liked. What she hated. How sometimes the cafeteria food was good, and sometimes it was bad. She even spoke about what teachers were the nicest and which ones scared her a little.

Just as Marisol was about to become an expert on all things elementary school, she heard Lola's voice come from somewhere out of frame. "Sweetie, go clean up your supplies from the kitchen table so we can eat dinner soon. Let me talk to Tía Marisol for a bit."

"Okay!" the little girl said happily. She slid off her bed and smiled at the phone once more. "Love you!"

"Love you too, Bug." Marisol smiled and was surprised to feel tears stinging her eyes. She didn't even know why she was crying, but something about hearing *I love you* with no strings attached was the best thing anyone had ever given her.

After a few hushed whispers and a shaky hand-off, her sister's face took up the screen. Lola's round face was smiling, though it was guarded, which was understandable. Over the past few years, their relationship had gotten better, especially after a year of therapy together. However, there were still things Marisol needed to work through before her sister could fully forgive her for the trauma she caused in childhood.

"Happy birthday, Mar."

"Thank you," she said softly, half wishing people would forget it was her birthday. She didn't want people to feel obligated to talk to her just because she was a year older now.

"Do you have any plans?" her sister pried, sounding just like Alice. What was everyone's obsession with wanting to know her plans today?

"I went to therapy."

"Well, that's good." This time Lola's smile was genuine. "I'm proud of you for going. I know it's not easy."

No, it definitely wasn't easy. Unlearning how to be a terrible person was never easy and never fun. Too many times, Marisol left a crying wreck, and by the time she got her emotions under control, she felt exhausted. She was putting in all of this work, and for what? For people to congratulate her accomplishments, but then never make an attempt at becoming part of her life?

She supposed there were other reasons, but those were

tougher to face. Like everything, it was easier to blame other people. Which was exactly why she was in therapy.

"So, what else? Surely therapy isn't the only plan you have," her sister asked again after a pregnant pause.

Without thinking through the decision to tell Lola, she blurted, "My therapist said I should get a tattoo."

"What?!" Lola sputtered, eyes wide. Her reaction was almost comical, if it weren't for the fact that Marisol was being serious.

"Well, I guess she didn't specifically say I should get a tattoo. She said I should do something I've always wanted to do but talk myself out of," she explained.

"And you've always wanted a tattoo?"

Marisol shrugged, feeling a little silly about it all. "I mean... yeah? I know it's not proper, or whatever, but I think it would look beautiful."

"I think so too," Lola said, surprising Marisol.

"You do?"

Lola nodded. "Yeah, I love seeing Javi's. We are planning on getting a couple's tattoo soon, once we decide on what that will be. Do you know what you want to get?"

Marisol didn't. She had only thought about the idea of getting a tattoo, not the actual tattoo itself. "I guess I haven't made up my mind yet."

"That's okay." Her sister shrugged. "Most places will have pre-drawn tattoos you can look at. Hey, how about I ask him if there's a shop he prefers? We can set you up an appointment."

"Oh, you don't have to do that."

There was a reason why Lola had never given anything of substantial value to Marisol, and that hung heavily between them. Marisol had not been a good sister. She was downright mean at times, to the point where Lola would run to her room in tears as a child. Even as adults, Marisol had said and done pretty nasty things.

It wasn't until Lola found Javi, and Marisol admitted she didn't want to stay married to Archie that their relationship started to shift for the better. They were still healing and would be for a while. But little by little, it was getting better. She hoped one day they might even be friends.

"But I want to," Lola said. "And, frankly, I don't trust that you won't chicken out and not schedule an appointment because you still think you need to please Mom."

Anger bloomed in Marisol's chest. Anger with Lola for chalking up her trauma to one simple thing, but also anger with herself because Lola was right. She didn't actually think she would go through with it if left to her own devices.

"Okay, fine," she relented easily. There was no point in arguing, and, frankly, she didn't have the energy to.

Lola grinned. "Cool. Great. I'll ask Javi, and then I'll schedule you an appointment. You better go because I'm making this your birthday present from me. Or do I need to drive over there and take you myself?"

Marisol rolled her eyes. "No, I think I'm capable of getting to a tattoo shop by myself."

"Good. Then wait for my text and enjoy the rest of your birthday."

Before Marisol could respond, Lola hung up. Her phone went dark, and she sighed, tossing it aside. She supposed there wasn't anything else to do but wait and watch reality TV to feel better about her own life.

Marisol put on one of her favorite shows about couples and all the drama leading up to their marriage before settling in for the night. Marital drama was entertaining when it wasn't her own. She tore open her veggie chips and popped one in her mouth. It wasn't the most glamorous birthday she ever had, but at least she didn't have to be paraded around a bunch of people who only cared about her name and status.

Not even a full hour later, her phone buzzed again. She picked it up to see two texts: one from her sister and the other from her father. She clicked on her father's message first. It was a simple happy birthday text, but she appreciated his effort to reach out. It didn't slip her mind that her mother had yet to contact her. She didn't expect her to, but still, it hurt.

She sent a quick thank you text to her father before opening up Lola's text. Her heart lurched with both excitement and nervousness as she read her sister's message.

> Appointment scheduled for noon tomorrow at Golden City Tattoos. Don't be late.

CHAPTER 3
Cisco

The closed door helped a little to block out the electric guitar playing through the loud speakers in his shop. Cisco had them installed a week before they opened Golden City Tattoos and had the foresight to not install any in the room he deemed his office. Five years later, he appreciated that decision more than ever because he couldn't imagine how much louder the music would be if he did.

The pads of his fingers gently thrummed against his antique wooden desk. It was a dark brown mahogany wood with built-in drawers on either side of him. It was a bitch to carry into his office because the damn desk weighed at least three hundred pounds and couldn't fit through the door. He ended up having to create a larger entrance to his office in order to get the desk in, but all that work was worth it. It looked and felt good.

He felt like a damn boss. Which he was.

Cisco glanced down at his work phone, wondering if the call dropped, but, no, they were still connected. His realtor was simply taking forever. Luckily for Ernesto, Cisco could be a patient man when he wanted to be. While he waited, his eyes roamed his dark, emerald-green walls, covered with framed pictures of favorite tattoos he had done over the years. There were even pictures of a younger, more eager-eyed Cisco, who, at twenty, opened his first tattoo shop in Albany, just north of his current shop in Berkeley.

He still had both shops today, entrusting his cousin to run the shop in Albany while Cisco focused his attention on the shop in Berkeley. It had been a good arrangement for years, but Cisco had gotten that itch again—the need to expand and start up another shop in a more populated city. San Francisco? Los Angeles? Santa Monica? He was leaning more toward San Francisco because it was the closest to Berkeley. That way he could easily juggle his time between the two shops and could respond promptly if a problem arose. Santa Monica and Los Angeles were far and probably too much of a risk.

"Found it!" Ernesto's accented voice came through his speakers. Cisco let out a sigh of relief, half afraid Ernesto had dreamed about this listing. "This one's in San Francisco. That's a good location for you, yeah?"

Even though Ernesto couldn't see him, Cisco nodded. "Yeah, it has potential."

"This one is located on Market Street. Busy street with lots of activity. The space is a little smaller than your Berkeley location. Fourteen hundred square feet. Recently renovated with a new central AC system, updated bathroom, and new tile floors. It's only been on the market a few days, but a spot like this is going to go fast. If you want to see it, we better make an appointment soon," Ernesto said. Cisco could hear him typing something on his keyboard, probably pulling up potential visiting dates.

"They have availability this week and next, but the sooner the better," he stressed.

Cisco tapped the trackpad on his laptop, and the screen came to life immediately. His calendar was the first item to pop up, kept current by Lyana, his receptionist and younger cousin. If he was meticulous, she was the goddess of organization. No paperwork or appointment had been missed with her running the shop.

A new, highlighted note had been added to today's agenda. He had checked yesterday afternoon to prepare for his schedule and certainly didn't see this appointment. It was vague. Lyana had written "small to medium tattoo at noon" with no other notes.

He guessed it was a new client since his regulars typically left detailed instructions for him. He didn't usually take on new clients, but seeing as today was an unusually slow day, and he was the only tattoo artist working, his cousin simply scheduled him. Cisco's gaze dropped to the clock on his laptop. It was barely eleven, giving him time to prep after the call.

Pushing the mysterious appointment aside, he checked his calendar. It was only Tuesday, but his schedule was full this week except for a large opening on Friday. "Can we do Friday afternoon?" he asked Ernesto. He didn't want to push it back any further. Friday would already put him at a disadvantage for being competitive when it came to putting in his offer.

"Yeah, Friday will do. I'll set it up for two. I can pick you up—"

"Nah, send the address. I'll drive myself." He didn't have a problem with other people driving, but he liked the freedom of driving himself. Plus, he had been in a car with Ernesto behind the wheel. If he didn't value his life or sanity, he might consider letting Ernesto pick him up. But considering last time, when

Cisco's knuckles turned white and went numb from grabbing the handle above the window so hard, he felt like this was a safer option.

Ernesto laughed, not even trying to change his mind. "Yeah, I'll send over the address Friday morning. In the meantime, I'll keep looking." And then the phone went dead. No goodbyes. No *talk to you later*. That was very much Ernesto's style. Cisco didn't mind it because he was never one for prolonged goodbyes.

Pushing himself up from his leather work chair, Cisco pocketed his phone and headed out of his office. The music from one of his favorite local bands blasted through the speakers when he opened the door. He liked his music loud, but not *this* loud. He had to be able to hear his clients, and right now he couldn't even hear himself think.

When Cisco rounded the corner that led to the main lobby, Lyana was lounging in her black and pink office chair, eyes closed as she mouthed the words to a song and band she claimed not to like. Cisco smirked. They were a newer Mexican indie band that hadn't gained a lot of popularity yet. He knew they would blow up soon enough though. They had that infectious sound that made you want to sing along.

"Ay, Tiny. Turn it down, will ya?" Cisco had to shout to be heard. Even though he enjoyed the band, he didn't need to enjoy them this loudly.

Lyana—Tiny—opened one eye and glared at her cousin. Cisco didn't take it personally because that was the nature of their relationship. They teased and bullied each other and called it affection. It was the only way he knew how to bond with his seventeen-year-old cousin. She leaned forward and turned the dial to quiet the music until it was at a more respectable level.

"Shouldn't you be doing schoolwork?" Cisco came up behind her to lean against the wall. Part of the agreement for Tiny working here was that she would continue her education online. She hadn't enjoyed her time in high school because teens are dicks, and her only safe haven was working at the shop on weekends. Her parents—his tía and tío—agreed she could keep working as long as she continued her studies online. They didn't care if she wanted to go to college one day, but they insisted she get her high school diploma, a decision Cisco agreed with completely.

"Yes, *Dad*." Tiny feigned annoyance. "You're supposed to be a cool primo."

"I am. A primo who makes sure you get your school shit done."

Tiny didn't hide her laugh this time. "It's definitely shit. But I'm done. Had to take a test in science. Got an eighty-five, which is pretty good. Yeah?"

Despite her tough exterior, Cisco knew his cousin held a lot of insecurities, especially when it came to school—because of her dyslexia. It made her feel dumb and caused her to struggle academically. However, switching to online had been the best thing for her because she could go at her own pace, didn't have the distraction of other classmates, and felt more confident in her work.

"That's fucking awesome, Tiny!" He grinned and reached out to squeeze her shoulder. "Told you those flashcards would work."

"Yeah, yeah, yeah." She smiled, shoving him off her. "I guess you are right sometimes, Mr. Cornell University."

"I keep trying to get people to realize that." He winked.

"Well, keep trying and cry to your therapist about it." Tiny paused. "How did your session go yesterday?"

Cisco never shied away from speaking about mental health. It was an important topic and shouldn't have a stigma attached to it. To normalize therapy, he spoke openly about Alice and his sessions with her. "Always good. Still working too hard, per usual."

Tiny scoffed. "Yeah, you being a workaholic is an understatement."

It was undeniable. Cisco had poured every ounce of himself into his career. Since college, his singular ambition had been to open his own tattoo shop, and he had done just that. Not only had he built a successful business from the ground up, but he had expanded once and was already eyeing another expansion. For him, success wasn't just about the money—it was about what he could do with it. Providing his family with stable jobs, sending financial help whenever a relative needed it —that was how he measured his achievements.

But that kind of dedication came at a cost. The relentless hustle weighed on him, leaving little room for anything beyond work. He wasn't married, had no children, and burnout had become an all-too-familiar companion. That was why he visited Alice once a month—to recenter himself, to unload the burdens he carried in silence. She was his anchor, the one person who kept him grounded when there was no wife or long-term partner to do so. Sure, there were flings, casual entanglements that burned hot and fast, but they never lasted more than a few weeks. Commitment required time—something he had in short supply.

Pulling himself from his wayward thoughts, Cisco remembered to ask about the mysterious booking on his schedule. "Hey, so tell me about the appointment today. I thought my first one was at three."

Tiny straightened up in her seat, tossing her bright blue

hair over her shoulder. It was the only vibrant color on her because she dressed like a typical punk kid, in all black. He didn't know how she could survive in an oversized hoodie when it was ninety degrees outside, but as a teen, he wore the same thing. Now, at his ripe age of thirty-three, he still wore black, but clothes that went better with the season. So, not fucking hoodies.

"Yeah, we got a call ten minutes before closing last night. A woman was making an appointment for her sister. She left her card on file, wanting to pay for her sister's birthday present or something," Tiny explained.

"Did she say what she wanted?"

"No, just that if she doesn't show up to call her."

Strange, but Cisco had stranger requests.

"Alright, then I'm going to get my station ready. Bring her back when she gets here and keep the music at a decent volume, okay?"

Tiny flipped him off. "Aye, aye, captain." She then went back to her computer, pulling up a game she played to pass the time while the shop was slow.

As Cisco walked away, he heard his cousin yell, "Oh, I restocked all your shit! Next time, tell me when you are about to be out of gloves. I just put in an order for more, but it'll take a while since you need the biggest damn size for your freakishly large hands."

Cisco barked out a laugh but otherwise didn't respond as he entered his station. It was a small room painted the same color as his office. He liked dark colors, especially green. Only a little of the wall showed because the rest was decorated with photos of family, friends, tattoos, musicians, and places he hoped to visit one day. Some would call his style cluttered and maximalist, but he called it perfection. It was nice being able to look out and be surrounded by things you love.

Honestly there wasn't much for Cisco to do. Tiny had already set up most of it. His equipment was cleaned and sitting out on the tray for him. The client's chair also smelled of cleaning supplies and was covered in a disposable protective layer. Tiny even had his gel and gloves out waiting for him.

He was truly spoiled.

Usually, this would be the time he'd sit down and make any finishing touches to the art, but he had nothing to go off of. Normally he didn't like going into an appointment with no idea about what his client wanted, but he had enough experience and tons of unclaimed art pieces that he was sure they'd find something for her.

In the meantime, Cisco grabbed his iPad to work on a few other sketches for some of his clients. He got lost in The Sinner's Web album as he waited for his noon appointment.

CHAPTER 4

Marisol

She should leave. This was a stupid plan made during a moment of false bravado. She could hear it now. *Marisol, what have you done to yourself?* Or *Marisol, no man will want you now.* Her mother would shame her until Marisol started to believe she was an idiot and should have listened to her mother to begin with. Clearly, her mother, who had been married to her father for over thirty years, knew a little about relationships and what men wanted.

Not that she was living her life for a man. It was just that her mother thought she should. Archie was proof of this, and she was still dealing with the fallout of that mistake.

But maybe she had been too hasty in her decision on getting a tattoo. She couldn't recall what possessed her to tell her sister about her secret desire, but she did, and now she was in this situation.

Marisol knew she looked odd, standing outside the tattoo shop, clutching her purse like a weapon. She looked between the shop and her car, her body unsure which way she should go. The phone in her pocket buzzed before a decision could be made, and she reflexively reached for it. She wasn't at all surprised to see her sister's name pop up.

> You better not chicken out. It's already been paid for. Think of it as a present from your niece and nephew.

Well, when she put it like that...

Times like these, Marisol wished she had a group of girlfriends to push her out of her comfort zone. Lola was the closest thing she had to a friend, but there was still so much trauma separating the sisters that couldn't be repaired overnight. Their hangouts usually took place at rage rooms where they could break shit and feel better about it.

But Marisol was trying to prove she could be an independent woman who could think and make decisions for herself, and getting this damn tattoo was the first hurdle.

She could do this.

Taking a deep breath, Marisol pushed open the doors to Golden City Tattoos and stepped inside—only to collide with a petite teenage girl.

The girl raised an eyebrow and smirked. "I thought you were going to stand out there all day. I was just about to come check on you."

Well, that's embarrassing. She hadn't realized anyone was watching her freak out, and she silently thanked the heavens she didn't go back and forth from her car to the shop like she really wanted to.

"I guess I'm a little nervous." She tried to convince herself it wasn't actually a big deal, and she most definitely wasn't about to bow out now.

"You don't say," the teenager said, deadpan. "You must be C's twelve o'clock. What's your name?"

"Marisol," she said automatically.

The girl nodded, went back behind the counter and clicked a few buttons on her keyboard. Finding whatever she was looking for on the computer, the girl nodded again. "So, looks like your sister called or something? Do you, like, have an idea of what you want to do?"

Marisol had a few ideas, but no reference pictures, and she lacked the words to properly describe what she wanted. She should have had something ready, but she hadn't honestly thought she would actually get to this point.

"Do you have something I could look at?" Surely they'd have a book of designs or something like her sister mentioned.

The teenager nodded. "Yeah, it's right over here." She gestured to a large black book at the end of the counter.

Marisol nodded and noticed the girl's name tag: *Lyana* with the word *Tiny* in parentheses. "Erm, thanks."

"Sure. Tell me when you find something you like. Then I'll tell C you're waiting on him." Lyana plopped back down on her chair and focused on her computer again, leaving Marisol to search privately.

She picked up the large book and settled onto a couch near the desk. Her sudden entrance into the shop had left her no time to take in her surroundings. Now, as she looked around, the receptionist area reminded her of a speakeasy. The room was dimly lit, with deep purple walls, black artwork, and a low-hanging black chandelier adorned with faux red candles. Despite the dark decor, the atmosphere wasn't eerie or gaudy. Marisol felt surprisingly at ease.

Soft rock music played through the speaker—a band she would never admit to liking but had discovered recently while listening to a local radio station. The soft rasp from the lead singer scratched her brain perfectly, and she took an instant liking to it.

Marisol crossed her legs and balanced the book on her lap. She slowly flipped through the pages. It was easy to spot designs she didn't like. Most with skulls, large animals, or super-intricate and time-consuming designs were not her style. She also didn't want something big that would take up her entire thigh—which was where she settled on getting it. It would be covered by her clothes, even the tiny skirts she had in the back of her closet. If a bit of the tattoo peeked out, she'd just be sure to wear jeans or longer dresses around her parents.

The more she flipped through the pages, the more confused and overwhelmed she got. She felt Lyana's eyes on her, silently telling her to hurry up. But every design she thought she loved, she would either find something small that bugged her about it or second-guess herself to the point where she ended up hating the tattoo altogether.

A floral design was a safe bet, but did she really want flowers for her first tattoo? Maybe as accents, but not the entire piece. There wasn't anything wrong with a floral tattoo, but it seemed too cliché to have as her first. She wanted something with a little more story behind it. She also liked the cute characters based on her favorite childhood movies, but she didn't much want to look down and see a character she loved when she was five on her thigh.

Marisol was losing hope fast and nearly closed the book until she came to the final few pages. Her fingers hesitated before tracing the design on the page. It was of a woman's bust, but not any woman. This was a sprite or maybe a fairy goddess. Her hair was composed of long, beautiful strands that turned into flowers and twigs. Her hand reached out, holding something that looked similar to a planet. Earth, perhaps. She was beautiful, but more than that, the goddess was fierce and confident, all the things Marisol pretended to be. And maybe one day she could be—just like the woman on the page.

"I want this one," she said. Her voice was the most stable and certain it had been since she entered the shop.

Lyana pushed herself away from her desk and rolled over to her in the chair. She looked down at the piece Marisol settled on and nodded. "Oh, nice. That one has been in there forever. I've been dying to see it."

Having Lyana like the tattoo filled her with a newfound confidence and solidified her decision. "Yeah, I really like it."

"Black or color?"

"Hmm?"

"Do you want to keep it black, or do you want to add color?" Lyana asked. "Honestly, if you ask me, I would keep it black. I think it'll look better."

Marisol had to agree. She didn't care much for colored tattoos. On other people, they were gorgeous, but she didn't want that style for herself.

"Cool, then sit here, and I'll tell C you're ready. He'll come and get you soon." Lyana took the book from her and disappeared around the corner. She heard muffled voices, one clearly masculine, but couldn't make out the words. She sat and waited, her leg bouncing up and down in a nervous habit, and soon pulled out her phone to read her book.

Lyana came back out just as another client came in asking about piercing. She eavesdropped on their conversation before she heard someone walk into the lobby. "Marisol?" a deep and sexy voice called out.

Marisol's head swiveled in time to see a familiar-looking man. He wore all black, matching the gothic aesthetic of his shop. His jeans were form-fitting, as if they were perfectly tailored for his body. Marisol knew good tailoring when she saw it, and those jeans were definitely fitted just for him.

His black t-shirt looked simple, but she bet if she touched it, she would feel luxury material. He also wore a black watch that probably cost as much as some of her most prized jewelry. Which was...a lot. He was subtle with his wealth though. To an untrained eye, he'd appear as just a regular guy who shops where he buys food.

Marisol was staring, and she tried to gaslight herself into thinking it wasn't because he was the sexiest man she had ever seen, arms and neck full of tattoos. No, she was staring because he looked so familiar. Like she saw him recently. Like...

The man in the waiting room. At therapy.

"We go to the same therapist," she blurted out because, apparently, years and years of trained conversations didn't exist when she set foot in a tattoo shop.

The man tilted his head, cocking a brow up. His deep brown eyes questioned her, but she saw the moment realization hit. His full lips twitched up in a smile, flashing the whitest teeth she had ever seen.

"What a small world," he said in a way that neither confirmed nor denied he remembered her. It wasn't like they had a conversation. Their eyes met briefly, and then she left as he was entering his session with Alice.

"If you're ready, I'll take you back." He gestured to the hallway behind him, presumably where his station was set up.

Marisol nodded and grabbed her purse before following the man back. He was tall with much longer legs, so Marisol had to fast-walk—in heels—to keep up with him. Luckily, she was professionally trained in the art of heel-wearing and could keep pace without faltering.

"I'm Cisco, by the way." He stopped at an open door, gesturing for her to go first.

"Marisol," she said and tentatively walked in. The room was painted a dark emerald green with art adorning almost all the wall space. There was a leather chair with a foot rest, obviously meant for the client, and a stool with wheels next to it. A tray of small glasses and what she assumed was the tattoo gun sat next to it.

Oh shit, this was happening.

Her heart pounded as she sat down, resisting the urge to bounce her leg. Instead, she distracted herself by fidgeting with her hair—a nervous habit. Cisco must have noticed her anxiety because he gave her an encouraging smile, which eased her tension, but only slightly.

"This is your first tattoo?" he asked, getting supplies from the various drawers he had in the room.

"Yeah." And probably last, but she couldn't say that for certain.

"Do you have an idea of where you want it?" Cisco grabbed the last of his supplies, dropping them onto the tray before taking a seat on the small rolling stool.

Marisol nodded and shifted her weight to her left side while rolling up her already short jeans shorts to her hip. "I want it here." She gestured to her thigh. "But not so big it takes up the whole area. I want to still be able to cover it up."

He nodded and finished putting on his black gloves. He reached out to touch her thigh, and the moment the vinyl gloves touched her skin, she jumped. Cisco immediately pulled his hand away.

Marisol felt her cheeks flush, embarrassed at her reaction. "Sorry. Go ahead."

Cisco didn't move at first, watching her closely. Whatever

assessment he was doing on her, she clearly passed because, in the next instant, he reached out for her again, brushing her thigh with a feathery light touch.

"Are you thinking you want it here?" He mapped out an area on her upper thigh. It was big enough that it wouldn't compromise the small details of the piece, but small enough it wouldn't encompass her entire thigh.

When she nodded, Cisco removed his hand from her thigh, leaving her feeling unexpectedly empty. He turned to his work station behind him, grabbing the outline of her tattoo. "Can you stand up for me?" he asked right before crouching down, looking far more scandalous than it actually was. Her thigh was almost eye level when he started placing the tattoo.

After a few moments of deliberation, Cisco pulled back and looked it over. "What do you think about that placement?"

Marisol knew shit about placement, but she couldn't think of a problem with it. "I like it."

He smiled at her, and something in her chest fluttered. Suddenly, she was acutely aware at how close and personal he'd be while tattooing her. She silently thanked herself for scheduling a waxing appointment not too long ago so her entire body was smooth.

"What is your pain tolerance like?" Cisco started to clean the area where the stencil would be placed. It was cold to the touch but not unpleasant.

"High, but I don't know what to expect either." She never experienced pain from a tattoo, so she didn't have anything to base it off. But, in general, she didn't hurt easily, which was good since her emotional pain tolerance was at an all-time low.

"Do you need something to dull the pain? I have numbing cream," he offered.

"No, I'm fine," she said, hoping that wasn't a dumb move.

"Well, if it gets too intense, we can take a break. Just communicate with me," he said.

If only he knew her communication skills sucked. Still, she nodded. Cisco prepared himself and his tattoo gun. The sound of it buzzing was a little unnerving, and she gripped the sides of her chair tighter.

She had come this far and couldn't turn back now. For a moment, a sickness bubbled low in her stomach as she thought about all the reasons why she shouldn't do this. She wasn't a spontaneous woman who just went out to get tattoos. Her mother would hate it. Her mother would make *her* hate it.

"You ready?" Cisco asked, one hand on her thigh and the other holding the gun. He was so close, she could smell his spearmint aftershave and woodsy cologne. It gave her something to focus on instead of her wayward thoughts and the sound of the tattoo gun.

"Ready as I can be," she mumbled, averting her gaze.

"I'll be gentle with you for your first time," he said.

Marisol's body grew hot at the implication of his words. It also effectively distracted her so she didn't feel the sting of the gun puncturing her skin.

CHAPTER 5
Cisco

The woman in his chair didn't even flinch when he started tattooing her. He'd had thousands upon thousands of clients in that exact spot, all claiming to have a high pain tolerance. Some of them did and only found mild irritation while he worked on them. Others twitched and whimpered so much, he didn't think he'd get through tattooing them. Sometimes he didn't. There were people walking around with half done or barely done tattoos on their bodies from him.

He didn't know what he expected from the woman in his chair, but it wasn't this.

His first impression of Marisol was that she was beautiful. No, beautiful was too weak a word to describe her. Ethereal. Timeless. Breathtaking. She had shiny black hair that hung past her chest, styled in relaxed waves. Her face was clear of any blemishes, and the light dusting of navy eye shadow made her brown eyes pop. Plump red lips made him linger before averting his gaze.

Her skin had the rich, warm hue of autumn leaves just

before they drifted from the trees, kissed by golden undertones that made her glow as if she had spent days in the sun. It was the kind of deep, radiant brown that people spent hours in tanning beds trying—and failing—to replicate. Cisco's sharp eye for luxury didn't miss the fact that Marisol was draped in designer labels, each piece a statement of wealth and exclusivity. Her outfit alone likely cost more than some people's rent, a silent but undeniable display of status.

Definitely not the type of girl he saw often in his shop. She seemed almost reluctant to be here. Every few seconds, her eyes darted to the door, and he wondered if she would bolt.

"You okay?" he asked, trying not to seem like he was prying. Just a tattoo artist checking in on his client.

He felt her heated gaze on him and tilted his head up. The moment their eyes locked, Marisol looked away. A girl like her usually had the confidence to keep his gaze and flirt with him. He was an attractive guy, after all. Or so the women in his life said, and they couldn't all be lying to him. Marisol was an anomaly, and that made her all the more interesting.

"What drew you to this piece?" Cisco wiped away the ink and plasma after outlining a flower. It always interested him to see what people were drawn to and why. Some had beautiful and sentimental reasons for choosing the tattoo they did, while others just liked the vibes. Both were valid reasons.

Marisol didn't answer right away. Maybe she was one of those clients who didn't want to talk at all during a session. He'd respect that, but it made for a tiresome and sometimes awkward session. Cisco was a talker. He liked getting to know people and finding connections. It wasn't hard for him to make friends because he found commonalities in whomever he spoke to.

Just when Cisco had written Marisol off as a silent client, she spoke. "The woman—is she a goddess?"

"Of sorts," Cisco said. "She just popped into my head one afternoon, and I had to get her down on paper. She does look and feel like a goddess, though."

Marisol nodded. "She does. She's confident. Beautiful. Powerful."

"Those are all good qualities in a woman," Cisco said.

"In anyone," Marisol amended. "But I wanted her. Maybe she'll..." she trailed off, sucking that bottom lip between her teeth. It awakened something deep inside of him.

"Maybe she'll what?" he prompted.

"It's stupid," Marisol said.

"I guarantee you it's not stupid. The feelings art evokes in us are never stupid."

Marisol hesitated and looked around the room as if making sure no one else was in here. Once she was satisfied they were completely alone, she said, "Reminds me that I could be those things too." Her voice was so soft, Cisco had to lean in closer to hear her. He could smell the floral scents from her perfume, a perfume he decided he loved.

At first, her words shocked him. How could a woman who looked like Marisol not feel confident and powerful? But he quickly disregarded that question because he knew the answer. Hell, he *lived* the answer. Looks were deceiving. Hadn't he been dealing with that his entire life?

To anyone who didn't know him, he appeared like a tatted Latino man who matched the stereotypes people had of men who looked like him. He'd heard it all before. Illegal immigrant. Cartel member. Uneducated. Player. Thief. The list went on and on.

It was these stereotypes that nearly ruined his entire life.

People saw what they wanted to see and nothing else. They wouldn't see that he graduated from an Ivy League school with a master's in business. Or that he opened and managed two tattoo shops with a third on the way, despite the wrench that someone tried to throw in his plans. People didn't see that because they would have to face their own prejudices, and no one wanted to tackle their internal racism.

"I think it's a great choice," he said after a moment. For the first time, he saw Marisol smile. It made her look younger, offering a fleeting glimpse of her true self before disappearing in an instant. He had a feeling Marisol didn't smile often.

They settled into a comfortable silence, letting the raspy vocals of The Sinner's Web fill the space. He hummed along to one of their new singles, nodding in time with the beat. When he glanced at Marisol again, he was surprised to see her tapping her fingers to the rhythm and quietly mouthing the lyrics.

"You know The Sinner's Web?" he asked, grinning.

Marisol's cheeks reddened. It was fucking adorable. "I know some songs, yeah."

"They're badass. Have you listened to their new album? I got the record last week, and it's been in the player nonstop at my house."

"You have a record player?" Marisol perked up.

"Yeah, right over there." He gestured to the black dresser with a brown box record player resting on top.

"Wow, I've always wanted to see one of those. They released a record? I've listened to the entire discography three times from start to finish. I think I like it better than their EP." When Marisol spoke of their music, her entire demeanor changed. She transformed into a music geek, gushing over her favorite songs. It was such a switch from the closed-off, somber persona she donned earlier.

"Their EP was great; it definitely got me invested in their music. But I think I agree with you. Their album just has a lot of soul," Cisco said.

"And trauma," Marisol said immediately. She paled when she realized the words that left her mouth. "I mean, it just feels like something that would resonate with people."

And what could she resonate with? It wasn't his place to ask, but he found himself wanting to know anyway. "Yeah, they sing about a lot of parental trauma."

There was the slightest change in Marisol's expression. Her face pinched as if she had just sucked on a sour lemon. Was this the trauma she was referring to? And the reason she needed to get this tattoo as a reminder of who she was or wanted to be? He knew he shouldn't get involved, but he couldn't get the message to his heart. That damn thing liked to take over, even when his brain told it to stop.

For the next hour and a half, their conversation revolved around The Sinner's Web—their favorite songs, the lyrics that resonated the most, and how the band's music seemed to be evolving. As the discussion flowed, they branched out to other artists with a similar sound, discovering even more common ground. Cisco was surprised by how closely their musical tastes aligned and how much knowledge Marisol possessed on independent artists.

Marisol even introduced him to a band he'd never heard of before. Intrigued, he immediately downloaded their album onto his phone, eager to explore their sound. When she mentioned her favorite song, he took a mental note, planning to listen to it later—preferably in a quiet moment when he could truly absorb the music and maybe, just maybe, understand Marisol a little better.

The bitter taste of disappointment churned his stomach

when he finished up the last of the shading. Marisol's tattoo was done, which meant she would be leaving soon. He didn't know why that thought upset him, but he felt it all the same.

"Ready to check out your tattoo in the mirror?" Cisco put the tattoo gun down and pushed his stool back, so Marisol could get up.

He offered a hand to help her out of the chair, and Marisol took it. Her soft hand fit into his perfectly, and he pulled her to her feet, coming chest to chest with her. Marisol gave him a timid, almost shy smile. Reluctantly, he stepped aside so she could see the finished product in the mirror.

She walked with a slight limp, which was to be expected after a needle dug into her skin and she sat in the same position for a long period of time. She kept her shorts rolled up so she didn't irritate her skin.

This was Cisco's favorite part. The part where his client got to experience seeing their tattoo for the first time. Their excitement always filled him with pride for his work. He was fortunate enough to never have any dissatisfied customers. He took his time to get to know his clients. Their likes and interests. He listened to them when they spoke and tried to capture exactly what they pictured in their head.

Marisol's situation was a little bit different since it was his design in the first place. He still took just as much care tattooing it as he would any other tattoo he did.

Marisol reached the mirror, never once meeting her gaze in it. Her focus was on her thigh, of the goddess Cisco created for her. A girlish squeal he didn't peg her capable of left her lips, and her eyes glossed over.

"Cisco..." she said his name with such reverence that he wanted to bottle up that sound and listen to it again while he was alone in bed tonight.

"Cisco, this is beautiful." She met his gaze in the mirror before turning around. "It's perfect. It's...wow. I can't believe I did that."

Cisco smirked. "Damn straight you did that. Fair warning, tattoos become addicting. Many people can't stop after just one."

She giggled. "Noted. Though I don't have plans for more. If I do, you're my man."

You're my man.

It shouldn't have meant shit to him. But the thought was planted in his head, and now he couldn't let it go. "Let me bandage you up and talk about aftercare."

Aftercare, for fuck's sake. His brain needed to not immediately go to the horny place it felt compelled to go to.

Pushing those thoughts aside for now, he catered to Marisol, making sure she was wrapped up properly before giving her instructions that detailed exactly what she needed to do over the next few weeks.

"If you have any questions, here's my number." Cisco dug through his pocket and pulled out his card. He searched for a pen before writing down his personal phone number on the back. "Text or call me anytime."

Marisol took the card from him and tucked it securely in her purse, alongside her aftercare instructions. "What do people normally tip for these things? I guess I should have looked that up before," she said sheepishly.

"Don't worry about it."

"No, I need to—"

"You really don't," Cisco cut her off. Then he had an idea. A brave—or stupid—idea. "How about you come with me to The Sinner's Web concert next weekend, and we will call it even?"

This was so unprofessional. He shouldn't be asking a client out, especially in such a shitty way. But he felt drawn to Marisol, and he was never one to ignore his impulses. Which either went really well for him—or very badly.

He hoped for the former this time.

"You...have tickets?" she asked like she didn't believe him. Which was fair.

Cisco got out his phone and scrolled through his email until he found the receipt. He showed her the proof for two concert tickets for next weekend at seven p.m. He had been planning on taking Tiny, but...he could make it up to her later.

"I've never been to a concert before." She glanced between him and the phone as if weighing his suggestion.

He tried to mask his excitement with a neutral expression, though he wasn't sure he pulled it off. "I couldn't think of a better first concert than this one."

"Can I...erm, think about it?" she asked.

Cisco tried to hide his disappointment. It wasn't a no...but it also wasn't a yes. He supposed it was the best he could hope for after springing it on a woman he just met.

"Yeah, of course. You have my number."

Marisol seemed surprised by his reaction, like she expected him to be pissed. She looked at him strangely before smiling. "Thank you. I'll be in touch," she said as if he had just proposed a business meeting rather than a date.

Just like that, Marisol walked past him and out of his studio. It wasn't until he heard the bell atop the door signaling she left that he realized he didn't have her number. All he could do was wait and hope she'd actually text him back.

He hoped she did because he had a feeling there was more to Marisol than met the eye.

CHAPTER 6
Marisol

No one told Marisol about the intense need to scratch the healing tattoo on her thigh. The need to dig her nails into her flesh and scratch the itch that'd been driving her crazy for the last two days was strong. Multiple times, she had nearly caved, but each time she looked down at the beautiful goddess on her thigh, she couldn't bring herself to do it. Even if that left her in agony.

Marisol studied the aftercare instructions Cisco gave her like she would be having a quiz on them at the end of the week. She had run out of the unscented lotion sample Cisco gave her, which helped the itchiness and the peeling of her tattoo. She was tempted to call him to ask what brand it was, but then she would have to give him an answer about the date.

Was it even a date?

Part of her wanted to go. She had never been to a concert before except a few orchestra concerts her parents dragged her to for charity, but those weren't exactly the epitome of fun. It was just another way to flaunt their money and parade their generosity around—because giving to charity only counted when others took notice of your good deeds.

But another part of her couldn't ignore the undeniable truth she was still—technically—married to Archie. The thought settled over her like a weight, heavy and unshakable. They were separated, their lives split down the middle, yet on paper, she still carried his name, still wore the title of his wife.

Did that mean she wasn't allowed to go on a date with someone else? Was there some unspoken rule, some invisible boundary she would be crossing? She had no idea how any of this worked. The uncertainty gnawed at her, a quiet, persistent whisper in the back of her mind, making her hesitate just enough to feel the conflict twisting inside her.

She was getting distracted. Bottom line was that, as much as she wanted to attend, she didn't know if she would actually say yes. She still had time to answer, even if she felt bad for stringing Cisco along in the process.

Marisol pulled up to her favorite beauty store that carried various skin care lotions, hoping she'd find something unscented with healing properties. The store was busy for a Thursday afternoon. *Did these people have a job to be at?* she wondered, annoyed by the number of bodies here. Technically, the same argument could be said about her, but she didn't have a job. Other than playing the role of the perfect daughter so her parents didn't cut her off.

"Can I help you?" A short, blonde woman popped out from seemingly nowhere. A pleasant enough smile was on her face, but it was her eyes that gave her away as they roamed Marisol's body. The woman was intimidated by her —probably due to Marisol's looks. She wasn't being vain when she said she was pretty. Marisol knew she was pretty. Hell, she spent countless hours to achieve this effortless beauty, which had been so ingrained in her because of her mother.

"No, I know what I'm looking for. Thanks."

At her dismissal, the woman gave her a fake smile and walked off.

After no more interruptions, she reached the skin care aisle and looked through the face washes and creams until she got to the body lotions. There were tons to pick from, ranging from tropical smells to earthy scents, which was great if she didn't need an unscented one. She had to search through dozens and move bottles out of the way until she spotted a single bottle labeled unscented.

It wasn't a brand she ever heard of, but she popped the lid open to smell. Nothing. Exactly what she needed. She was tempted to look around and do more shopping, but the hem of her shorts rubbed her tattoo and was getting annoying. She was ready to go home and change into a robe.

Marisol rang up her purchase. The damn lotion was expensive, so she hoped it did the trick. She carried the small black bag to her car, gently tossing her purchase and purse in the passenger seat before getting in. Another warm day in Berkeley meant she quickly turned on the car and put the AC on blast.

One thing about Marisol was that she wasn't going to sweat. It was gross.

Just as she was contemplating whether she would stop and pick up something for lunch, her phone rang. Her mother's photo flashed across the screen. She wasn't expecting a call, but she assumed her mother was calling to talk about some upcoming event she would undoubtedly drag Marisol to. Especially now that Marisol was no longer a part of the family business and in the midst of a divorce, her mother found new ways to guilt her into doing what she wanted. She was tempted to let it go to voicemail but decided against it because the woman was persistent. She wouldn't stop pestering her.

"Hello, Mother," she answered finally.

There was movement on the other line before her mother's voice filled her car's speakers. "Marisol, darling, how are you doing?" Her mother always sounded slightly annoyed and disinterested every time she spoke, and this time was no different. Didn't matter that she was the one who called.

"I'm fine. Just...shopping. Is there something you need?"

"Well, no, actually. Not me. But I do have a favor to ask of you, dear."

Marisol tensed. She never liked her mother's "favors." They usually meant meeting someone who had the personality of a garden gnome or attending one of her friend's functions as a "representative" for their family.

"Did you hear me? I said I need to ask you for a favor." Her mother's sharp tone cut through her thoughts.

"Yes, sorry. What do you need, Mother?"

"Now that we're back from vacation, your father has to go to the San Francisco store tomorrow to inspect it one final time before opening. Unfortunately, I have a massage I scheduled weeks ago that I simply cannot miss. I know you are no longer working at the family business, but would you be a dear and accompany your father tomorrow? I know it would mean a lot to him, and me too, dear, to have you involved again."

It took everything in Marisol not to groan. Even though her mother couldn't see her, she refrained from rolling her eyes because somehow it would get back to her. The family business was something of a contention between them. One would argue that it was the first time Marisol ever defied her family.

Her family owned a winery that was outsourced to multiple restaurants, liquor stores, and various other companies. She and Archie were supposed to take it over, but when she announced her impending divorce from him, she also said she would no longer be an active participant in the business. Her father was sad but understood. Her mother, on the other hand, was pissed. Ever since then, she found ways for Marisol to be involved in her sneaky way. This was no different.

It was another way her mother had her claws in her, pulling all the strings as if she were a puppet.

If she were a different woman, she would say no. But she wasn't a different woman, and this was her mother. One who, despite how awful she could be, was the woman she craved approval from the most. At least that was what her therapist said.

"Sure, I guess I can go—"

"Oh great! Your father will pick you up around nine in the morning. Goodbye, darling." Her mother made kissing sounds before the line went dead, abruptly cutting off the conversation once she got what she wanted. Marisol was left feeling like she just got whiplash.

Before she could fully process what happened, her phone rang again. Thinking it was her mother calling back to add on to her little "favor," Marisol answered without looking. "Hello?"

"Marisol."

Her blood turned to ice, a sharp chill creeping down her spine. She mentally cursed herself—why hadn't she checked? More than that, why hadn't she blocked his number when she had the chance? The answer gnawed at her. There was no good reason, nothing she could justify beyond the flimsy excuse that she might need to contact him about the divorce. But deep down, she knew better.

Gritting her teeth, she forced herself to speak. "Archie,

what do you want?" She prayed her voice didn't betray the unease curling in her gut.

Archie was her ex-husband. Or he would be—if he ever bothered to sign the damn papers. Somehow, in that delusional little mind of his, he still believed they were together, as if their marriage hadn't already crumbled into dust.

"You didn't show up at the work mixer I texted you about last week." His voice echoed throughout the car and made her shiver, but not in a good way. If she were honest, Archie had never made her feel good in any aspect.

If it had been up to her, she would have never married him.

"Why would I go to the mixer with you, Archie?" She forced her voice to be even so as not to incite any more hostility.

"Because you are my wife, Marisol, whether you like it or not. As my wife, you need to be by my side for events like these. People are going to start talking," he said, lecturing her like she was an insubordinate child.

Why couldn't this man get it through his head that they were done? Had been done for a while now, and nothing would change that fact. It was the one area of her life that she was pushing back on, and so far, she had both her father's and her sister's support.

"Let those people talk. If they are dumb enough to think I'm still with you after two years of separation, then I don't know what to tell you. Have you forgotten that we are in the middle of getting a divorce? If you would just sign the damn papers, all of this would be over."

A throaty laugh played through the car speakers, the laugh of a man who found no amusement in his situation but was determined to get the outcome he desired. "Yes, so you say.

But, Marisol, we both know you can only stay away for so long."

"Excuse me? I don't know what you mean by that, but—"

"I'll talk to you later, Marisol. And I forgive you this one time," Archie interrupted. The line went dead, and music from her playlist played quietly in the background.

What. The. Fuck?

Archie had always been an asshole, but never to this extreme. It had only truly started this last year, once he realized she was serious about leaving him. She had tried to find some decency in Archie, especially when everyone seemed to love him. What was she missing? Her mother was in her ear the entire time to make sure Marisol didn't screw it up with Archie. She wanted them together. Even though her sister had met and dated him first.

The look of absolute horror and betrayal on Lola's face when Archie said he was breaking up with her to date Marisol would forever be etched into her brain. She had hurt her sister in the past, but never to that level.

Granted, it worked out for Lola in the end because her sister ended up finding the love of her life, and now she and Javi had two kids together. But it didn't erase all the terrible things Marisol did to her. Even if she was only going along with what her mother wanted, she still went along with her every time.

She didn't have the capacity to deal with Archie or her problems with her sister today. She boxed up that conversation, mentally putting it on a shelf to deal with later at therapy. Right now, she needed to get home, get out of these damn shorts, and lather herself in this overpriced lotion.

And that was exactly what she did.

CHAPTER 7

Cisco

"Alright, I'm gonna stay up here and give you time to check the space out." Ernesto leaned against the wall, positioning himself underneath the shop's AC vent. Sweat rolled down his agent's forehead at an alarming rate, but that was what Ernesto got for wearing a three-piece suit during a heat wave.

Cisco left Ernesto to fan himself as he walked through what was once an office building. There were remnants of clunky desks and ancient-looking computers littering some of the space. Besides the few remaining pieces of old technology, the property was vacant, giving Cisco a blank canvas to imagine what his shop could look like.

There were four distinct areas, plus a receptionist area. He could hire four new artists, all specializing in different areas. Line work, shading, color, and maybe cover-ups. A piercer would be nice to have as well.

The location for this shop was ideal, surrounded by restaurants, bars, and local shops. He may have to field a few drunks attempting to get tattoos, but what parlor didn't deal with that shit? It was a small price to pay for a location in the heart of the city.

As it was, the building was in good shape. He'd have to paint the walls to match his gothic aesthetic. Right now, they were a horrid beige color that made him want to claw his eyes out. Ernesto mentioned the building recently got new tile floors, but he would replace the tile with dark wood flooring. As far as projects went, it seemed straightforward and something that wouldn't break the bank.

By the time Cisco made it back to the front, Ernesto had lost some of the redness to his cheeks and was no longer sweating buckets. His realtor smiled. "So, what do you think? Good property, no?"

"It's a damn good property," Cisco agreed. The floor-to-ceiling windows behind Ernesto looked out onto the busy street. It wasn't even a weekend, and there were still crowds of people coming to and from the various businesses. A tattoo shop would thrive under these conditions. The asking price for this property was steep, but the evidence as to why was outside.

"If you are seriously considering this, then you're gonna need to make an offer and fast." Ernesto always told it as it was and didn't sugarcoat anything. It was one of the reasons Cisco liked working with him so much. Another being Ernesto was a proud Mexican man who fought hard for his clients, especially the brown men who got passed up time and time again for their white counterparts. It was all a part of business, no matter how shitty it was.

"What are your thoughts about the place?" Cisco trusted Ernesto's professional opinion.

Ernesto gestured at the window to the crowds walking by. "This is a prime location. It's different from your other two, meaning you're going to get a new clientele and probably a steady flow of them. The space is fantastic. With a few renos to put your stamp on it, you'll have this place up and running in no time. If it were me, man, I'd put my hat in the ring for this one."

It was a damn good location, and the space was perfect to take on a few new talented artists. Both Golden City Tattoo shops could run themselves at this point and have an established clientele. It would allow Cisco to spend more of his time at this location to get it on its feet and train his staff, at least until he found a shop manager. He had more primos who would be all too willing to take the position.

His decision was made. "Make an offer," he told Ernesto.

The man's lips curled up in a smile. "Good choice, man. We'll put in asking price, all cash like normal?"

Cisco nodded. "I'm willing to go up in price if it becomes a bidding war." For a location like this, he imagined he'd be paying a little more than the asking price, and he was willing to dish out the extra funds if necessary. It would be worth it if it secured this shop.

Although everything was happening quickly, and Ernesto was already walking to the door, this moment was not lost on him. Ten years ago, if someone would have told him he'd have two successful tattoo shops with a third on the way, and be part owner of a music venue, he wouldn't have believed it.

Ten years ago, Cisco was in a much different place, both mentally and physically. A major event threatened to upend his entire life and take away his chance of a future. Even after everything came to light and he was free of the demons attempting to ruin his life, the damage was already done. It took him years to restore himself.

And now he was a first-generation college graduate with two, almost three successful business endeavors. His immigrant parents didn't like tattoos, but they were still fiercely proud of him. Cisco thought he was getting his mom more on board with tattoos, and he secretly hoped he would be able to give her a small one. He'd happily risk his father's wrath. It would be worth it.

The sweltering heat hit his body the moment they stepped out of the building. The weather didn't seem to deter the groups of people walking down the sidewalk. The sushi restaurant across the street was particularly popular, with a line starting to form on the street. A large handmade sign indicated it was happy hour and advertised all their happy hour deals.

"Look, you'll be next to a popular restaurant and a wine store that's opening soon." Ernesto gestured to the stucco building next door. It looked like the building was pulled out of a picturesque town in Italy and moved here. A trellis with leafy vines decorated the front of the store. By the window was an arrangement of colorful potted plants. The curb appeal of the wine shop was hard to resist.

"Too bad wine sucks," Ernesto mumbled under his breath.

As if summoning the winemakers themselves, the door opened on the shop, chiming a bell from up above the door frame. An older, stout white man stepped out first. His salt-and-pepper hair—or rather what was left of it because of his receding hairline—was cropped close to his head, neat and tidy. He was clean-shaven and wore neatly pressed brown trousers with a bright yellow polo shirt. He looked as if he could be on his way to go golfing. The man exuded wealth, reminding him of someone's rich grandpa who enjoyed spoiling his grandchildren.

Then a woman stepped out behind him. She was younger, with a darker complexion the color of clay. He nearly looked away until he caught her features in his peripheral vision. Long, dark hair covered her face, but Cisco didn't need to see it to know those long, gorgeous legs belonged to Marisol.

Who had still not answered him about the concert.

Before he could fully think out his plan, Cisco changed directions and started to walk toward the mysterious older man and Marisol. "Hey, where ya going?" Ernesto asked, but Cisco ignored him. Neither the man nor Marisol took notice of Cisco until he was right in front of them.

Cisco watched all the color drain from Marisol's face, her eyes widening at his abrupt appearance. He couldn't blame her for her reaction. She probably thought she was free of him.

"Hi," was his brilliant greeting. Now the attention of the older man was on him too. He didn't seem mad, just curious.

"Hi there. Are you here about the opening?" the man asked.

Cisco didn't understand what he meant until he saw the red and white "Help Wanted" sign hung precariously on the window.

"Oh, no. Actually, I'm interested in purchasing the building next door." Cisco gestured to the neighboring shop.

The man stuck out his bottom lip and nodded as if Cisco had just gotten a right answer on a test. "You don't say? What business are you in?"

"Tattooing. Looking to open my next tattoo shop here." Cisco waited for judgment to follow.

To the man's credit, he only looked more intrigued. "Fascinating. What does that entail?" He looked ready to hear Cisco's full business plan. Talking about his business was not the reason Cisco approached the two of them. He wanted to speak to Marisol, who had still not acknowledged his presence other than shock.

He didn't know how to get out of this conversation and

was about to share his business plan with this strange man before Marisol found her voice. She gently touched the man's arm, and he turned to face her. His face softened as he smiled.

"Daddy," she started, answering Cisco's unasked question about their relationship. "Do you mind waiting for me in the car? Cisco is a...friend. I want to catch up with him really quickly." She batted her long eyelashes at her father, who nodded.

"Travis Roberts," he said, extending his hand.

Cisco took it. "Francisco Ramos, but you can call me Cisco."

"It was nice to meet you, Cisco," he said and let his hand drop. He leaned over to kiss Marisol's forehead before heading to a black Bentley, leaving the two of them alone.

Marisol rounded on Cisco. "What are you doing here?" she asked accusatorially, as if he planned on following her.

"I really was here to look at the shop next door," he said. "I had no idea it was next to"—he looked back at the wine store and gestured to it—"this."

"Yeah, my father owns a winery and has outsourced to local shops for years. This is his first brick and mortar shop," she explained, eyes darting between Cisco and the car. The windows were tinted, but he'd bet her father was watching their entire interaction. It explained why Marisol was so stiff and looked ready to bolt. She had been tense in his chair, but eventually eased up. He doubted he'd get the same reaction from her now.

He had a unique opportunity at hand, and although it wasn't the ideal time, he didn't want to waste it. "About next Saturday—"

"It's fine if you want to take someone else," Marisol interrupted. "I know you were just being kind."

Being kind was opening the door for her or picking up something she dropped. No, Cisco wasn't being kind. He was interested. "No, the offer still stands. I would like for you to go with me."

"Oh," she said softly, an undeniable smile ghosting her lips.

Of course, he could be interpreting her nervousness for reluctance, and maybe she was not interested in going out with him. That would suck, but he would accept her no.

"I...still haven't had time to check my calendar. Can I let you know tomorrow? I have your number still."

He supposed it was a good sign she hadn't thrown his card away. Still, he couldn't help the disappointment that took over. "Sure. I'll talk to you tomorrow then."

"Tomorrow," she agreed. "Goodbye, Cisco." Marisol offered him a tight smile before she walked away from him. Her short, fitted skirt hugged her ass perfectly. It was long enough to cover her tattoo though, which was what she wanted. Even when she slid into the front seat of her father's car, she took great care to keep her thigh concealed. She shut the door with a resounding thud.

Cisco didn't move back to his car until the Bentley drove down the road, taking Marisol and her answer about tomorrow further away.

CHAPTER 8

Marisol

If Marisol had friends, big life decisions would be much easier. Dates shouldn't have fallen under that category, but any deviation from her norm fell under major decisions. Choosing for herself didn't come naturally, no matter how much she willed it.

Thoughts of her mother plagued her mind, taking up residence within her soul and tainting every decision of her life. Her mother's approval was at the forefront of everything. It was easier to simply go along with what she said because it made life easier. Even if that chipped away at parts of her until she was nothing but an empty shell, content to be pushed along by someone else.

So, yes, friends would make this decision a lot easier so they could psych her up and tell her it was okay to go on a date with a man her family—specifically her mother—would not approve of because he did not fit into the image she had molded for their family.

Although her relationship with her sister had improved, they didn't talk about men or dating. Not since Marisol married Archie, Lola's ex-boyfriend, and destroyed her sister's trust. Now they stayed on more neutral topics, like Lola's children or weekend plans. Despite not going in-depth about their lives, Marisol still enjoyed the time she got to spend with Lola. It made her think of all the time she missed out on as children, but it gave her hope for the future.

With no friends and her unwilling to call her sister about this matter, Marisol only had one other option. Heading into her formal dining room, Marisol sat down on a white upholstered chair and opened her laptop. She pulled up her email, found the link sent to her and clicked on it. Her face filled the screen while she waited for her call to be answered. She didn't have to wait long.

On the second ring, a new face filled the screen. Her gray hair was piled into a neat bun atop her head, and her glasses sat on the bridge of her nose. She squinted, mumbling something under her breath. "Can you see me?" Alice asked, poking at the camera.

Marisol smiled. For as good as her therapist was in person, she lacked the proper knowledge of online therapy sessions but was getting better. At least this time, she was able to send the link and log on to her own session.

"I can see you just fine. You don't need to poke the camera." She laughed.

Alice stopped assaulting the camera and sat back in her black leather chair. "Oh, good. It's good to see you again, Marisol. How are you doing? You don't normally call last-minute sessions."

The warm smile Alice reserved for her always put Marisol's nerves at ease, even if her mind was a whirlwind of anxiety. "Thank you for meeting with me on such short notice."

"Anything for my favorite client."

"Are you allowed to say that?" Marisol asked, raising a brow.

Alice just winked at her. "So, what did you want to talk about? Oh! Did you get that tattoo for your birthday?"

There was a playful gleam in Marisol's eye as she stood up and raised her cotton shorts.

Alice gasped as she leaned closer, her eyes taking up the entire screen. "Oh, Marisol, it's beautiful! Look at that line work. Oh, wow. I expected a little flower or something, not this beautiful piece. It's big!"

"It is, but it's easy to conceal too. Only Lola knows I got it. She's actually the one who scheduled the appointment for me. I don't think I would have gone otherwise," Marisol admitted.

"How sweet of her. It's a great present for you. She took the time to hear what you wanted and gave it to you. Has she seen it yet?" Alice asked.

Marisol rolled her shorts back down and took a seat. "Only on a video call. She liked it too. But, uhm, that's kind of the reason I scheduled this meeting."

"Oh? About your sister?"

"No, not Lola." She shook her head, suddenly feeling foolish. Maybe it wasn't the right idea to call Alice. She wasn't a relationship guru. She couldn't tell Marisol what to do or—

"Marisol, come back to me. I know that look. You're doubting our call. But that only confirms this call is completely necessary. Tell me what has you worried," Alice said gently. Her voice had a soothing quality that made Marisol take a deep breath.

"Well, while I was getting tattooed, the artist—his name is Cisco—and I got to talking. We like the same music and connected over a band we both like. I had a fun time talking to him, and by the end of it, he…" She hesitated as nerves started to take over.

"And what happened by the end of it?" Alice inquired, a small smile on her lips.

Marisol fidgeted in her chair. Her leg bounced up and down in rapid succession, a nervous habit that drove her mother crazy. "He asked me out. At first, I thought he might have been joking, but I ran into him again yesterday, and he's serious," she said so quickly, her words ran together.

Thankfully, Alice was able to understand her chaotic speech. "Did he? And what did you say?"

"I didn't give him an answer. But he gave me his business card, and I told him I would text him an answer."

"And have you?"

Marisol bit her lip. "No."

"Ah," she said. "Well, have you not answered because you don't want to go and don't want to upset him, or have you not answered because you want to go but are afraid of what your mother will say?"

"That one," she said. "The last one."

It didn't matter that Marisol was thirty years old. It didn't matter that she had lived apart from her mother for nearly ten years. And it didn't matter that she told herself time and time again that her mother wasn't the end-all, be-all. She had not yet figured out how to break the toxic cycle they had developed over her life.

"What about him makes you nervous your mom won't like him?" Alice asked.

"What wouldn't she like? He's a tattoo artist full of tattoos. He wouldn't exactly fit in at the country club."

"So, he's full of tattoos and a tattoo artist. Is that all you can tell me as to why she wouldn't like him?" Alice tilted her head to the side.

Marisol shrugged. "I guess I don't know much about him."

"Precisely," Alice said as if she just came to some earth-shattering conclusion. "Appearances can be deceiving, Marisol. We've talked about this. You aren't your mother. You are allowed to get to know people because, if you pass up someone simply because of the way they look, you could be passing up on a chance at true happiness. This isn't your mother's life. This is your life, Marisol. You are working on taking that back.

"So, I want you to listen to your gut. If it is telling you to give him a chance, then I think you should take him up on his offer. However, if you truly do not want to date right now, there's no shame in telling him you aren't interested. Whatever you choose, make sure it is a decision you aren't going to regret a week from now," Alice said. "The best part is that you don't have to tell your mother anything. You're thirty, Marisol. You are allowed to make your own choices."

"I needed to hear that," Marisol said softly. It was like she needed permission to do something for herself. Just like the tattoo. This was different though. She hadn't dated anyone since Archie. Their divorce had been pending for over two years now, and in that time, she had not met anyone else. Not even her mother, who once had a list of guys she wanted Marisol to meet, approached her about dating. It was strange, actually. She had thought that since she was divorcing, her mother would be dying for the chance to choose her second husband, but she had been unusually quiet in that aspect.

"It's okay to take risks and try something different. Plus, a free meal is a free meal."

"Alice!" Marisol laughed at her cheeky response. Alice only winked.

Their conversation ended soon after that with a promise to see her in person next week. After teaching Alice how to hang up, Marisol was left with nothing but her phone and a choice.

She couldn't overthink this. She needed to be bold and brave. To be confident like the woman in her tattoo. Repeating that mantra over and over, she grabbed her phone and typed in his number. Before she lost her courage and backed out, she typed her response and hit send.

> If the offer still stands, I would like to go with you to the concert next week.

She read and reread the message a hundred times before she realized she didn't tell him who it was. Right before she could type that out, she received a text.

> I'll pick you up next Saturday at five. Send me your address.

CHAPTER 9
Cisco

Marisol's apartment was located in the middle of downtown, towering well above the other buildings in the area. A tall linebacker of a teenage doorman greeted him at the entrance and opened the door for him. "Are you visiting, sir?" he asked, voice cracking on the last syllable.

"Picking someone up."

"Got it. Well, feel free to wait in the lobby. We can ring them if you can tell me their name, and I'll let them know you are here," he offered.

"Marisol Roberts." Cisco already texted her, but in case she hadn't seen her messages.

He walked over to the small lobby with a few white chairs and a black couch. A table was set up behind the couch with small glass cups and a pitcher of icy water. A bowl of fruit, mostly apples and pears, sat next to it. Cisco hadn't eaten, opting to get something at the concert or after. In truth, he couldn't eat because of the anticipation of seeing Marisol tonight.

He didn't know what it was about this complicated stranger that intrigued him, but he wanted to peel back every complex layer until he found the core of what made her *her*. He was surprised he heard back from her, and even more surprised Marisol agreed to join him for the concert.

Tiny had taken the news of not going to the concert tonight pretty well. She teased him relentlessly about his date, considering it had been a while since he had taken anyone out. Tiny also demanded he make it up to her by buying her and her friends pizza for their monster horror marathon they were having tonight. Who knew three tiny teens needed five pizzas?

An elevator chimed behind him, and Cisco turned in time to see Marisol walk out. He thought she looked beautiful before, but the woman approaching him made his heart stop.

She was dressed in all black, a far cry from the outfits he had seen her in before. Her shirt was an off-the-shoulder crop top that laced up the front. A red strapless bra peeked through the laces, pushing up her breasts. The tight leather skirt was almost indecently short, but showed off her tattoo, which appeared to be healing nicely. It looked damn good too. Her hair was done, mostly straight with a slight curl at the end. The outfit was complete with black leather booties.

For a second, he forgot how to breathe.

"You look beautiful," he said in a way of greeting.

"I know," Marisol said, straight-faced. Her red lips twitched up, breaking the façade. "Thank you. You look really good too."

Cisco wore black fitted jeans with a dark collared shirt and a brown bomber jacket. The days were warm, but nights in Berkeley had a chill to them. If Marisol was concerned about this, her outfit didn't show it. He was glad he decided to bring the jacket in case Marisol needed it for later.

"You ready for tonight?"

This time, Marisol couldn't hide her smile. Her face lit up, showing a more playful side to her. "I'm so excited, but also nervous. I don't know what to expect."

"Expect fun. Are you hungry? We can eat before," he suggested.

But Marisol shook her head. "Too nervous. Can we eat after? I'm also going to need a drink. Or maybe two."

He nodded once and gestured to the door. "Drink it is, then. Let's go."

THE VENUE, Lucky Rabbit, was nestled on the other side of town, about fifteen minutes from Marisol's house. Already, the night life was in full swing, forcing Cisco to drive at snail speed so he wouldn't hit any drunk pedestrians fucking around on the road. Luckily, the parking lot was policed by a security guy, shooing away anyone not here for the concert.

Cisco pulled up to the valet, tossing the keys to the young man salivating over his car. "This is it?" Marisol asked, her voice laced with uncertainty. Her grip on the door handle turned her knuckles white.

Lucky Rabbit wasn't much to look at. It was a cinderblock building painted black with an obnoxious pink rabbit smoking a cigarette. Two bouncers manned the door, checking tickets and IDs of patrons. The crowd entering Lucky Rabbit varied in age from teenager to middle-aged rocker dads. The Sinner's Web was a small band, so the location of the concert made sense and added to the whole indie, grunge vibe the band was known for.

"Yeah, they play here a lot." Cisco parked the car, leaving it on for the valet driver.

"Oh," was all Marisol said, not making an attempt to get out. Not until Cisco got out and opened the door for her. He offered Marisol his hand, but she hesitated. He didn't think it was from not wanting to touch him but being completely out of her element.

Honestly, it was adorable.

"Hey." Cisco crouched down so he could be eye level with Marisol. Her large, honey-brown eyes stared back. She tried to remain stoic, but the way her eyes darted from side to side and the tight grip on her purse gave her away. He didn't think Lucky Rabbit was a place she was accustomed to. It made him wonder exactly how glamorous a life she lived. If her condos were any indication, he could guess.

"Are you uncomfortable?" Cisco asked.

"This just isn't a place I would normally go. It's...different," she said, confirming his suspicions. "The places I go don't look like this."

"I imagine it's very different. But it could be a fun different." Cisco offered her his hand. "Want to be different together?"

That made Marisol smile, and Cisco wanted to capture that moment. It made him feel like he just won an award and was gifted with a trophy. "You're convincing," she said and took his hand.

Cisco coaxed her out like a timid dog. She stayed glued to his side as he led her to the entrance. The bouncers knew him on sight, and Darrell—the head of security—nodded at him before letting him and Marisol through.

"Hmm, didn't realize I was out with a big shot."

Cisco knew Marisol was teasing, but he still shrugged. "I'm part-owner."

"You own this place?"

"Partly." Cisco laughed at Marisol's stunned expression. "I like music. I can't sing worth a shit, but I can provide a venue for those who can." Plus, the cash flow was nice and allowed him to provide for his extended family.

"A tattoo shop owner and a music venue owner. Should I know anything else?" Marisol asked.

"I once owned a hot dog stand, but then my cousin crashed his car into it. That business didn't last long." He earned a laugh from Marisol. It was a sweet sound he wanted to hear again.

The moment they stepped through the entrance, they were greeted by the smell of cigarettes and weed. Already a large group of people had arrived. This was a sold-out show, so by the time the concert started, the number of people would double. There was standing room only, no places to sit on the main floor. Marisol seemed to notice this as well and pursed her lips together.

"It's a big crowd," she said, gripping Cisco's hand tighter. She hadn't dropped it, even though they were inside now. Not that he was complaining.

"I take it you don't want to be in the pit?" Cisco mused.

"The pit? What the hell is the pit?" Color drained from her face. He felt bad for how uncomfortable she was, but he hoped he could make tonight more enjoyable for them.

"I'll show you later. Let's get a drink, and I'll take you to my favorite spot." When she nodded, Cisco led her to the bar and ordered whatever local beer they had on tap. He offered one to Marisol, who immediately took the glass and drank down half its contents.

Damn. She was more nervous than he thought. Was it a crowd thing? Or something deeper?

Still, he kept faith that the spot they would be watching the concert from would ease some of those nerves. "This way." He pulled her past the bar and back toward a closed-off area. The bouncers there let them pass without a second thought but stopped the two drunk men who tried to follow them in, claiming they were with "the dude with the brown jacket and his hot chick."

He felt the urge to turn around and smash his fist against the drunk man's stupid face for calling Marisol the "hot chick," but he didn't think that would make a good impression on a first date, no matter how good it would make him feel.

Ignoring the drunks behind them, Cisco gestured for Marisol to go up the stairs while he followed behind her. The second story balcony was small, overlooking the first floor and giving them the perfect view of the stage. There were a few high-top tables with chairs, but the best thing was that no one else was on the balcony. The only other person who could have been up here was his cousin, Santiago, who was the co-owner of Lucky Rabbit, but he and his partner were in Vegas for their five-year anniversary.

This VIP section was equipped with a fridge full of drinks and snacks, as well as their own private bathroom. Back in his teenage years, Cisco would have thought being on the balcony was the worst thing ever because he wasn't in the middle of the pit, jumping and swinging his fists with the rest of them. But as a thirty-three-year-old man? That sounded like a fate worse than hell. There was no amount of pain meds that would make him feel good the next day.

Ah, the joys of aging.

The tension that had been coiled in Marisol's shoulders

seemed to ease once they escaped the overwhelming press of the crowd. Her grip on her purse loosened, almost as if she were letting her guard down. Cisco wanted her comfortable so she could enjoy the concert without always looking over her shoulder when someone got too close. She took a deep breath, letting the quiet of the empty space settle over them before scanning the area. Once she seemed to realize they were alone, she placed her purse down on a nearby table.

"Are we going to be alone up here?" she asked, her voice tinged with both curiosity and caution.

"Just the two of us. Figured it was better than being down there." He gestured to the ever-growing crowd below. Everyone was pressed up against each other, with only a modicum of space toward the back of the venue.

"Thank God," Marisol muttered under her breath as she dragged a chair closer to the balcony ledge. With effortless grace, she hopped onto the seat, her movements causing her tits to bounce, which he deliberately avoided acknowledging. Settling in, she crossed her legs, the shift in position revealing a glimpse of her tattoo—a dark swirl of ink against her skin briefly catching the light.

"That's healing good." Without thinking, he reached out to feel the raised skin, pleased to feel it moisturized. "Has it been itchy?" Realizing his fingers lingered on her thigh, he pulled them back.

Thankfully, Marisol didn't seem upset he touched her without permission. "Like a bitch. How come no one ever warned me?"

"It was in the care package I gave you at the end." He smirked. "You telling me you didn't read it?"

"Oh, I read it. It mentioned slight itchiness. That's a lie. I've never wanted to dig my nails into my skin more. It's frustrating." Marisol frowned, an adorable pout on her face. Cisco shouldn't have found it so endearing, but he did.

"Ahh, I'm sorry. Next time I'll make sure to write an appropriate description."

"You're teasing me."

"Maybe a little." Cisco smirked.

The corners of Marisol's lips twitched up in a smile. Her gaze dipped down to his lips, lingering before moving back up. "I don't like a tease."

No, he imagined a girl like her wouldn't. A spoiled daddy's girl who got what she wanted.

Cisco didn't get a chance for rebuttal. The lights in the venue dimmed, followed by excited screams from the crowd. Moments later, the sound of the bass drum thumped a rhythmic beat. He felt it in his chest as if it were his own heart beating loudly for all to hear. The electric guitar played a single note, and the stage lights flashed as a group of four took the stage.

Pasión Rebelde was a band Cisco recently started to listen to. When he heard they were opening up for The Sinner's Web, he was excited by the prospect of seeing them perform. The drummer, guitarist, and lead singer were proud Mexican-American women, and their bassist was the lead singer's husband. They opened with their single called "Mundo Nocturno." It was a heavy metal song sung in both English and Spanish about living in someone else's shadow.

Cisco turned to take in Marisol, hoping she was enjoying it. She bobbed her head, hair bouncing around her. To his surprise, she was silently singing along to the song. "You know them?" he asked, impressed. This woman was a well of musical knowledge.

It was dark, but he swore he saw her brown cheeks redden.

"Yeah. Just a few of their songs. I really like this one. It's on my shower playlist."

And now Cisco was picturing Marisol in the shower. Fuck, he needed to get his shit together.

"You're going to have to show me this playlist," he said.

"If you want, I can play it on the way back to my house." It was a shy offer, as if she expected him to turn her down. Maybe she wasn't as spoiled as he initially thought—like she had heard no often in her life.

"Only if I can sing the ones I know. I'm a great singer."

Marisol laughed. "You literally told me how horrible of a singer you are when we got here."

Cisco shrugged. "I've changed my mind."

She rolled her eyes at his response, feigning annoyance, though he could see the playfulness in her eyes. For the rest of the set, he was distracted by her excitement. It was contagious. He got up twice to get them another round of drinks and snacks. This would be his last beer since he was the driver and wouldn't put Marisol's safety at risk.

By the time Pasión Rebelde played their last song, Marisol was cheering loudly. It was such a switch from the serious, no-nonsense façade she donned when uncomfortable. Letting loose made everything about her more vibrant.

"Is there another band before The Sinner's Web?" Marisol was out of her chair, bouncing on the balls of her feet, sipping on her beer.

"Nope, they are next." Cisco pushed off his chair to join her, leaning against the balcony. Marisol wasn't drunk yet, but she was definitely starting to feel good. He made a mental note to cut her off so she didn't wake up tomorrow with a killer headache.

Marisol let out a girlish squeal. "Ugh, I'm so excited. You know, I don't ever do these types of things."

"Going to rock concerts?"

"Yeah. The classical shit my parents dragged me to was a snooze fest, and full of pompous aristocrats. There are only so many violin solos I can sit through. Plus, I have to do it sober," she whined, like that was the worst thing in the world. It honestly didn't sound appealing to him.

"And then we go to these pretentious afterparties—"

"Parties can be fun," he interrupted.

"Not these. It's a bunch of rich assholes bragging about how rich they are." She paused before adding, "Sometimes the food is good though."

Cisco could empathize with her. Having money made many people arrogant, which was why he never made his wealth his personality. In fact, in many ways he rebelled against the image of wealth. He wasn't the richest man by a long shot, but he had more than enough to live comfortably, invest in his business, and take care of his family. Taking care of his loved ones was his biggest motivator in every aspect of his life. From going to an Ivy League school, majoring in business, to opening his own shop.

He worked his ass off for what he had. Not for the sake of simply having money, which was nice, but to provide for those he cared about.

"Sorry, you probably think I'm just a spoiled brat complaining about stupid shit," she said flippantly.

"I don't think that at all," Cisco replied automatically.

Marisol furrowed her brow, glancing at him. "You don't?"

"Nah, I think people treat you like a princess but demand things from you without asking your opinions on the matter. I think you go along with it because it's easier than fighting."

Judging by the way Marisol's gaze dropped and the way she bit her lip, Cisco knew his assessment was pretty spot-on.

But he didn't bring her out here to be her therapist. She had Alice for that. He invited her to have a good time. They could save trauma bonding for their next date...if she agreed to see him again. Which he hoped she did.

"Need something else to drink? Water or soda?" he suggested, changing the topic.

"Water would be nice." Marisol relaxed at the change in topic.

Cisco grabbed two waters from the mini fridge before handing one to Marisol. She thanked him then pointed to the stage. "What are they doing?"

Cisco watched the guys in black change out instruments. "It's a set change," he said. "Basically, this crew takes down the last band's instruments and sets up the next."

"Ah, okay. Are they part of the band's crew? Or do they work here?" she asked, genuinely interested.

"A bit of both. The band's crew know what their band likes and how to set it up. The crew here can be more manpower to help. A few of the guys are my buddies. I tattoo them."

Marisol strained her neck as if to get a better look at the men working. Most of their tattoos were on full display, but with the dim lighting, it was hard to make them out. "You're really talented. How long have you been a tattoo artist?"

"I started when I was around seventeen? Maybe eighteen. Learned from my tío. He owns his own shop down in Texas, and every summer I would vacation there, learning from him. He was damn good. He's retired now because of his eyesight, but he still gives me advice from time to time." Cisco smiled, thinking about how his tío Armando always brought a flood of good memories from summer and the brutal Texas heat.

"What about you? What do you do?" Cisco asked.

Marisol just shrugged. "I used to work at my father's winery. But currently, I only help out when needed. Sometimes I'll help my sister at her bookstore, but other than that, I don't have a dream job like yours. I'm not sure what I would do, but I'm really organized. So maybe event planning? That could be fun."

Marisol seemed like a woman with a Type A personality. He could see her thriving when it came to events because she would plan for everything and make sure the event went on without problems. "Well, I know who to call if I decide to do a grand opening at my next shop."

Marisol flashed him a wide smile that sent heat straight through his body. She didn't get the opportunity to respond to him though because the house lights dimmed once again, and The Sinner's Web theme music started to play and pump up the crowd.

"Oh my god, is it time?" Marisol squealed and reached out to touch his arm.

Her excitement was infectious, and Cisco couldn't help but grin.

"It's time," he said, his voice tinged with anticipation.

Marisol's fingers tightened around his arm, her grip firm with childlike wonderment. A charged energy rippled through the air as the lights dimmed, and for a brief moment, the crowd held its breath. Then, one by one, the band members stepped onto the stage. The silence shattered—cheers erupted, a deafening roar of applause and screams filling the venue as the audience came alive.

CHAPTER 10

Marisol

"We are The Sinner's Web, and we want to hear you scream, California!" the lead singer yelled into the mic, followed by a chorus of screams and chants from the crowd. Not even Marisol was immune to the excited energy coursing through the crowd untethered.

A euphoria of music filled her body and couldn't be contained. She screamed with the rest of the crowd the lyrics to the band's most popular song. For the first time ever, she allowed all her walls to break down so she could enjoy her favorite band without any restraints. The booze in her system also did wonders to help boost her confidence.

Next to her, Cisco bobbed his head along with the drums, singing every word alongside her. He was right. He was a terrible singer, but so was she, which made it all the more fun. When he noticed she was laughing at him, he proceeded to amp up the goofiness and jump—dance?—around. He reached for her, attempting to get her to join him.

Marisol laughed at first, trying to push him away as thoughts of what her mother would think if she saw her now plagued her mind. She wouldn't recognize her daughter singing out loud to an underground rock band. But was that such a bad thing?

She was already here, disappointing her mother. Might as well go all out. Marisol matched his energy, jumping and pumping her fist to the beat while she sang like an angsty teenager who was finally let out of the house. In many ways, it felt like that.

The Sinner's Web played all her favorite songs and never once lost their energy. Neither did the audience as they belted out every song. A few people from the crowd below started to crowd surf, something Marisol had only ever seen in movies. It looked fun, but she could never have that many hands roam all over her body. Especially in places that should only be reserved for the bedroom. It made her even happier that Cisco was able to get them up on the balcony. It offered a perfect view of the stage without having people pressed up against her the entire show.

She only had Cisco pressing up against her, and she quite enjoyed that. Through his clothes, she felt the hard body that lay underneath and spent an embarrassing amount of time wondering what he looked like without them. Was this a normal reaction? Because she never thought about Archie naked, and he had been her husband.

Pushing all thoughts of Archie aside for now, Marisol took Cisco's hand and allowed him to spin her to one of the band's more pop-ish songs. Everything about this night was amazing. From the drinks, to the company, and, of course, the music. Their set lasted for close to an hour and a half, but it wasn't enough. She wanted more, and the sour taste of disappointment poisoned her when the band played their last song. Even after The Sinner's Web exited the stage, the chants still echoed across the room.

"Marisol, did you hear me?" Cisco pulled her out of her funk.

"No. Sorry, what did you say?" She gave him her full attention.

Thankfully, Cisco didn't seem upset. "I asked if you were ready to meet them."

"Meet who?"

"The band?"

"What band?"

With the patience of a Catholic saint, Cisco said, "The Sinner's Web."

"Wait." Marisol put up her hand, letting her slow brain process the words. She didn't think she heard him correctly. "We are going to meet the band?"

"They probably don't have a whole lot of time, but enough time to take pictures and sign something if you want," Cisco said, oblivious to the excitement building inside her.

"Are you serious right now?"

Cisco paused, looking at her oddly. "Uh, yeah? Do you not want to meet them? Because we don't—"

"No, of course I want to meet them!" Marisol interrupted. "Oh my god, but will they let us?"

"Half-owner, remember?" He smirked. "Comes with a few perks, but we gotta hurry before they head out."

Marisol only nodded, afraid that, if she tried to speak, her voice would betray her. Cisco took her hand as if it were the most natural thing in the world, his grip warm and steady, and guided her down the stairs. The first floor was still packed with people grabbing last-minute drinks or picking up band merchandise. Cisco didn't hesitate, maneuvering her through the crowd with ease, his hand a reassuring anchor as they made their way toward a roped-off section near the stage.

A woman stationed at the entrance caught Cisco's eye, offering a quick nod before pulling back the barrier to let them through.

Backstage was a whirlwind of activity. Crew members bustled about, carrying instruments, breaking down equipment, and exchanging quick words as they passed. Two doors at the far end of the space stood propped open, leading outside, likely to where the van was parked.

Cisco didn't stop there. He continued deeper into the backstage area, bringing her into a room filled with scattered folding chairs and a long table stocked with bottled water, energy drinks, and an assortment of snacks. But it wasn't the setup that made Marisol's breath hitch—it was the people lounging around the room. Not just any people.

The Sinner's Web.

Never in her life had she been starstruck. Marisol had encountered many high-profile people and minor celebrities who ran in the same or similar circles her parents did. But she had never met anyone she admired or connected with their art like this before. It gave her pause because, what did she do? What did she say? She didn't want to say something that would keep her up in the middle of the night, wishing for the floor to open up and swallow her whole.

Fortunately, Cisco didn't seem to have the same reservations. He confidently strolled up to the group of musicians, who all turned his way. A man she recognized as the lead singer stood up, reaching to shake Cisco's hand.

"Ayy, brother. Good to see you again," he said.

Again? Cisco had met these men before?

"Miguel, it's been a while. Fucking solid show tonight," Cisco replied.

"Muchas gracias." Miguel ran a hand through his sweaty hair, which would have normally grossed Marisol out, but for a rockstar, she could make an exception.

Cisco dropped Marisol's hand. The loss of his warmth disappointed her until she felt his hand on her back, gently urging her forward. "This is Marisol. It was her first concert."

"Really?" Miguel asked, surprised. "Damn, that's some pressure. Did we disappoint?"

"Oh, no! You guys were amazing. You're like, my favorite band. I listen to your album all the time in the car." Marisol winced. She spoke too quickly, sounding like an excited groupie and not the calm and collected adult she was trying to be.

Miguel chuckled. "We're honored to be your go-to car album." He then gestured to the other guys sitting around, clearly trying to catch their breath from their set. "This is Tito, Matías, and the bastard gasping for his breath is Óscar."

Óscar flipped him off, throwing a half-empty plastic water bottle at Miguel, but he missed terribly and hit Tito's chest.

"The fuck, man?" Tito frowned, grabbing the water bottle and smacking Óscar on the head. Óscar flipped him off too, and pretty soon they were all flipping each other off and hurling insults at one another. It somehow ended with laughter breaking out amongst them.

Men were fucking weird.

"You coming to the party with us, Cisco? You can bring your girl too," Matías asked, and Marisol felt her cheeks redden.

She wasn't Cisco's girl, but the thought was appealing. Coming home to a hot tattooed man every night? She could think of worse things. But it was just a date. The first one she had in a long time after her marriage. And even before then, if she were being honest. She and Archie didn't date. They made appearances.

Guilt coiled low in her belly at the thought of Archie. A man she was still technically married to. Didn't matter that they were separated and had been for a while, or that Marisol held no love for him—on paper, she was a married woman. Something she should probably tell Cisco sooner rather than later...but now didn't seem like the right time.

"Nah, we're going to head out for the night. We just wanted to stop and get a picture," Cisco said.

"That's fine, pero we're all sweaty," Matías said, and all heads swiveled toward Marisol. "You don't mind, do you?"

Sweaty, stinky men didn't usually do it for Marisol, but she wouldn't care if they had rolled in glue and feathers. She was getting a picture with her favorite band. "I don't mind," she assured.

Cisco looked around before stopping an employee who just dropped off water bottles and asked her to take their picture. The woman nodded and moved to stand in front of them. Cisco came around and put his arm around Marisol, pulling her close to his chest. She used to hate when Archie did this because it felt too possessive. But when Cisco did it, it felt respectful. Comforting even.

The rest of the band crowded in around them and, boy, could she smell each and every one of them. She hoped these men at least showered before attending their afterparty.

"Smile," the woman said. For the first time in a long time, Marisol's smile was pure and real. Her cheeks hurt from it, not having exercised those muscles enough. This night would go down as one of her most favorite nights of her life.

Once the woman took a few pictures, she handed Cisco

back his phone. "Thank you," he said, quickly checking over the pictures. Marisol caught glimpses of each photo and barely recognized that smiling woman. "I'll send you these," he promised.

"It was really good to meet you all," Marisol said to the band. It was brief, but that didn't make it any less perfect. Each member offered her a polite smile and shook hands with Cisco before he led her out back.

Only once they were outside, away from The Sinner's Web, did she let out the excited shriek she had been holding since the moment she saw them backstage. "Ohmygod!" Her words came out rushed. "They were so nice! Do you get to meet the bands often?"

Cisco grinned, his handsome face taking on a boyish quality as he flashed his teeth at her. "I do. It's pretty cool, huh?"

"Uhm, yeah! I would be meeting all my favorite bands if I were in your position," she said.

"You are welcome to come with me to any show. I'll always give you the VIP treatment." Cisco flagged down the valet and handed the guy his ticket. He jogged off, promising to deliver it quickly.

Cisco then turned back to her, taking a step closer. Marisol's breath caught in her throat, catching a whiff of his cologne. Cedarwood and mint. Her body heated up, which was pathetic. It should take more than proximity and a good cologne to turn her on, but clearly her body had different thoughts.

"I had fun tonight," Cisco said.

"So did I." And she did. More fun than she'd had in so long.

"Can I see you again?" he asked.

Marisol opened her mouth to say she would think about it but promptly closed it. That was what she always did, wasn't it? Say she would think about it and then convince herself she wasn't allowed or didn't deserve to do something she really wanted to do. And she really wanted to see Cisco again. She found herself drawn to him and was desperate to learn more about the man who kept surprising her around every corner. To hell with the consequences, she wanted to see him again.

"Yes." She watched a beautiful smile spread across his lips. "I would like to see you again, Cisco."

She was acutely aware of their proximity. Her chest nearly brushed his. She had to angle her head up in order to see him properly. He hovered over her, licking his lips. It would be so easy to stand on her tiptoes and eliminate the distance between them until their lips were pressed together. If she were a brave woman, she would do just that.

But her bravery sobered up half an hour ago.

The moment passed just as quickly as it came. Cisco's car pulled up beside them, and it took a moment for him to move. He lingered there and seemingly made his decision because soon he leaned down and pressed a faint kiss to her cheek.

It was perfect.

It was not enough.

"Let me take you home, Princesa," he said and opened the car door for her. She had been called princess before and normally hated it. Usually, it was to mock her or remind her how spoiled she was. But not the way Cisco said it. It was... different. Kind.

Not wanting the night to end, but knowing it had to, Marisol got into the car and let him drive her home. For the entire car ride, she couldn't think of anything else but his lips on her cheek.

CHAPTER 11

Marisol

Even for a Sunday, Sunset Diner was unusually crowded. Navigating between tables and weaving through the throng of diners felt like an Olympic event as Marisol hurried after the hostess. She was convinced the hostess was practically sprinting to their table. Of all days, she had chosen to break in her new boots today, and they punished her for it with every step, squeezing her feet uncomfortably as she jogged to keep up.

"Here you go. Your waitress will be with you soon," she said and then disappeared back into the crowd before Marisol could thank her. Not that she could blame the poor woman. The line behind Marisol was out the door. Sunset Diner's food was good, but she wasn't sure if they were line-out-the-door good.

Taking a seat at the table, Marisol pulled out her phone to see a text from her sister, Lola. Today was their monthly "break shit" day, as Lola deemed it, where they would go to a rage room and break shit. But Javi and Fabian were having a father-son day. Marisol didn't know what a father did with an infant for a father-son day, but things like that were important to her sister's husband. However, that left Camilia with Lola to have a mommy-daughter day. Their first stop was having lunch with Marisol.

> Parking. A billion people here. Will be in shortly.

Marisol read the text from her sister and was about to respond when another text came in. Not from her sister this time, but Cisco. Her heart skipped a beat before she opened the text. He sent her a picture of him in front of a mirror wearing The Sinner's Web shirt he randomly found in the back of his closet. But that wasn't what caught her attention. It was his arms—his very muscular and tattooed arms—that awoke something primal deep within her.

He looked damn good. It was silly to miss a guy she barely knew and had seen yesterday, but she did. She missed Cisco, which was largely due to last night being one of the best of her life. She had looked at the picture Cisco sent of the two of them with the band at least a hundred times. She almost set it as her phone wallpaper but was afraid someone in her family would notice and start to ask questions. Questions she didn't know how to answer yet.

> Guess who is going to be playing the entire The Sinner's Web album on repeat today and possibly piss Tiny off?

> And Tiny is...?

> My cousin. Lyana. You met her at the shop.

Ah, yes, her. Images of her nametag resurfaced from her

time at the tattoo shop. She smiled at the thought of the teenager complaining to Cisco and the two having an all-out music war in the shop.

Before she could respond, another text from Cisco came through.

> Last night was fun. I want to see you again soon, Princesa.

"What are you smiling at?" a familiar voice broke through her Cisco fog, and Marisol jumped, quickly blackening her screen. She looked up to see her sister approaching, tilting her head down to stare at Marisol as if she could will an answer out of her.

"Nothing," Marisol said a little too quickly, which only made Lola raise her brow more. "Just a funny video I saw."

"Hi, Tía!" Camilia smiled, coming up to hug her. The genuine excitement on her niece's face always made her breath hitch. What would it be like if most people in her life looked as happy to see her as Camilia did? She certainly wouldn't be as fucked up as she was.

"Before we sit, I want to see your tattoo." She came around the table, looking put-together for a mom of two. She wore tight jeans, showing off her curves that their mother always tried to hide or make Lola feel insecure about. Her mother constantly bashed Lola for her size and put her on all kinds of crazy diets, which she would make Marisol do as well to keep her "thin and desirable" figure.

Both of them were working on that in therapy still.

"It's mostly healed now." She pulled up her dress slightly for her sister and niece to see.

Camilia gasped and reached out to gently touch Marisol's tattoo. "She's so pretty. Does it still hurt?" her niece asked curiously. "Mamá Lola always rubs special lotion on my cuts when I get hurt."

Marisol's features softened. "Well, that's because you have a good mommy."

"Oh, yes, she's the best. And I have the best daddy too," Camilia said before claiming one of the chairs at the table for herself.

"It does look beautiful. I'm so glad you went through with it." Lola took a seat next to her daughter.

"Thank you for setting it up and paying for it. You didn't have to do that," Marisol said.

Lola just waved her words away. "It's your birthday. I was happy to. Besides, I've never really given you anything big for your birthday. It was past time."

The waiter took this opportunity to come by and ask for their drink order, dissolving the awkwardness Marisol felt over her sister's comment. Lola ordered a Coke Zero, Camilia opted for juice, and Marisol said water, even though coffee sounded much better.

"So, what else did you get for your birthday?" Lola asked once their waiter left.

Marisol had a brief moment where she wondered if she should tell Lola about Cisco and going out to a concert last night. It hadn't technically been for her birthday, but it was close enough. A big part of her wanted to keep Cisco a secret for now. Something only for her until she figured out where Cisco would fit into her life and if he even stayed in her life.

So, she shrugged. "I ordered takeout. Caught up on a few shows. Mrs. Baker gifted a beautiful pair of earrings. Dad sent me a flower arrangement, and Mom...bought me a gold membership at my gym."

Lola scoffed. "Typical Mom response. I swear, that

woman…" she trailed off, turning to look at Camilia, who stared at her wide-eyed.

Unlike her daughters, Camilia loved her grandmother. Lola and Marisol were fiercely protective over Camilia and made sure their mother didn't pull the same shit on Camilia she did to them as kids. Their mother didn't see her grandkids often but was usually on her best behavior when she did.

"Anyway, I'm glad you had a good birthday. Did you spend it with any of your friends?" Lola quickly changed the subject in hopes Camilia wouldn't pry too deeply about Grandma. Her sister had made it very clear she wanted her daughter to make her own judgments.

"They were busy, which was fine. It was nice to spend the day by myself," Marisol said. It was only half a lie. She did enjoy not being bothered by anyone, but she didn't want to admit to her sister that she had no friends outside of Lola.

Her sister was smart, though, and had always been able to read her better than anyone in her family. Lola pursed her lips, and Marisol knew she was in for a lecture. Thankfully, she was spared by the waiter, who came by again to take their order. Both Camilia and Lola ordered banana pancakes, and Marisol ordered a veggie omelet with turkey bacon, pretending to not notice her sister's reproachful glare at her food choice.

Not that Marisol could blame her. Turkey bacon kind of sucked, but Marisol was a creature of habit. She had always ordered this and didn't have the mental energy to choose something else.

Once their waiter left, Marisol was no longer safe from her sister and whatever she had brewing in her head. "Your friends are busy often," she mentioned casually, baiting Marisol like a trained fisherman.

"Our schedules don't align." She shrugged.

"They never seem to unless it's an event where all Mom's friends will be. Ever think that you may want to consider new friends?"

Oh, Marisol considered that quite often. The problem was that making friends as an adult was hard. Especially when she didn't go to work, have any hobbies that involved other people, or go out to bars. Did people even meet friends at bars? She was so far removed from social life, she wouldn't even know where to go to make friends. Maybe thirty-year-olds hung out at Michael's or Target.

"You're alone a lot, Tía," Camilia said, adding salt to the open wound. She spoke with all the innocence only a child could possess, so really Marisol couldn't be too wounded.

"She's not wrong, you know." Lola's words weren't unkind, but it did little to squash the embarrassment—and resentment—brewing inside her. It was easy for her sister to say things like that. She spent her whole life making connections outside the family while Marisol was forced to grow up fast and learn how to make herself into a pretty accessory her mother could tote around at will.

Needless to say, there wasn't a lot of time to make friends.

"I think I have a solution for you though," Lola went on.

"Oh, do you?" Marisol was unable to keep the bite out of her tone. If Lola or Camilia noticed, neither commented on it.

"I do. I was taking Fabian to his doctor appointment yesterday, and the nurse and I got to talking. She mentioned that, on the weekends, she volunteers at the animal shelter. You know the one off Sulphur Springs Road?"

"Yes," she said tentatively, not sure if she liked where this conversation was headed.

"Well, they are having a free pet adoption next weekend

because they are at capacity. I think you should go check it out and get—"

"I'm going to stop you there," Marisol said, putting her hand up. "There is no way I'm bringing a dog home. Do you understand how labor-intensive a dog is? I'll have to take it out multiple times a day. Forget traveling. I'd have to be home to let the dog out and feed it. And there's no way I'm picking up dog poop. Besides, dogs don't like me."

"That's not true. You don't like dogs. Which is fine," Lola said quickly before Marisol could interrupt. "I wasn't talking about a dog though. I feel like you would do well with a cat."

"A cat?"

"Yes, maybe a kitten, though they are a lot of work," Lola said.

"Mamá Lola, are we going to get a dog?" Camilia asked cutely, just as their food came. Marisol's veggie omelet looked drab compared to their sweet, buttery pancakes.

"Your father wants one soon, but I want Fabian to be a little older," she said before looking back at Marisol. "You like cats. This could be a good thing."

She had one cat sweatshirt as a preteen, and she was still not living it down. "I like the thought of a cat," she mumbled. But the real thing? She'd have to clean the litter box, take it to the vet, and make sure it had food and water. Granted, these things were much easier to do than caring for a dog, but it still seemed like a big commitment.

But, on the other hand, it might be nice not to come home to an empty condo day after day. A pet would have no choice but to like her. Probably.

"You should at least go. What's the harm in checking it out?" Lola asked, dabbing at the syrup running down her pink lips.

"I guess I could check it out...if I don't have anything else going on." She didn't, but Lola didn't need to know that.

Her answer pleased her sister because Lola grinned and got out her phone. "Okay, I'm going to text you all the info. And for once, don't tell Mom you are thinking about getting a pet. You know she'll just talk you out of it if she knows."

Just like their mom denied them pets growing up, not wanting to take care of another "thing."

"I rarely call Mom up to chat." And this would be one thing she definitely wouldn't mention if she did.

A moment later, her phone buzzed as Lola's text came in. "Pet Adoption Extravaganza" flashed in gaudy colors across her phone. These people seriously needed to hire a better graphic designer.

The "Extravaganza" would take place next weekend with promises of free dogs and cats, though donations were welcome. Apparently they had well over three hundred pets all looking for their "fur-ever home."

Was she seriously considering doing this?

CHAPTER 12

Marisol

I think my sister wants me to get a cat.

Cats are nice. I'm more of a dog person.

Yeah…but I don't know if I'm a cat person. Definitely not a dog person.

Knew there had to be something wrong with you. 😊

I'll let you know if I have a new fur baby tomorrow.

Name it Lil Cisco.

Gross.

The air was ripe with the fresh scent of piss and shit. There was no escaping it, even in her car. The smell permeated the air and slipped through every opening and crevice. Why the hell was she here? She didn't even think she wanted a pet, and yet here she was, at nine in the morning, parked by an old, smelly building with a line out the door.

It was because she felt like she owed it to her sister. Like coming here would somehow make her feel better about how badly she treated Lola growing up. The thought of turning around and driving back home was tempting...but she was already here. It would feel like a waste not to go in and at least check it out.

With her mind made up, Marisol got out of her car. The scent was only worse out in the open, but she hoped she'd eventually get used to it. That or pass out from the fumes.

By the time she made it to the end of the line, it had started to move, and people were heading inside. Excited children with their parents spoke animatedly about the pet they would soon adopt and whose bed they would sleep in tonight. A few older women stood in a cluster, all discussing if they should get a cat or kitten. From the sounds of it, the discussion was getting heated.

To say that Marisol felt out of place was an understatement.

She slipped in between the empty spaces of people, making her way inside. The room was small but open. Two doors on opposite sides of the room led to two different areas. One for dogs and the other was marked cats. The boisterous barks from the dogs made her happy she didn't need to go through that way to get to the cats. Already she was overstimulated and overwhelmed and didn't want to add anything more to the mix.

Most of the crowd seemed to be going left toward the dogs, which left the right wide open for her to sneak through. The sounds were muffled the moment she stepped through the door into a white room filled with plexiglass cages. Soft purrs and meows followed her the further she walked into the room. Most people stayed toward the front where all the small kittens were, which left the back completely open for her perusal.

Marisol had never seen so many cats in her life, in all different colors and various sizes. She saw a gray cat with white whiskers. According to the sign on his cage, his name was Mr. Whiskers. Mr. Whiskers had a more extensive hair routine than her, judging by how shiny and luscious his coat was.

She didn't stop at Mr. Whiskers. There were tons of other cats to see, and Marisol took them all in. The same group of older women—apparently having decided upon an older cat— crowded some of the cages in the back. She maneuvered past them, toward the end of the room.

The cages back here were mostly empty, with only the occasional sleeping cat. Eventually, she didn't come upon any more, but something possessed her to make her way to the end, just to say she went through it all. Marisol was about to return to the entrance when something caught her attention.

Easily mistaken for a white cloth or small blanket, a short-haired white cat peeked its head up. Ocean-blue eyes stared back, assessing her. There was no name on the cage or anything that marked the cat as available. Feeling drawn to the lonely cat, Marisol took a step closer. The fur on the cat's back stood up on end, making her pause.

Tentatively, Marisol reached out, placing her hand at the small opening in the plexiglass. At first, the white cat did nothing but hiss. She should have pulled back and left. There were hundreds of other cats that were far friendlier, but none of them intrigued her quite like this one. She couldn't put her finger on it. Maybe because this cat was alone, away from everyone else. It wasn't getting any attention and had to defend itself because no one else was around to do it for them.

That cat reminded Marisol a lot of her.

It was as if the cat came to that realization at the same time. Slowly and cautiously, it got up and approached Marisol. She didn't move, keeping her hand where it was to let the cat decide. Soft fur soon brushed her fingers as the animal moved closer to the glass. Then a new sound appeared. Not hissing but soft, low purring.

Marisol looked around, but she didn't see any volunteers. No one was paying her any mind at all. She hesitated only slightly before reaching for the lock and unlatching it. The door opened, and blue eyes stared back at her as if to say, *well, what now?*

"You better not bite," Marisol muttered and reached for the cat. She winced once she had her hands around the animal, waiting for it to attack her, but it never did.

"Okay, this is good. We're good," she murmured and pulled the cat to her chest, gently rubbing its little head. The soft purrs only got louder. "Well, hello there. This isn't so bad, right?" she asked, talking to herself. The cat closed its eyes and lay against her.

"Wow, that's impressive," a female voice said from behind Marisol.

Marisol jumped at the sudden noise. Her heart pounded loudly in her chest. She felt like a little kid who was just caught doing something wrong.

The woman in front of her was roughly her age, with short-cropped black hair that contrasted starkly with her pale skin. It should have looked off-putting, but it worked on her, giving her a gothic vibe.

"I'm sorry, I didn't see anyone over here and—"

The woman waved her words away, showing off the numerous gold rings adorning her fingers. "Oh, don't apologize. We encourage guests to play with and pet the animals to make sure you're a good fit. I'm just surprised because she has not let a single person touch her since she arrived."

Ah, so the cat was a girl.

"Mostly she stays in the back of her cage and hisses at any of the volunteers who try to help her," the woman explained. "Which is why we have her back here all alone. We tried moving her up to the front, but she would fight anyone who tried to touch her. We didn't want any potential families getting bitten or scratched either."

"What happened to her?" Marisol asked. There was a reason this cat acted out. It wasn't a natural response, which told her she hadn't had the easiest upbringing.

"Sadly, we don't know much about her," the woman said. "We got her about a month ago. She was left at our entrance in a small makeshift cage. She was really dirty and lethargic, so we managed to get her cleaned up and fed, but since then, we haven't been able to approach her."

"Did she come with a name?"

The woman shook her head. "No, unfortunately. We've been calling her Snowball though."

Snowball. She liked that. More surprisingly, she liked the cat. Damn Lola.

"What is the process of adopting?" Marisol asked.

As if understanding her, Snowball began to purr louder. She leaned forward and licked Marisol's hand with her scratchy tongue. It was gross, but also kind of cute.

"There's some paperwork to fill out and a quick pet safety lesson," she said.

Marisol looked down at Snowball, who was content in her arms. Was she really going to do this? She thought about leaving Snowball behind, and the thought was physically painful. She couldn't leave this cat alone, always on the defense every time someone walked by. That was no life at all.

"I would like to adopt Snowball."

The woman grinned, her pretty face brightening. She clapped her black-manicured hands together. "That's wonderful. Follow me, and we will get you and Snowball ready to go. Did you hear that, Snow? You have your *fur*-ever home!"

Snowball appeared unbothered by her joy.

Marisol followed the woman out of the cat room, through a door she missed at the end of the room. It led to an office space with a few other volunteers and people adopting pets. The woman took the last available computer and sat down, gesturing for Marisol to take a seat on the wooden chair.

"Do you have your ID on you?" she asked.

Marisol shifted Snowball's weight to one arm and dug through her purse until she found her wallet. "Yeah, here it is." She passed the ID over.

"Marisol Roberts. That's a pretty name," she said. "I'm Stella. Been here for about two years volunteering. My partner says I like animals more than people, which is accurate. People suck. Pets give us undying love and devotion."

"People can be...complicated," Marisol agreed, which seemed like an understatement.

Stella passed Marisol a clipboard with things to sign and fill out. Most of it was simple. Her name, where she lived, if she ever had a pet before. The last page was an acknowledgment for responsible pet owners, detailing exactly what she needed to do to care for Snowball.

"I'll give you a copy of the last page," Stella said once Marisol handed her back the paperwork. "It details Snowball's diet and records. Like I said earlier, we don't have any of her history before she came to the shelter, but we've been told she is roughly five years old, and we managed to get her up-to-date on all her shots. You'll still want her to get into a vet soon for assessment. Do you live in the area?" When Marisol nodded, Stella searched through the messy desk until she located a yellow paper.

"Here, take this. These are vets and clinics we recommend in the area. It's a good place to start if you don't have one you like going to. Do you have any questions for me?"

"Yeah, what type of food should I be feeding her? Is one brand better than the other? I'm new to this," she admitted reluctantly, afraid Stella would deem her incompetent and take Snowball away from her. She just met the little white cat, but already she was forming a bond with her. As irrational as it seemed, she was excited, albeit nervous, to take Snowball home.

"On the back of the 'How to care for your cat' paper, we wrote down what we have been feeding her here and potential wet food you could also give her. You really want to avoid artificial preservatives and carbohydrate fillers. The packages will list all the ingredients, but if you use the one we have been giving Snowball, you should be fine," Stella assured.

There were so many other questions Marisol had, but she didn't know where to start and didn't want to overthink the situation. She would figure it out or enlist her sister's help since Lola was the reason she was getting a pet in the first place.

Stella excused herself before coming back out with a box carrying case. There were air holes at the top, and Marisol was horrified when it was placed in front of her. The very first thing she would buy Snowball was a proper carrying case, because this just seemed inhumane. It wasn't, but Snowball still deserved better.

"One last thing," Stella said as Marisol placed Snowball in the box, saying a silent apology to her. She looked up just in time to see Stella hand her a neon-green paper. "I don't usually give this to everyone, but you seem to have a way with animals that would be greatly appreciated around here."

Marisol took the flyer and read the bold words at the top: *Volunteers wanted.*

"You don't need to answer right now, but we would definitely love to have you on the team. You have the right vibes that would fit in with the rest of us, and clearly you have a way with animals.

"Our number is on the front." She pointed to the contact information. "I'm here every Thursday through Monday. Just call and ask for me if you have any questions. Feel free to drop in too. I really hope to hear from you, Marisol." Stella's smile was genuine and friendly, reminding her of a gothic golden retriever.

It felt nice to be wanted, and that was nearly enough for Marisol to agree, but her father always told her to take time to think through decisions and not act on impulse. She figured that would apply to this situation as well. "Thank you. I'll let you know soon."

Stella seemed content with her answer and smiled. "Do you need help out?"

The offer was kind, but Marisol shook her head. "I got it."

"It was good to meet you, Marisol. I hope we hear back from you soon. Just take this door here, and the parking lot will be to your left." Stella went to open the door for her.

Marisol gathered the paperwork, hoping she remembered everything, and then grabbed Snowball, who meowed from the box. *I know, I'll get you out soon,* she thought.

"Thank you for your help," she said as she passed Stella.

"Happy to. Have a good day and enjoy your new family member!" Stella called before the door shut.

Walking quickly, Marisol fumbled for the keys and unlocked the door. As soon as she was inside with the AC on, she opened the box up. Snowball jumped out of it with an annoyed meow. She walked in circles on her seat before plopping down, looking regal and comfortable within her car.

Then reality sank in, and, holy shit, Marisol just adopted a cat.

"Fuck," she groaned and reached for her phone. Her finger hovered over Lola's number to call her and demand she help Marisol with everything Snowball would need. But then she scrolled back up and clicked on another name. She hadn't seen him since their date, but they had been texting pretty much every day. So, calling him now wouldn't be weird...right? Before she could talk herself out of it...

He picked up on the second ring. "Texting wasn't good enough for you anymore, Princesa?"

She ignored the warmth that went through her body each time Cisco called her Princesa. "I adopted a cat!" she blurted.

"Hey, that's awesome. You weren't sure if you'd actually get one today," he said, ignorant of Marisol's rising panic.

"Is it awesome though? Or did I just make a stupid decision?" she asked, unable to keep her anxiousness out of her voice.

"Marisol—"

"I mean, where do I even go to get Snowball food? Would Trader Joe's have it? That's where I get my food. And what about a litter box or toys? Cats need toys, right? I don't know any pet stores around. Fuck, maybe I jumped into this too quickly."

There was silence on the other end of the phone that went on so long, Marisol had to make sure the call didn't drop. It didn't. Then, finally, Cisco said, "Send me your location. I'm coming to get you."

CHAPTER 13

Cisco

"This isn't Trader Joe's." Marisol angled her body to get a better look at where Cisco had taken her. She was correct. This wasn't Trader Joe's. Because Trader Joe's wasn't a pet supply store, and Cisco feared for the cat if Marisol was left to her own devices. That was why he left work to come help her. Definitely no other reason.

It was a perfect day for Cisco to leave work early. He intentionally didn't schedule any clients since he was going to help Tiny with inventory. His cousin wasn't thrilled to be left to deal with the work by herself, but the extra two hundred dollars he promised made her a little less mad at him. Especially after he mentioned how much he enjoyed Marisol's company, and how he hoped this could turn into something serious one day.

"Someone must be twitterpated," Tiny had said before he left.

"What the fuck is that?"

Tiny rolled her eyes at his lack of pop culture knowledge. "Have you never seen *Bambi*? You know, *twitterpated*," she stressed again like repeating the word would somehow make him understand.

It didn't.

"Trader Joe's doesn't have what you need," Cisco said as he unbuckled himself. He reached over to unhook Marisol's seatbelt, but the cat—Snowball, apparently—hissed at him from her lap and swatted at his hand.

"Lovely cat you found," he mumbled.

Marisol smiled, happily petting Snowball, who leaned into her touch and purred loudly. "She's mean and hates everyone. That's why I like her."

"I'm glad you bonded with a demon cat." Since Snowball was now officially distracted, Cisco risked his hand and quickly undid Marisol's seatbelt for her. The soft laugh he earned from her made it worthwhile.

"This is a boutique pet store. It has all the freshest ingredi-ents and accessories spoiled pets will need. Tiny has a chihuahua, fucking terror that she spoils rotten. The damn thing eats dinner on a gold plate. She gets all her pet stuff here," he explained.

"Snowball should find this satisfactory then. Can you get my purse? Stella, the woman from the shelter, gave me a list of things she'll need," Marisol said. "Snowball can come inside, right? Since it's a pet store."

Cisco nodded. "Yeah, you can put her back in the box—"

"I will not put her back in the box. She hated that thing! I'll just carry her," Marisol argued, but before Cisco could reply that it might not be the safest option, she was out of the car with Snowball in her arms. It gave him the perfect view of her ass as she dipped her head before stepping out. If he were a better man, he'd look away and not ogle her body while her back was toward him. But he was, in fact, not a better man.

Not wanting to be left behind, Cisco got out of the car and quickly caught up to Marisol. On instinct, he placed his hand on her back, searching both ways for cars before crossing the street. He had set foot in Tiffany's Pet Co. before, so he was familiar with the layout and knew the cat stuff was toward the middle of the store.

"Oh, this is perfect." Marisol moved away from his grasp and headed toward the row of beige carts. Instead of a seat for a toddler, there was a small space for animals. She placed Snowball down, quickly making sure she was comfortable before rejoining Cisco. Her shoulder brushed against his, and he didn't imagine the way her cheeks reddened at the contact.

He took a smug satisfaction in knowing he could make this beautiful woman blush for him. Pushing his luck, he placed his hand on her back again and waited for her reaction. Marisol leaned into him. It was subtle, but he felt it.

Since their first date, he had been eager to see her again. He regretted not kissing her the night he dropped her off, but he hadn't been sure how sober she was. He wanted her to remember their first kiss, and he didn't think it was the right time. At least that was what he thought at the time. Looking at her painted red lips, pouty and begging to be kissed, he hated himself a little for missing the opportunity. He wouldn't pass it up again.

"So...where do we go?" Marisol's voice broke through his fog. He had been staring, and she noticed, judging by the sly upturn to her lips. He was caught red-handed but didn't have the decency to look ashamed.

"You have your list?" he asked.

With her hands now free, Marisol searched through her little pink bag he was holding, pulled out a wrinkled paper and handed it to him. "This is the food she needs. That's all that's on there, though."

"Then food first." He gently urged her forward. Tiffany's was not busy, only the occasional dog owner with their expensive dog snaked between the aisles. The cat aisle, full of various prestigious brands to choose from, was empty. Colorful bags of cat food lined the shelves, ranging from grain-free to carnivore food and everything in-between.

"Damn, who knew cat food was such a lucrative business?" Marisol ran her hands down a purple bag designed for outdoor cats.

"You're going to need this one." Cisco located the indoor, grain-free cat food with gut health. Whatever the fuck that meant for cats. It wasn't a particularly large bag—for the price, he would have liked it to be twice the size. Still, he put two in the cart. He then moved on to the wet food and grabbed the chicken and veggie one listed on the paper.

"Those look heavy," Marisol commented, looking at him with long black lashes.

"I'll carry them for you, Princesa. Don't worry." He winked.

"A chauffeur and a grocery boy? If this is your idea of a second date, you are doing great," she teased, eyes shining with mirth.

"Is this a second date?" he teased back. "Because if it is, I want to take you to lunch after this."

"Well, I suppose I can schedule you in. I'm dreadfully busy. Laundry to be done. Dishes to be washed."

"That's very domestic of you," Cisco joked.

"Actually, Mrs. Baker does it for me. She's wonderful."

"And Mrs. Baker is?" Cisco asked, raising a brow.

"My maid," she said simply.

Of course she had a maid. He didn't fault her for it. He had a bi-weekly cleaning company that scrubbed his house from top to bottom. He wasn't a messy person, but his time was limited, so this helped keep his house in order. Strangely enough, it also helped with his mental health. There was just something about a clean house that eased pent-up anxiety.

He didn't know Marisol well...yet, but he believed she had enough pent-up anxiety to deal with.

"Could Snowball come to lunch with us? I don't want to leave her alone yet. We could get her a carrying case?" Marisol suggested, gently brushing the cat's fur with her red-manicured nails. He thought briefly of those nails being dragged down his back while he...

Yeah, no. Definitely shouldn't be thinking of that.

"Yeah, I know a place. Let's grab the last few things she needs," he said.

Marisol allowed him to take the lead, which Cisco was all too happy with. He found her a self-cleaning litter box with odor-free litter. Marisol seemed particularly thrilled about that. To him, it looked like a little cat spaceship Snowball could shit in. After a quick Google search to look at reviews, he noticed they were overwhelmingly positive, which helped justify the hefty price point.

"Oh, I want to get one of those scratchy post things. Cats love those, I think," Marisol said once they entered the toy aisle. Toys overflowed the shelves, from squishy mouse toys to fluorescent fish on a stick. It took a bit of searching until they came upon the cat towers, all equipped with multiple cat scratching posts. He didn't know so many different types of towers existed.

"Hmm, what do you think, Snowball? Which one do you like the most?" Marisol scratched Snowball behind the ears.

Snowball looked up, cast a glance around, and put her head back down, clearly uninterested.

Cisco couldn't offer any words of wisdom. He never owned a cat in his life. Marisol inspected each tower. The short, small ones and the large towers that looked like they trained cats for the kitty Olympics. After a moment of deliberation, she pointed to a tower with three different stories and two scratching posts. "I think Snowball will like that one the most."

"Can't disappoint Snowball," he quipped before leaning down to pick up the box. "Fuck, this thing weighs a ton," he grunted as he maneuvered the box into the cart.

"Do you think it'll be easy to put together?" Marisol asked. "I'm not good at building things, but my brother-in-law is."

"I'll put it together for you."

"Oh, you don't—"

"What else does Snowball need?" Cisco cut her off. He already planned on helping her put the cat's equipment together, so he didn't want to hear her protests.

The last things they picked up were a few other furry toys and a food and water dish that could be programmed to feed and water at certain times of the day. Cisco led them to the front where he started to place everything onto the conveyor belt. He watched the price skyrocket just after two things and was once again left baffled at how much it cost to raise a spoiled pet.

"The total is four hundred and forty-eight dollars even," the teenager behind the register said. His eyes lingered a little too long on Marisol, specifically her chest, before Cisco promptly stepped in front of her, glaring.

The boy blushed and quickly looked away.

"Just one second," Marisol murmured, searching through

her purse, but Cisco already had his wallet out and handed over a black card.

Marisol's head jerked up just in time to see the teenager swipe Cisco's card. Her lips parted in silent surprise before closing abruptly once she realized what he was doing. Her honey-brown eyes met his. "You didn't have to pay for this," she said with a hint of accusation. As if by him paying, it would allow him to hold something over her. Not for the first time, it made him wonder what the people in Marisol's life were like if she was this suspicious about everything.

"I didn't," he agreed. "But the thing is, I'm trying to impress this beautiful woman's cat so she'll like me."

The faintest of smiles played on Marisol's lips. He watched her hesitate, freezing in place before making her mind up and leaning toward him. She pressed a gentle kiss to his cheek. "Thank you. Snowball appreciates it."

It was a swift kiss, a ghost of a kiss. Yet her lips seared his skin, implanting themselves on him. He felt like a damn peacock, standing up a little straighter and puffing out his chest to attract the females.

"Just Snowball?" He smirked.

Marisol winked at him, just as the teenager said, "Thank you, sir. Have a good day," and handed him back his card.

Figuring out how to fit everything in his car was a game of Tetris where he stacked cat items precariously upon one another, hoping they didn't get too jostled around on the drive to lunch. By the time he was finished packing the car and putting away the cart, because he wasn't an asshole who left carts in random places in the parking lot, he was particularly ravenous.

"How do you feel about pizza?" Cisco asked once he slid into the driver's seat.

"People who don't like pizza are psychopaths or aliens. Probably both," Marisol said, deadpan. She shimmied in her seat until she was facing him. "Actually, I was thinking we could get our food to go? Eat at my house while we—well, you —put together Snowball's things? I just really want to get Snowball home and adjusted."

He would be lying if he said he wasn't curious about what Marisol's house looked like. What she came home to every night. It seemed like an intimate look into her soul, and he was a desperate, greedy man who needed to know everything he could about her.

"Sounds good to me. I know the perfect place."

Mario's Pizzeria was bursting at the seams when Cisco opened the door for Marisol. The hostess looked frazzled as she attempted to find tables for abnormally large parties. Despite it being just the two of them, plus Snowball, the woman looked at them as if she had just seen the Grim Reaper coming to collect her soul.

"I'm sorry, ma'am, we don't allow cats in the restaurant," she said, body tensing as if waiting for impact.

"We are headed to the take-out counter. We won't be long," Cisco said, and the hostess visibly relaxed.

"Oh, of course. Just around the corner. Enjoy the rest of your day." She smiled before quickly greeting another large party wanting a table.

Cisco worked as a waiter during college, and he knew how grueling it could be. He grabbed a twenty from his pocket and slid it over to the hostess, who looked like she was about to cry at the gesture. "Thank you so much," she mouthed before taking a family back to their table.

"That was kind of you. She looked stressed," Marisol said, frowning.

"Working with the public is stressful." Cisco placed a hand on her back and led her toward the take-out counter. "Do you have a favorite pizza?"

"I usually just get pizza with veggies. But I'm open to maybe trying something different," she said.

"Then I'll surprise you." Cisco gently squeezed her hand and headed over to the counter. The man working there, in contrast to the hostess, looked calm and at ease. Granted, Cisco was the only one there, so he imagined being calm would be easy under those circumstances.

Cisco scanned the menu before spotting the roasted tomato sauce pizza with garlic, sausage, spinach, and chunks of mozzarella. He added on buttery garlic sticks because no pizza lunch was complete without them.

Just as he took out his card to pay, he heard a masculine voice behind him ask, "Marisol? What are you doing here?"

Cisco's head swiveled to the side to see a man around his age. He gave off a posh vibe and held himself like any white man with an exorbitant amount of privilege. He was dressed in designer slacks with a button-up shirt, rolled up around the arms. Cisco wondered if it was this man's version of casual-wear. His golden-brown hair was styled so not one hair was out of place, making him look like an extra at a frat party.

He turned just in time to see the expression on Marisol's face drop and all color drain from her face. It was as if she was staring at a ghost—an evil, vile ghost. The hair on the back of his neck stood on end as he tensed. He closed the space between himself and Marisol, framing his body to conceal hers.

"What's wrong?" he questioned. Not *are you okay?* Because he knew she wasn't.

"Marisol, who is this man?" the annoying, agitating voice answered from behind them before Marisol could speak.

He looked over his shoulder just in time to see the disgusted look in the stranger's eyes as he took Cisco in. Black jeans. Black shirt. Tattoos covering every available space on his body except his face. He knew what people saw when they looked at him, and it was never anything good. They thought him a low-life thug who wanted to start trouble.

"Who are you?" This time the question was directed toward him. The man's blue eyes traveled over his body, sizing him up before meeting Cisco's glare. The man stood straighter, narrowing his eyes to appear tough, but Cisco saw the under-current of fear in his expression.

"Archie, not here. Go away," Marisol said, a tremble in her voice. He had never heard her sound so small or unsure before. Was that fear? Anger? Something else? His temper flared. He didn't know this man—Archie—but he didn't like him.

"Not here?" The man laughed humorlessly. "Then where, pray tell, should we have this discussion? Color me surprised when I'm having lunch with friends, only to find my wife with another man."

His body went rigid. The happy sounds from the restaurant's patrons all faded away until he heard nothing but the ringing in his ears.

Wife? Did he say wife? The word repeated over and over in his head like an obnoxious mantra. Marisol was a married woman. He had taken a married woman on a date and was about to help her put Snowball's things together. Where would she have taken him? Surely a married couple would live together—did she just hope her husband wasn't home so she could sneak in Cisco like a forbidden fruit she just had to taste?

Hurt and confusion must have shown in his expression because Archie smirked at him. Weird reaction for a man who just found his wife cheating.

"Oh, for fuck's sake." Marisol pushed past Cisco, Snowball still in her arms as she approached Archie. She stood just a few inches shorter than him, but that didn't stop her from getting into his face. "I am not your wife. I haven't been your wife in the last two years. If you would hurry up and sign those damn divorce papers, we would both be free. I do not and will never want you, Archie."

Archie's lips twisted into a maniacal smile, like he had an ace up his sleeve they didn't know about. "Whatever you say, Wife. I'm sure I'll see you around shortly. In the meantime, be careful who you spend your time with. You never know who is watching." With those cryptic words, Archie left, disappearing into the throng of people.

He vanished as swiftly as he came. His abrupt departure uneased Cisco.

He stared after Archie as he left, both confused and irrationally annoyed. His anger only grew when he saw Marisol visibly shake, her bottom lip quivering. "Marisol..." he said, reaching for her.

Before he could make contact, Marisol stepped away. "I'm going to wait in your car." Without waiting for a response, she hurried around the corner and out of sight. She left Cisco alone with his thoughts and anger, wondering about the hostile history between Marisol and Archie.

CHAPTER 14

Marisol

Don't cry. Don't cry. Don't cry. Marisol repeated the mantra all the way through the busy restaurant and out to Cisco's car, which he mercifully left unlocked. She felt the eyes of everyone she passed bore into her, judging her every move.

Who saw that altercation? How was Archie going to spin this one? What did Cisco think of her?

The first tear rolled down her cheek. Followed by another and another until she couldn't hold back the dam any longer. Silent sobs racked her body as she clutched Snowball to her chest like a life support. Her cat purred once, licking Marisol's face. It was both gross and strangely comforting.

Every time she thought she found something good in her life, there was always someone else there to pull the rug out from under her. To remind her that she had very little autonomy when it came to her own life and future. There was always someone else pulling the strings like a puppet master, and she had no choice but to go along with it. It was just easier that way.

Archie was a man who thrived on control—meticulous, calculating, and unwilling to let anything slip through his fingers. He cared about appearances just as much as her mother did, maybe even more. It was one of the reasons she suspected he was deliberately dragging out the divorce.

The Roberts name wasn't just a name; it was a legacy, a symbol of power and prestige that carried weight in their community. Being tied to the family meant influence, doors opening that otherwise remained closed, and a level of respect that couldn't be bought—only inherited. Before Archie married into the Roberts family, he was just another wealthy man, someone with money but no real standing among the elite. But now? Now he was a wealthy man with connections, someone whose presence commanded attention simply because of the name he was attached to.

And he wasn't about to give that up. Letting her go meant losing his grip on the very thing that had elevated him beyond just another rich businessman. Prestige, power, influence—it was all wrapped up in his marriage to her, and Archie would fight tooth and nail before he let any of it slip away.

Marisol wasn't sure how long she had been alone, but when she heard the door open to her left, she quickly dabbed at her eyes. It did little to hide the fact that she had been crying. Her makeup was a lost cause at this point; she just hoped she didn't look like a clown. She certainly felt like one.

Cisco got in, the car instantly filling with his piney scent, but also the Italian herbs and marinara from the pizza. He leaned back to place the pizza in the small back seat. How he found a spot that wasn't cluttered with her cat purchases, she didn't know.

The silence hung heavy between them when he turned back around to grip the steering wheel. She knew she should say something. Anything to defuse the tension and explain herself, but the words wouldn't come. She was scared and didn't like this feeling one bit. Things were quickly spiraling out of control, and she no longer had the reins on this situation.

"I'm sorry."

"You're married?"

They spoke at once, both meeting the gaze of the other. Marisol couldn't make out what Cisco was thinking. He wore a mask of indifference. The only sign that pointed to his anger was the way he gripped the steering wheel so hard, his knuckles were turning white.

Her story with Archie was a long, complicated one that she rarely got into with anyone other than Alice. Mostly because she knew Alice couldn't judge her and wouldn't share her story with anyone else. Not that she was worried Cisco would share her story with others, but it didn't make it any easier to talk about. She should have told him about Archie before she agreed to the first date. The fear of him turning her down immobilized her.

"Technically? Yes," she whispered, just as Cisco cursed in Spanish under his breath. His mask slipped, and she could see the anger and hurt displayed on his face. It spurred her on to say more because she couldn't have Cisco getting the wrong impression of her.

"But we have been separated for two years. Married for three. Honestly? I wanted to divorce him the moment we married, but I stayed with him one year out of fear. Fear about what others would think." By others, she meant her mother. Always her mother.

"The moment I asked for a divorce, I signed the papers. He has yet to sign anything because it wouldn't look good for his image," Marisol said, tears prickling her eyes once again. "I'm working with my lawyer to finally be rid of him, but Archie is a powerful man, and my mother adores him. She doesn't want me to divorce him because it would look bad on the family, and my hands are tied, Cisco. I'm trying so hard to be free of him, but I feel like I'm the only one fighting for me."

The heaviness settled in her chest, and she felt like she could no longer breathe. She didn't want to cry. Not in front of Cisco or anyone who wasn't Alice. She had to be composed. Proper. Perfect. Never let anyone see that mask slipping. Those were the words her mother beat into her brain over and over throughout her life.

But a person could only take so much. Be told how to feel and act for so long until something inside of them fundamentally broke. She refused to cry in front of anyone. She hated showing that level of vulnerability, but to her absolute horror, tears flowed freely down her face again. The more she tried to fight them, the harder they fell.

"Fuck, Marisol..." Cisco's concerned voice rang out. At least she thought he sounded concerned. She couldn't be certain because she didn't want to spare a glance and risk crying even harder.

Stop. Fucking. Crying.

Muscular tattooed arms wrapped around her, pulling her into a hard chest. Snowball hissed before jumping from Marisol's arms to sit on the dash, tail swatting at the window. She melted into the embrace. When was the last time someone hugged her while she cried? Too fucking long ago.

"I'm sorry, Princesa. Do you want me to go back in there and punch his fucking face?" Cisco asked in all seriousness.

It was such a wild and violent thought that Marisol couldn't help but laugh. It was borderline hysterical, but she chose to ignore that. "As appealing as that sounds, the fallout wouldn't be worth it." Maybe. Probably. Though it would make her feel a lot better to see someone punch Archie in his too-perfect nose. Give his plastic surgeon a run for his money.

Finally, mercifully, the tears stopped. Cisco's hand ran up and down her back in comforting strokes. She felt his hot breaths against her shoulder. There was no reason for that to turn her on, but something coiled low in her belly. Heat rushed her body in every place that Cisco touched her. She had just been crying over her ex-husband, and now she was practically purring for Cisco. Maybe she truly was as broken as she thought.

Cisco pulled back a moment later, keeping his hands on her shoulder. She could only imagine what she looked like to him. But the way Cisco looked at her had her forgetting about everything wrong with her appearance. He looked at her like she held the secrets of the universe, with reverence and awe. Who knew it took a girl crying to get that kind of look from a man? Maybe she needed to rethink her whole no crying thing.

"Does he bother you often?" Cisco asked, still searching her face for answers.

Marisol just shrugged. "Only when it's convenient for him and inconvenient for me. Like now." She was playing it down. Some weeks she would hear from him every day. Sometimes she would go days without hearing from him, and she would think he was finally giving up, but then he or her mother would try to rope her back in.

"I'm sorry, Cisco. I should have told you. This was not how I wanted you to find out. And his behavior was awful. I'm so sorry—"

"Nah, Princesa, you don't apologize to me for a man's behavior. If he does anything to upset you or try to take advantage of you, you tell me." Cisco looked intensely at her, making Marisol blush.

It wasn't a question, but she nodded anyway. "Okay."

"Okay," he repeated. Cisco let his hands linger on her side a moment longer before wiping the last few remaining tears from her face. "Now, I'm going to take you back to your car, and then I'll follow you home so you can boss me around. Sound good?"

How could she say no to that?

"I don't like it there. Try moving it back to where it was. It's growing on me now," Marisol mumbled, holding her hand over her mouth to hide her chewing. Cisco was right: the pizza was amazing, and Marisol was indulging in her second piece—a luxury she often denied herself—while bossing Cisco around in her home.

He was the one who asked for it. She simply obliged.

Plus, she couldn't help but admire the way his muscles strained against the tight fabric of his shirt. Or the way his shirt would ride up, exposing the delicious abs he hid underneath his clothes. For all of Archie's faults, he kept up with his body, but it paled in comparison to the quick glimpses she got of Cisco.

Honestly, she didn't care where the damn cat tower went. She just enjoyed the free show Cisco was unknowingly putting on.

After the run-in with Archie, she was convinced Cisco would be done with her. She couldn't even blame him. Who would want the type of baggage she brought with her? Archie was...a lot. And so was her mother, though he didn't know that yet.

Hell, *she* was a lot. It would have been the perfect opportunity for Cisco to cut his losses, drop her off, and never see her again. But that wasn't what happened. If anything, seeing Archie made him more eager to get to her house. Whether to check to make sure he didn't truly live here or make sure she was safe, Marisol didn't know. She had a feeling it was the latter, though.

Cisco grunted as he pushed the tower back to the original spot. Truly, it was better there with the perfect view of the outside. Snowball would enjoy that. "Perfect." She smiled.

Cisco wiped his brow and looked over the last thing he needed to put together. "Where do you want the litter box?" He cut into the box with the X-Acto knife Marisol found in her junk drawer.

She hadn't considered where she would want that bulky box. Certainly somewhere out of sight.

"The guest bathroom down the hall and to the left should be fine. Do you need my help?" Marisol was about to get up when Cisco stopped her.

"Nah, I got this. Put on a movie for us to watch. I'll be done soon. Try to leave me some pizza, yeah?"

"No promises there," she hummed, taking another bite of the garlicky pizza.

The smile Cisco aimed at her was panty-melting, forcing her to squeeze her legs together. The bastard noticed her not-so-subtle movement and smirked. With one last heated glance, he carried Snowball's litter box to the guest bathroom.

What was it about this man that made her hot all over? Marisol had never been an overly sexual person, which made dating Archie easy. Sex had only lasted a few minutes, and she could just lie there. She supposed it felt good...sometimes; other times, it felt like a chore she just wanted to get over. Even as a teen and during college, she had never been drawn to sex like most people her age were.

She didn't even lose her virginity until she was twenty-five, to a man she had been dating for a year. She thought that was perfectly acceptable, but apparently it was late according to conversations she overheard. Still, Marisol never felt like she was missing out.

And then Cisco. He just looked at her. With his dumb tattooed body and his dumb smirk, and suddenly she needed to change her panties. Her body flushed in ways she didn't think she was capable of, and she craved...something. Him? His body? The connection? She felt like it was a mixture of the three.

What would it feel like to have Cisco in her bed? *Naked* in her bed. The thought alone made her breathless. She wanted to see every tattoo on his body and trace them with her finger. She wanted to kiss his body all the way down to his hip until she was confronted with his co—

"Done!" Cisco's voice penetrated her dirty thoughts. Her head snapped up just in time to see him walking back into the living room and sinking down on the couch next to her. His thigh brushed against hers, but he didn't move to give her any more space. Good, she didn't want him to.

"I think you've earned a piece of pizza." She smiled and passed him the box.

Cisco took one look inside and gasped, offended. "What is this?"

"What is what?" Marisol wrinkled her brow, trying to peer into the box, but Cisco jerked it out of her view.

"This!" He shook something limp in front of her, and it

took Marisol a moment to realize he was shaking a piece of her uneaten crust at her. "You are an adult, Marisol. How can you not eat the crust? It's the best part."

"One"—Marisol held up a perfectly manicured finger—"the crust is not the best part. And two, wait until you see how I eat my sandwiches."

"I don't think I'm ready for that." Cisco feigned repulsion before popping the entire pizza crust into his mouth, stunning her. "You don't know what you're missing," he murmured around the food.

"I think I'll be fine." Marisol chuckled, rolling her eyes.

Snowball meowed from her perch on the windowsill as if agreeing with Marisol. The cat had adjusted quite easily and quickly to her new house. It felt like Snowball had always been here. She still wasn't sure about Cisco, but the curious cat had watched his work as if supervising his every move.

Marisol couldn't help but think how well Cisco fit in here too. Their conversation was easy. He didn't ask her any more about Archie, which she appreciated. They simply talked about their favorite music and the concert. She didn't speak much about herself, because, really, there wasn't much to say, but she enjoyed learning everything she could about Cisco.

She learned he spent most of his weekends at Lucky Rabbit to discover new bands and often tattooed the employees. That most of his employees were family, and he enjoyed having a family business. He went to a prestigious college for business while tattooing and working at a restaurant on the side. Cisco liked to travel and recently went to visit family in Mexico. It was all fascinating, and she soaked it up.

But time was a thief. After they ate their way through the pizza—her without the crust—and finished the second movie of the night—which they paid very little attention to—Marisol looked at the time. She was disheartened to see that it was almost eleven, and she had a therapy session in the morning. Normally her sessions were on Mondays, but Alice had a last-minute function she needed to attend and didn't want Marisol to have to wait another week before being seen. She greatly appreciated that.

Cisco seemed to notice the time too because he angled his body toward hers and took her hand. It felt like the most natural thing in the world. "When can I see you again?"

It was a surreal experience to want to be seen again. Not only wanted, but for someone to *need* to see her again. She contemplated the right response. She didn't want to be seen as too eager and come off as clingy. But she also didn't want to wait too long to see him again.

Fuck it, she was going to risk sounding clingy.

"I have therapy tomorrow, but after?" she suggested, hoping she didn't sound as desperate as she felt.

"I'll pick you up from Alice's office," he said automatically, like it wasn't a crazy idea to see each other again so soon.

"I'll have my car, so why don't you meet me here?" she suggested.

"I'll take care of it."

"But how—"

"Princesa, I'll take care of it. Let me pick you up, okay?"

How could she argue with that? And why the hell did it make her swoon to be taken care of like this?

"Okay," she said softly, unable to hide her smile.

"It's late," Cisco said, looking at the front door as if it personally offended him.

"It is."

"I should go."

"Probably," she agreed.

His eyes dipped to her lips. Unknowingly, she ran her tongue along her bottom lip, wetting it. Cisco's pupils dilated. "I'm going to kiss you before I leave, Princesa."

"Okay," Marisol said breathlessly. Her heart pounded loudly in her chest as an invisible string pulled her closer.

She didn't have time to be self-conscious about her breath or if she was a good kisser because Cisco's lips were on hers. It was soft, but mighty. She felt the kiss throughout her entire body. Kissing had never been like this before. Never made her feel lightheaded and wanted all at once.

But it was too fast. Too light. Just as quickly as it started, it was over. Marisol's eyes fluttered open in time to see Cisco staring—admiring? She had half a mind to pull him back and feel his lips on hers for longer, but she held back. She couldn't muster up the courage.

"I'll pick you up tomorrow."

"Okay," she said because apparently that was the only word she was capable of.

Then all too soon, Cisco was gone. Snowball took over the place where he had been and snuggled up to Marisol's side. She knew she should go to bed, but her body was still alive with the thought of their kiss.

CHAPTER 15

Marisol

There was no way Marisol was going to leave Snowball alone during her first full day at the house. Since it was her sister's idea, Marisol felt it was only right that she call Lola for help—to which her sister replied with a surprised, yet excited scream and hung up. Marisol took that as a confirmation, so she started getting ready to meet Alice.

Twenty minutes later, there was a knock on her front door. She barely answered it when her sister barreled past her and into her condo, dragging her husband, Javi, behind her. Snowball was in good hands, even though she didn't seem overly fond of Javi. Must be a men thing.

Smart cat.

Lola pried, trying to get Marisol to talk about her plans for the day. Marisol told her she had a therapy appointment—which was true—and she needed to run errands. It wasn't as if she was hiding Cisco... No. She was very much hiding Cisco. But not for the reasons people might think. She wasn't ashamed of him. She simply wanted to keep this slice of happiness to herself for a little while longer. However, in the spirit of working on her relationship with her sister, she let her know that she had a date.

It was the wrong fucking thing to say though, because her sister demanded to know everything. Who was he? How did they meet? Had they been out before?

Marisol kept her answers vague, trying to give her as little as possible without lying to her. Thankfully, Javi saved her by reminding Lola that Marisol was going to be late for her appointment if she didn't leave. Lola was clearly not happy but acquiesced.

After promising to keep in contact, Marisol left the house with enough time to stop for coffee on the way over. Alice's office was abnormally chilly when she arrived, but clearly her therapist didn't agree. She came out in a knee-length skirt and a short-sleeve shirt. She was also fanning herself with a makeshift fan created from computer paper.

"Never get old, dear. Hot flashes are the worst." Alice stepped aside to allow Marisol to walk through. She cursed the thigh-length black dress she wore, wishing she thought to put on a snowsuit before leaving the house.

Graciously, a blanket was awaiting her when she walked into the room. She sank down on her usual spot on the sofa, unfolding the blanket to drape over her bare legs. She was well aware this could quite literally be her comfort blanket for the duration of their session.

"The last time we spoke, you mentioned you were debating going on a date. Did you ever come to a decision?" Alice asked, ever the professional. She wasted no time getting down to the nitty gritty of it all. Marisol appreciated this approach because there was no time for bullshitting.

She still couldn't believe it was only last week that she went on her first date with Cisco. It felt much longer but also like no time had passed at all. Her feelings for him had developed quickly and only grew stronger. She was both thrilled and terrified. Mostly terrified, but she tried not to stew on that fact for too long.

"I did and agreed to the date."

If Alice was surprised by this, she didn't show it, but she did smile from ear to ear. "Did you? And how'd it go?"

"It went really well," Marisol admitted with a sheepish smile. "He took me to a concert to see a band we both enjoy. It was probably one of the best days of my life."

"That sounds lovely. Do you plan on seeing him again?"

"I have actually. He helped me pick out things for Snowball."

"And Snowball is?" Alice asked, reminding Marisol she hadn't yet filled Alice in on that new development in her life. That was a rarity because she told her therapist everything and practically in real time.

Marisol recapped the last few days. How Lola suggested she check out the shelter during free adoption day, to finding Snowball and how they clicked immediately. How Cisco came to pick her up and shop for everything Snowball needed. And finally ending on how they ran into Archie, but the day wasn't ruined by him. It was still horrific to see him.

"Wow," Alice said once Marisol finished her updates. "You've been through a lot in these last few days. I imagine seeing Archie was hard, especially while you were out with Cisco."

Marisol couldn't help but shift uncomfortably. That moment had sucked, and for a second, she believed Archie had ruined everything. Hell, she thought Cisco believed the same thing. Unlike Archie or anyone else in her family, though, Cisco listened to her explain and chose to believe her. Not only did he choose to believe Marisol, but he also sided with her and promised to help her if Archie became a problem again.

"It wasn't pleasant, but it didn't end badly. Cisco came back to my house to put together Snowball's tower and litter box. We spent the evening together." She conveniently left out the kiss. She told Alice most things, but there were certain things Marisol wanted to keep to herself.

"I want to circle back to the shelter. You mentioned meeting someone named Stella? Can you tell me more about the flyer Stella offered you?" Alice asked, crossing her legs and balancing her notebook on her lap.

"She gave me a flyer that talked about volunteering. Stella encouraged me to check it out. Said I might be a good fit." She shrugged.

"Did she specifically say why you'd be a good fit?" Alice inquired.

"Oh, I think it's because I was able to connect with Snowball. She thought I might be able to connect with other stubborn animals, I guess."

Alice wrote something down in her notebook. "And what do you think about volunteering?"

"I haven't really thought about it," Marisol replied honestly. She had forgotten about the interaction until this moment. "Why?"

"Well, to me it sounds like something you'd excel at."

"Why?" she asked again, unable to hide her confusion.

"Because it highlights your strength." Alice must have noticed the confusion written across Marisol's face because she added, "There's a lot of organization and planning that goes into volunteering. Those are two things you excel at. You've also been wanting to meet new people with similar interests as you who aren't part of your parents' crowd. Well, I can't think of a better start than the people you volunteer with."

"So, you think I should volunteer?" Marisol raised a brow. She had not been expecting to talk about this. Hell, she didn't even consider it, but now the thought had bloomed.

"That's a decision you need to make, but I think it could be a good way to spend your days. The last time you did something out of your comfort zone, you got asked out on a date by a guy you are clearly connecting with. This might be another good opportunity for you. At the very least, it would give you an excuse for when your mother calls for some last-minute 'favor.'"

Once again, Alice provided a perspective she hadn't thought about. Marisol was never good on the spot, and when her mother randomly called for a favor, she had a hard time saying no. Partially because she couldn't come up with an excuse, and partially because she didn't want to disappoint her.

It seemed like a selfish reason to start volunteering, but she couldn't bring herself to feel bad about it.

"I'll think about it," she said, falling back on her go-to answer. Commitment was just too...final.

Alice nodded encouragingly. "Have you heard from your mother recently?"

Marisol shifted uncomfortably in her seat. Slowly, she shook her head. "No, it's been more than a week since I last heard from her." She hated talking about her mother. Her mother was like Beetlejuice. Say her name three times, and she would be summoned. She didn't like hearing from her, but it was worse when she didn't hear from her. It made her anxiety spike. It was a lose-lose situation.

"Do you think she's getting the sense you are no longer

interested in giving in to her demands?" Alice asked, not unkindly.

Once again, Marisol shrugged. If her mother saw her now, she would chastise Marisol for her rudeness. "No. I'm sure she's busy, and I'll hear from her soon." Sounded like a problem for a future Marisol.

Alice poked around at the subject for a little while longer, but Marisol wasn't receptive to her probing. Call it avoidance, but these last few days, Marisol had experienced levels of peace and joy she wasn't accustomed to. She was unwilling to give that up.

The remainder of the session passed quickly, with neither of them bringing up the topic of her mother again. However, Alice took a moment to reinforce her suggestion of Marisol volunteering, believing it could be a positive experience for her. Though unsure, Marisol assured Alice she would think about it.

"That's all the time we have today, Marisol. Did you need to schedule another meeting this week, or would our scheduled meeting for next week suffice?" Alice asked, pushing off her chair.

Marisol followed in pursuit. "Next week should be fine."

Alice took the lead, opening the door to the waiting room for her, and immediately stopped in her tracks. "Oh." Her eyes widened. "Cisco, was I expecting you today? I don't remember seeing you on my calendar."

A deep voice that filled her body with butterflies replied, "You weren't. I'm waiting on her."

Marisol rounded the corner to see Cisco, dressed in his usual black jeans and a button-up black shirt. Matching blacks. It was a small detail, but an important one. From here, she could smell his cologne. It wasn't overpowering, just a light earthy smell she had come to really like. Sitting next to him was Tiny, his cousin and the teenager who ran the front desk at his tattoo shop.

"Oh, I see." Alice smiled, winking at Marisol. She felt like a teenager getting picked up at home by the boy she liked. It was...nice. Odd, but nice. "You two have a good rest of your day. I'm going to meet my daughter for lunch." She beamed before closing the door behind Marisol, leaving them alone in the waiting room.

Cisco looked Marisol over before meeting her gaze. He smiled, both flirty and sweet. "All black after just adopting a white cat? Brave move, Princesa."

"You're one to talk," she quipped.

"I only look good in black," he said, though she seriously doubted it.

"It's true. Otherwise, he's ten times uglier," piped up Tiny. Cisco shot her the finger, but Tiny just shot it back. Both of them grinned at each other, the love and playfulness for one another evident.

"Can I have your keys?"

"Hmm?" Marisol asked.

"Your keys, Princesa. For your car. Remember, I'm taking you out?" He ignored the fake gagging from Tiny.

Right. Keys. Date. Marisol searched through her purse before handing them out. Instead of Cisco taking them, Tiny grabbed them. The girl was obviously old enough to drive, but that didn't ease Marisol's nervousness about giving her keys over to a teen driver.

Tiny assured her, "I'm the best driver in the family."

"Only because she drives like a grandma and avoids highways," Cisco said.

"Shut up." She flipped him off again before turning her

attention back to Marisol. "I'll be careful. Please don't make me ride with this idiot again. All he does is talk about you and how pretty you are and how much he wants to kiss—"

"Okay!" Cisco interrupted. "Always fun hanging out with you, prima, but you gotta go."

"Yeah, yeah, I'm gone. Don't forget to Venmo me!" she called as the doors slammed behind her.

"I promise she really is a good driver." Cisco took Marisol's hand.

She ignored the warm flush that went through her body. "If she crashes, you owe me a new car."

"I'll buy you whatever fucking car you want. Now let's go. I have something fun planned for us." Cisco didn't offer further explanation as he led her out of the building and to his car.

"Where are we going?" Marisol's curiosity got the best of her.

Cisco opened the passenger door for her and said, "Dancing."

What?!

CHAPTER 16

Cisco

When he was thirteen, Cisco's mother signed him up for salsa classes. What awkward teenage kid wanted to take dance classes? Certainly not him, and he hated it. He was one of the only boys in the class, and none of the girls were interested in dancing with him. He had been a scrawny, awkward kid, so he couldn't blame them. His early teenage years were not kind to him, and he lacked the grace and poise salsa classes demanded.

It wasn't until his early twenties that he acquired an appreciation for dance in any form. It helped that he gained more control of his body because he wasn't a lanky teenage boy anymore. Dance was sensual and commanded a lot of trust between partners. This was one area Cisco wasn't sure Marisol was completely on board with. She was guarded, and that often came across as standoffish. He was quick to see through the cracks in her armor though. There was more she was holding in and not telling him.

Marisol held her emotions close and kept people at an arm's length. He wanted to completely shatter that barrier between them, and there was no better way than the closeness dance provided.

He found out last week that a speakeasy downtown was holding a beginners' salsa lesson for partners. He had never purchased tickets faster, even though he didn't talk to Marisol about it beforehand. Part of him knew, if he asked her beforehand, she would immediately shut down the idea. Maybe keeping it from her was shitty, but he couldn't bring himself to be too sorry about it.

"What is this place?" It was the first thing Marisol asked since he picked her up and dropped the bomb about going dancing. Honestly, though, she took it better than he expected.

The two of them stepped into Rosa's Hideaway, a cozy speakeasy-style bar and restaurant that felt like a step back in time to the Roaring Twenties, though with a few modern touches. The dim lighting cast a warm glow over the rich mahogany furnishings, while vintage jazz music played softly in the background. The lounge area featured a handful of plush brown leather couches, inviting guests to sit and relax. Nearby, several high-top tables offered additional seating, their polished surfaces reflecting the soft amber glow of the antique-inspired chandeliers. Toward the back, a small cleared space with large speakers stood ready for dancing, promising a lively atmosphere as the night unfolded.

"This is Rosa's," Cisco said, leading her to the bar. "Do you want something to drink?"

"Am I really going to have to dance?" she asked him.

"You are," he said, unable to hide his smug satisfaction.

"Then I'm going to need a vodka tonic. Heavy on the vodka."

Cisco ordered their drinks before leading Marisol to one of the leather couches. Light, jazzy music played in the background, adding to the ambiance. A few other couples and groups had already arrived and were speaking amongst themselves.

Marisol took a seat, crossing her legs before taking the offered drink. "You know, I expected lunch when you said you wanted to see me again."

"That would be predictable, Princesa. I don't like predictable," Cisco mused, taking a drink of his whiskey. He loved the smoky taste and the way it burned his throat as it went down. "Besides, this gives me an excuse to touch you."

He watched as the flush in her cheeks deepened. She tried to hide it behind her glass, but she couldn't hide from him. Her gaze swept across the room, quietly assessing the other patrons. Her painted fingers tapped against the couch, her knee bouncing to its own rhythm—a habit he'd come to recognize whenever she found herself in an unfamiliar setting. Her eyes lingered on him when she thought he wasn't looking.

He noticed. He always noticed.

"If you want to touch me, there are better places for you to do that," Marisol said, her heated gaze traveling up and down his body before locking with his. "But I suppose this will do."

Visions of him running his hands along the curves of her naked body played in his mind. The whimpers of pleasure he desperately wanted to rip from her lips. Her moans he wanted to capture in a kiss. This line of thinking went straight to his cock, and the last thing he needed right now was to start dancing with Marisol with a raging hard-on.

Trying to covertly readjust himself, he cleared his throat, attempting to find a safer and tamer topic. "Have you danced before?"

Marisol nodded. "I was put into dance lessons the moment I learned to walk. Or at least that's how it felt. My mom wanted to be sure I didn't have two left feet and embarrass our family at my dad's events. I'm not sure I was ever as good as she wanted me to be, though."

"Did your dad have a lot of events?"

She laughed, but there was no humor in her voice. "Tons. It felt like I was going to one every week. My sister could sometimes get out of it, but I never could. Turns out years of formal dance training wasn't needed at these events. People mostly just stood around, talked and sipped on their wine."

He wondered what it would be like growing up like that. Where every weekend was already planned for you, and you were expected to play a part. Cisco had a great childhood, albeit humble. His parents didn't have much, considering they immigrated to the States at only eighteen years old. But he never thought about all the things he didn't have growing up in California; he only thought about the fun and love his parents gave him.

He got the impression that, from a young age, Marisol had a job to perform, and her parents—specifically her mother—made sure she pulled her weight.

"I will say, on the rare occasion I did dance, none of my partners were as cute as you," Marisol said coyly, still hiding the glass in front of her beautiful face, obstructing his view.

Cisco's lips twitched at the corners before pulling into a grin. "You think I'm cute?" he teased.

"I think you're alright," she said playfully. It wasn't a side he saw a lot of, but he fucking loved it.

"Nah, Princesa, you already said it. I'm cute as hell."

"I take it back; you're a nightmare." She swatted at his chest.

But Cisco grabbed her hand and brought it up to his lips, pressing a soft kiss to it. The tone switched from playful to intense so quickly. "You look beautiful," he murmured. "So damn beautiful."

Marisol's breath hitched, pupils dilating. Her gaze seared him from the inside out, and he was drawn to her like a moth to light. She wet her lips, and that was the only thing Cisco could pay attention to. He wanted to kiss her. To taste her. He wanted to—

"Buenos tardes, mis amigos," a feminine voice broke the trance.

He was so close to kissing her again. Their last kiss had been too short, too soft. He wanted more, but if he kissed her now, he wouldn't be able to stop.

Marisol gathered herself before him and pulled back. He followed suit, turning his body to see a woman in a brown knee-length dress. She smiled at the few people sitting around with drinks in their hands. There weren't many. Maybe twenty at most, but enough to make the small room feel crowded.

"My name is María, and this is my partner, Savi. We're going to be your dance instructors tonight," the woman said, smiling at the room.

"Do we have anyone familiar with salsa dancing?" the male instructor—Savi—asked the group.

A few people, including Cisco, raised their hands.

"Ah good, we have some experts here tonight." María laughed. "For those of you who don't know, salsa is a Latin American dance. It combines many dance styles together to create energetic footwork, quick hip movements, and fluid turns. It's both precisely fast and elegantly slow. Think of it like fire and ice."

"It's a romantic dance," Savi added. "You'll be up close and personal with your partner, learning each other's bodies and movements. This is supposed to be fun and sensual. Take a few moments to finish your drinks and then join María and me on the dance floor."

There was a polite round of applause for the instructors before everyone went back to their drinks. A few people glanced at Cisco but quickly averted their eyes. He didn't mind the stares because, half of the time, it was to admire his tattoos. Other times it was full of judgment, but he didn't give a fuck about what a stranger thought of him.

Except for Marisol.

When he turned around, she scowled at him.

"What?" He looked down, making sure he hadn't spilled something on his shirt or ripped his clothes.

"Nothing," she said, though it was clearly something. He let the silence settle between them until Marisol blurted out, "I mean I can dance, but I've never done this style before."

Ah, so she was nervous. He could work with that.

"No problem, just let me lead you." Cisco shrugged. "You'll do fine."

"And when I fall on my ass or embarrass myself, I'll remind you what you just said," she shot back.

"I'll protect that pretty ass, Princesa, just trust me." He grinned. "I'm not going to let you fall."

"You promise?"

Cisco made the motion of crossing his heart with his finger. "Swear."

She looked at him intently before finishing up her drink, placing the empty glass on the table. She reached out for his hand. "Fine. Let's do this. But I reserve the right to hold this against you if it goes badly."

"You can hold whatever you want against me. It would be my honor." He winked, taking her hand and leading Marisol out on the dance floor with the rest of the patrons.

CHAPTER 17
Marisol

She didn't have enough to drink to mentally prepare herself for being pressed up this close to Cisco. She had been under the delusion that they would ease into such an intimate dance, but clearly the instructors didn't subscribe to the same school of thought.

"We are going to start with the basics. It'll look like this," María said. Savi took her hand and placed his other high on her hip. They counted the eight beats out loud as they moved in sync with each other, ending with Savi pulling María to his body, dipping her. His hand traveled to her thigh, and the two were locked in such an intense stare that Marisol felt like she was intruding on something.

An excited murmur went through the onlookers as they faced off with their partners. If Cisco could hear just how fast her heart was beating, she would be mortified. She didn't hide her nervousness well, though, because Cisco started to sway his hips, overly dramatizing the movements.

"You can't tell me this doesn't turn you on." He did a weird little thrust that had her laughing out loud.

"I will do anything for you to stop doing that." She grinned.

His eyes darkened, a goofy grin forming on his lips. "I think a kiss would stop me."

A kiss might stop him, but it would definitely heat her body and leave her wanting more. "Play your cards right, and you might just get one."

He grasped at his chest, panting. "Ah, Princesa, you wound me."

She highly doubted that but didn't get a chance to say as much because they were approached by Savi. The man was pretty, dressed similarly in all black. Judging by the perfection of his unblemished skin, he had an even more extensive skin-care routine than Marisol. She had half the mind to ask.

"And how are you two doing?" he asked in a slightly accented voice. Cuban, maybe. "Do you need me to demonstrate the dance again? I'd be happy to for Marisol."

Cisco's hold on her tightened as he pulled her closer, nearly flush against his hard chest. "We are doing fine." There was an unmistakable hardness in his voice that wasn't there before. Her body tingled at the possessiveness of it. Normally, she would be pissed if anyone felt entitled to her, but clearly her body felt differently when it came to Cisco.

Marisol leaned into him, just to see what he'd do. A shaky breath left his lips, revealing just how much she was affecting him too. Good. She didn't want to be the only one unhinged when it came to the other.

Savi didn't appear offended. If anything, his smile only widened. "Ah, my apologies. I see there is no need for my assistance here. Your chemistry is"—he brought his fingers up to his lips and kissed—"so good." He winked at them before moving toward the older couple next to them who argued over hand placement.

Once they were alone again, Marisol looked up at Cisco through her lashes. "We're doing fine, are we?" She couldn't help but tease.

Cisco, who looked ready to pounce on poor Savi, relaxed his body. No signs of his annoyance lingered when he smiled at her. "We are. You're in capable hands. I'm a pro."

"A pro?" she mused.

"Mhm, yup. You're looking at a two-time junior runner-up in dance. Runner-up because the kid who always won was the child of the owners." He chuckled.

"Good. Now prove it."

Cisco took that as a challenge. The room filled with the sound of a Spanish love ballad and the counts from both María and Savi as they guided people through the dance. Turns out, Cisco wasn't lying about being a runner-up. He was good. Damn good. Marisol didn't have time to feel self-conscious or silly at the quick footwork or the way her hips moved awkwardly during the parts she was least familiar with.

None of that mattered with Cisco because he didn't make her feel like she had to be perfect. She could stumble through a move, and he wouldn't get mad or berate her for her incompetence. He laughed with her, guided her through the steps she couldn't master with patience, and never once made her feel small.

This was how it was supposed to be. Not something she had to hide back her tears or stress over because she desperately wanted to impress her mother. No, she felt light on her feet. She was having *fun*. Her laugh was genuine, and her mouth hurt from smiling too much.

One hand stayed in his the entire time, while her other

touched different parts of him. His arm, shoulder, chest, and back. Each new place, she discovered something new about his body. How his muscles would flex each time she dragged her nails down his arm. The way his eyes never strayed from her, no matter what they were doing. This close, she could make out the tattoos creeping up along his neck.

Then he pulled her close again, her back pressed against his chest. She felt the heat of his breath against her neck. She had to remind herself to breathe. It just became increasingly more difficult when his hand ran down the flat expanse of her stomach to her navel. Her head tilted back to meet Cisco's sultry eyes.

This man was breathtaking. His tattoos didn't just add to his appeal; they deepened the sense of mystery surrounding him. Intricate black and gray designs covered his forearms, a mix of bold geometric patterns and delicate, swirling script that hinted at stories only he knew. A serpent coiled around his wrist, its sharp eyes watching, while a compass rested on his biceps, as if guiding him toward something greater.

Who was this tattooed entrepreneur with a kind soul? He was everything she had never allowed herself to want. Everything her mother despised. From a young age, Marisol had been pushed toward a specific kind of crowd: the sons of wealthy businessmen, heirs to old-money dynasties, men with influence in their communities. Politicians. Lawyers. She had met them all. Which was why her mother had loved Archie so much. He checked so many of the boxes she wanted in a son-in-law. But none of these men had ever made her heart race the way Cisco did.

She was raised to believe that her mother's wants and needs were her own, and she didn't try to fight it. Not when she broke her sister's heart. Not when her own heart was breaking. She was just a doll to be used.

But this doll wasn't made of porcelain any longer.

She was learning how to fight back and make her own path in life, even if she still felt like she had so much further to go. Cisco was a man she picked for herself, despite her fears and the voices in her head telling her this wasn't what her mother wanted and would cause a fight. Cisco was worth the fallout of a relationship she wasn't entirely certain she still wanted. A man she hadn't known for long already knew the true her better than anyone else.

The thought was both scary and strangely exciting.

He continued to look at her like she was the only woman worth seeing. That did something to Marisol, stirred a feeling inside her she thought went dormant a long time ago. Her body was no longer her own. She felt like the world was moving in slow motion as she leaned up and closed the distance between them. Her lips molded to his, a current of electricity running through her body the moment they touched. She was hungry for more, and she didn't want to deny herself.

Her lips parted, a low, needy sound leaving them. Cisco's tongue found hers, mingling in a moment of heat. She wanted more. Needed more. She nearly deepened the kiss when she heard Savi somewhere behind her shouting directions at a couple. Reality hit her hard, and she pulled back as if shocked.

"Uh, sorry. I don't know what came over—"

"Get your ass back here, Princesa." Cisco didn't let her get far. He grabbed her around the waist and pulled her back, his lips slamming against hers. There was no hesitation on his behalf. He kissed her like this was the last time he would ever kiss her. His tongue brushed hers, and she moaned, though he swallowed it up. The room faded until there was nothing but her and Cisco.

Cisco, the man who was slowly breaking down her walls.

Heat pooled between her legs. Who knew she could get so turned on by a kiss? Granted, this wasn't just any kiss. It left her panting and breathless, desperately wishing they were alone and not in the middle of a speakeasy with other couples.

Reluctantly, they broke away from each other. Marisol was seconds from stripping them both, consequences be damned, but the loss of his lips on hers was like a bucket of cold water. Effective, yet annoying.

A sly grin spread across his lips. "Why did I bring us here? Fucking stupid. Let's go back to your house."

"Cisco!" She laughed, swatting at him when he attempted to pull her away from the others dancing...or what they considered dancing. The jerky movements and questionable footwork made her wonder what tempo they were chasing. She felt much better about the small imperfections in her own footwork.

"And that's our time, dancers!" María said cheerfully, her voice breaking through the music. Savi cut the sound and moved to stay at her side. "Everyone did amazing, but it's most important that you had fun. Did everyone have fun today?"

Applause and cheers met her question. Cisco wrapped an arm around Marisol and pulled her close. He leaned down to whisper in her ear, "Now, can we leave?"

"Now we can leave," she agreed, taking his hand and allowing him to lead her out of the speakeasy. Her body was still thrumming with pent-up energy. She couldn't remember the last time she felt like this after a date. Hell, she couldn't even remember the last date she went on before Cisco. Now she actually felt a pang of sadness it was coming to an end.

"Can we do this again?" she blurted when they got to his car.

Cisco opened her door, raising a brow. "Go on a date?"

"No. Well, yes, but I meant dancing. You're really good at it. And it was...fun."

"You don't have to say 'fun' like you regret the word." He laughed. "But I'll take you whenever you want to go. You looked beautiful, and you were the best partner I've ever had."

Marisol hid her blush by quickly getting into the car. The Sinner's Web was playing softly on the radio. It helped ease the sudden nerves that took root inside her. They were going home. Cisco was dropping her off. Did he expect to come up with her? And if she agreed...what did he expect to do?

Her stomach churned. It wasn't as if she had thought about...*that*. After all, she was seconds away from stripping him in the middle of a public place and having her way with him. But that was in the heat of the moment, and now she was back in reality.

It wasn't that she didn't want to. She did...maybe more than she cared to admit, but the thought still scared her. Happiness was in her reach, but was it truly attainable or just a moment in time that would end?

"Hey, Princesa, you okay?" Cisco's hand reached for hers, and she jumped.

Marisol hadn't even heard him get in. The concerned look on his face told her this wasn't the first time he tried to get her attention. "I'm fine," she lied. "Just tired."

"You are a bad liar, Marisol," Cisco said, but he didn't sound upset. He sounded...almost understanding, which didn't make sense since he didn't know what she was thinking.

Before she could spiral any further, he quickly added, "Let me get you home so you can rest."

Cisco pulled out of the parking lot and took off in the direction of her house. Unlike her, who had to GPS the Walgreens down the street, he had her home memorized. Their drive was quiet, though not awkward, as they listened to their favorite band.

Ten minutes later, he pulled up to the front of the building and reached over to unhook her belt. "Did you have fun tonight?" He searched her face for any signs of doubt.

She gave him none. "Tonight was fun. Like, really fun. Thank you."

"You're welcome." His voice was gruff, holding back emotion she couldn't quite place. Did he not want this date to end any more than she did?

"Can I see you tomorrow?"

Cisco offered her an apologetic smile. She braced herself for rejection. "I can't."

Her body sank with disappointment. She felt like an idiot, especially when her eyes began to sting. "Right. Of course."

"Marisol, look at me."

She really didn't want to, but he placed his hand under her chin and tilted it up. "I can't," he repeated. She opened her mouth to snap at him and let him know she heard him the first time, but then he added, "Because I'll be meeting with my realtor tomorrow about the property we toured. The one by your father's shop? I don't know how long it'll be, but I don't want to keep you waiting. Let me see you this weekend. All weekend, preferably."

There was no fighting back the smile and the relief in her features. "This weekend you're mine, then."

"Ah, Princesa, I fear I'm already yours." He smirked and leaned in to kiss her. It was soft and quick. It still left her breathless when he pulled back. "Now, walk that pretty ass up to the door so I can make sure you get home safe. Tiny said your car is in the parking lot, and your keys are at the front desk."

He truly did think of everything. "Thank you," she said again. With great reluctance, she got out of the car. She turned back once to wave one last time before heading up to her front entry. The nighttime doorman smiled at her, opening the door.

By the time she retrieved her keys and checked the lobby window, Cisco was gone.

CHAPTER 18

Marisol

My feet are sore. You think it's because of how many times you stepped on them?

Excuse me? That was one time, and it's only because you have giant feet.

Well, you know what they say about big feet. Big d...

Finish that and I'll block your number.

Big dumb shoes. What did you think I was going to say?

You're lucky you're cute.

Just cute?

....

> Okay, okay. Don't admit it. I'll admit I miss you, Princesa. I'm seeing you this weekend. Tell Snowball I'll see her soon.

When the phone rang again, Marisol had just stepped out of the shower, tying her fluffy pink towel around her body. Snowball was curled up in her sink, sleeping soundlessly. Her white tail brushed against Marisol's phone with each lazy sway.

She could only laugh. Didn't she just finish talking to him an hour ago? It thrilled her that any spare moment he got, Cisco's first instinct was to call her. Without checking, Marisol answered her phone, putting it on speaker so she could dry off.

"Aren't you supposed to be in a meeting?" She laughed.

There was a pregnant silence on the other end of her phone before a very different voice than Cisco's greeted her. "I'm not sure what meeting you're referring to, but no."

Marisol's mother's voice filled her bathroom. Not even Snowball was immune to the sound of Luciana Roberts' contempt. She jumped off the counter and retreated into the bedroom, just as Marisol wished she could do. Silently, she cursed herself for answering the phone without checking to see who was calling.

"Mom. Hi," she said breathlessly, wishing the cell phone towers all over California would spontaneously combust so she'd have an excuse to drop the call.

"Were you expecting someone else?" her mother asked in a way that hinted she knew more than she was letting on, but how was that possible? The only person in her family that sort of knew about Cisco was Lola, but even she didn't know much. Not that she spoke to their mother much anyway.

"No, sorry, you just caught me off guard."

"Off guard?" her mother scoffed. "What was it you were doing?"

Marisol gritted her teeth, taking deep breaths. "Just got out of the shower. Is there something you need?" she asked with forced patience Alice would be proud of.

"No need for the attitude, dear. I'm simply calling to invite you over on Friday for family dinner."

Ignoring the comment about her attitude, Marisol quickly scrambled for an excuse to get out of it. This weekend she wanted to reserve for Cisco, and she'd much rather spend time with him than suffer through an awkward family dinner. The thought of it made her stomach twist—enduring endless jabs about her appearance and the inevitable mention of Archie. Her mother would press for details, prying relentlessly until Marisol was forced to come up with a reason to escape.

It was always easier to refuse over the phone, where distance gave her a layer of protection. But standing just feet away, face to face, made it infinitely harder to hold her ground.

"This weekend? I...I wish you would have told me earlier. I'm busy."

"Surely that can change?" her mother challenged. "After all, Lola and Javi will be here. Along with my grandchildren. It wouldn't seem right not to have my eldest daughter here too. I would love to invite Archie, but seeing as you two are...not on the best terms, I'll be happy with just you coming."

Pretending her mother didn't mention Archie, she focused on the fact that Lola was coming. It was a rare day in hell when Lola agreed to be in the same room as their mother—or, as she called it, "exposure therapy." She felt compelled not to leave her sister there alone to fend for herself. Sure, she had her husband and their father...but Marisol was her big sister. A shitty sister, but still. She felt the least she could do was suffer alongside Lola.

It didn't make sense but somehow eased her regret.

"Maybe I can move things around—"

"That's so good to hear, dear. I knew you'd make the right choice. I'll see you on Friday." Without waiting for a response, her mother hung up, leaving Marisol flustered.

"Wonderful," she muttered, placing her phone back on the counter.

The old Marisol would have let that one interaction ruin the rest of her day. She wouldn't have even bothered getting dressed and would have gone straight back to bed.

Before her mother called, though, she had planned on giving Stella from the shelter a call. After her last session with Alice, she felt confident in her decision to volunteer. She still wouldn't consider herself a pet person—besides Snowball— but it would be a nice way to meet people.

She finished up in the bathroom, pulling on silk red shorts and a black Sinner's Web shirt. She put her hair in a loose braid before leaving her bathroom and heading to her living room. Snowball meowed at her when she sat down on the couch. She waited on Marisol to wrap herself up with a fuzzy blanket before moving to sit on her lap.

"Where did I put her number?" Marisol wondered out loud, doing a quick search of her coffee table before finding the crumpled-up paper with Family Pet Shelter's number on it. A picture of a cartoonish man and woman holding a dog and cat smiled up at her.

"They seem happy," she said to Snowball.

Snowball just blinked at her and then put her head down, promptly falling asleep.

"Right, I'm on my own," she muttered and ran her finger over the numbers. Before she could talk herself out of it, she pressed call and put the phone to her ear.

Each ring made her heart pound faster. Not only did she hate talking on the phone, but she hated talking on the phone to strangers. She always felt awkward and felt the need to fill in any silence with ramblings. Suddenly, the phone stopped ringing, and loud barks assaulted her ear, followed by a cheery voice. "Thanks for calling Family Pet Shelter; this is Stella. How can I help you?"

"Hi, Stella. This is Marisol Roberts. We actually met the other day. I don't know if you remember me—"

"Marisol! Yes, you adopted Snowball. How's she adjusting?" Stella asked, genuinely curious.

The cat in question happily lounged across Marisol's lap like she owned the damn house. Affection for the white furball swelled in her chest as she petted the top of her head. Snowball purred immediately.

"I would say she's adjusting very well. Like she's always been here."

Stella laughed good-naturedly on the other end. "Yup, that about sums up cats. Once they find their person, they are locked in for life."

"Thank you again for helping me with the adoption," Marisol said. "I was actually calling about the volunteering you mentioned. I'm wondering if you still need volunteers?"

"Desperately!" Stella said. There was shuffling on her side, and then a door closed, blocking out most of the barking. "We have many areas we still need help in. What skills do you have?"

"Oh, uhm, I'm organized," she said lamely, not realizing

she would be interviewed on the spot. "Planning and delegating. I also am good at both written and verbal communication. I have a lot of contacts in a lot of different fields."

"Contacts?" Stella asked, intrigued. "Like contacts who may or may not be interested in donating to a good cause?"

If there was one thing her parents' "friends" were good for, it was giving away money that would make them look like good people.

"Oh, yeah. I've helped organize a few donation galas, and they are all eager to outbid each other," Marisol said.

"Wow. I think you just became my best friend. I've been wanting to put some sort of fundraiser together for the shelter, but I'm in over my head. I'm good at loving on pets, but trying to put something together of that magnitude honestly leaves me curled up in a ball."

Marisol knew how stressful it could be. Every tiny detail needed to be planned, and any mistake reflected poorly on the person who organized the event. She wasn't sure if it was all the years of constantly striving for perfection or the countless hours she spent organizing her schedules, but she loved planning events. Anything from large galas to raise money for whatever charity her parents were interested in at the moment to the baby shower she planned for Lola. It made her feel good to see people enjoying something she put together.

"We can talk about your goals for the event, and I can start drafting ideas," Marisol suggested.

"I would love that. We will be meeting next Tuesday. Would you be able to make the meeting? I can introduce you to the rest of our team, and we can discuss the fundraiser." Marisol couldn't see Stella, but she imagined the petite woman bouncing excitedly in her chair. She gave off golden retriever energy, which contrasted greatly with Marisol's black cat energy.

But even black cats needed their people.

"Sure. I'll be there," she said.

"Great! Marisol, I can't thank you enough for calling me back. I think you are going to be a great addition to the team. Is this a good number to text you from?" Stella wondered.

"Yeah, it is."

"Great. I'll text you the info. Oh, we usually meet at a restaurant downtown. Super chill, and everyone can order what they like. Anyway, I'll text you all this information. Thanks again for reaching out. I'm excited to get to know you more."

"I'm excited too." And she was, which was the weird thing. She genuinely looked forward to meeting these people and offering her expertise.

Stella thanked her again profusely and promised to send over the information as soon as they got off the call. Marisol hung up, feeling something akin to pride growing in her chest. This was another step in taking charge of her own life and making her own decisions.

Granted, she never thought taking charge would bring her to an animal shelter, but she liked it. If the rest of the volunteers were half as nice as Stella, she figured she'd get along with them well enough. Maybe even make friends who weren't affiliated with her parents at all.

"I did it, Snowball. Think Alice would be proud of me?" she murmured, rubbing her cat's head. Snowball purred, licking her hand as if to say *good job, Mom.*

Her phone buzzed on the nightstand with an unfamiliar number. It was Stella with the information about the meeting. It was held at an unfamiliar location, but she was excited to try out something new. Usually, she stayed with her "safe" restaurants. Places she's been hundreds of times and could order the same thing without looking at the menu.

"After that, I deserve some wine," Marisol said, moving from under Snowball, who yipped before jumping off her lap. She got up and headed to the kitchen where she stored her small wine fridge. After selecting one of her father's wines, she poured herself a glass.

Her mind wandered to Cisco and what he was doing right now. It was strange to miss someone you just saw, but there was an unfamiliar ache in her chest that hadn't been filled since last night. The strong connection forming between them both scared and excited her. She didn't think anyone had ever made her heart beat as fast as Cisco had. He could barely touch her, and already she felt like she could melt into a puddle at his feet.

Marisol took her wine and sat on the couch, deciding to spend a lazy day inside. Before she knew it, she was eight episodes deep into *Love is Blind* and dozing off.

Her condo went dark, only the glow from the TV providing any light. After hours on the couch, her body hurt—the joys of turning thirty and getting weird aches and pains in parts of your body you didn't know existed.

After pushing herself off the couch, Marisol went to her living room window, cracking it ajar to let the cool night air into her apartment like she normally did when the weather was nice. She called for Snowball, but the cat stayed curled up on the couch.

"Suit yourself," she muttered and walked back to her room.

Her head barely hit the pillow before she fell fast asleep.

CHAPTER 19

Marisol

The thought of coffee was the only thing that got her out of bed. Slipping on her fuzzy pink slippers, Marisol grabbed her robe and headed into the kitchen. The fancy but complicated machine sat out on her counter with a sticky note from Mrs. Baker on how to run it.

After a minute of fumbling through the instructions, she finally managed to get the coffee machine working. The soft hum and slow drip of brewing coffee filled the quiet kitchen, a welcome promise of caffeine. Letting out a small sigh, she rubbed the last traces of sleep from her eyes and turned toward the pantry.

Snowball's breakfast was next on the list. She reached for the bag of cat food, shaking it lightly as she stepped back. The absence of her feline companion in bed that morning hadn't gone unnoticed. Snowball was probably curled up on the couch, basking in a patch of sunlight, completely unbothered by the world waking up around her.

"Snowball! Time to eat," she called and popped open the can. Last time that had been enough for Snowball to come running into the kitchen, meowing her head off. Marisol barely had time to put her bowl down before Snowball attacked it.

This morning was different.

Snowball didn't come running in. She didn't dance around Marisol's feet or meow her annoyance because Marisol was taking too long to prepare her food.

"Snowball?" she called again, this time walking into the living room. She quickly scanned the room, but no signs of Snowball. Was the window open wider than it was last night?

Cold fear and dread froze her body as she took a step closer to the window, looking out at the balcony. She remembered cracking it last night, but just enough to let in a breeze. She would remember if the window was a third of the way up. Something had to have pushed it up...or a certain cat who managed to wiggle underneath and run free.

Fuck.

Dread pooled low in her belly. This couldn't be happening. She stepped away from the window and looked in every spot Snowball usually hung out in. Her bed, the couch, the litter box, food bowl, and even her closet. For an hour, she ripped through her house, not caring about the mess she left in her wake. Each corner she turned or small alcove she searched, she hoped Snowball would be lounging lazily, oblivious to her manic search.

"Snowball!" she cried out in frustration, stubborn tears she could no longer control rolling down from her eyes.

Snowball was gone.

And there was only one reason for that. Because she was fucking stupid and opened the window last night. Once again proving she thought of no one else but herself. She crumbled to the floor, heartbroken.

What made her think she was capable of caring for and

loving Snowball when she couldn't care for herself and failed as a big sister? It was clear to everyone but her that she was a shitty caretaker and had no business trying to fill that role. It backfired every time.

Her phone buzzed in her pocket, scaring her out of her dark thoughts. She had half a mind to ignore it, but something made her look to see who was calling her. Cisco's name flashed across the screen, and she held back a sob.

Her thumb skated over the answer button and pressed down. Marisol brought it up to her ear, but she couldn't find the words. Each time she opened her mouth, a sob threatened to escape.

"Marisol?" Cisco's worried voice came from the other end. "Princesa, are you there? What's wrong?"

The dam shattered at his words, raw and filled with concern. He fucking cared. He was worried about her. No one had ever cared before. Not like this.

She had spent a lifetime having her feelings overlooked, her struggles dismissed, her pain unseen. She had learned to endure, to carry it all alone because there was never anyone to share the weight. But now, faced with genuine care, with someone who actually saw her, she didn't know how to hold herself together.

So, she didn't.

The walls she had carefully built crumbled, and all she could do was break down.

There was some rustling on the other side, and Cisco cursed. "I'm coming over. Unlock your door, Princesa. I'll be there in ten. Stay on the phone with me. You don't have to talk."

She heard the sound of a car unlocking, followed by a door closing. He was really on his way to her.

Marisol managed to pick herself off the floor. She rubbed her eyes, trying to clear her vision as she made her way to the front door. With a click, the front door was unlocked for Cisco.

Eight minutes later, she got a text from the front office about a visitor and cleared Cisco to come up. A few moments after that, she heard urgent footsteps coming down the hall, followed by her door swinging open. Cisco stood there, eyes wide, with damp hair as if he had recently gotten out of the shower to rush over here.

Marisol could only imagine what he thought about the scene before him. Her red-rimmed, puffy eyes were full of tears. Her house was in shambles, everything out of place, tossed thoughtlessly to the ground, and furniture overturned in her haste to find Snowball.

Cisco said something in Spanish she didn't understand but didn't sound good. In three long strides, he crossed the room and took her into his arms. She didn't fight; Marisol melted into his embrace. She couldn't produce any more tears, but the impending doom fell over her, casting darkness all around her.

"What happened here? Marisol, are you hurt?" Cisco pulled back enough to search her body, looking for any wounds. He probably thought this was a damn home invasion for how disastrous she left her house. She couldn't blame him for thinking that.

"Snowball…" she finally managed to croak out. "She's gone."

A tiny flicker of relief passed through Cisco before his body tensed again. "Are you sure?"

"Of course I'm sure. Do you think I normally keep my house looking like this?" she snapped and instantly regretted it. "Sorry…I didn't mean…I'm just…"

"No apologies necessary. I'll help you find her. Is she chipped?"

"I...don't know. I didn't ask." *Stupid, Marisol, stupid,* she chastised herself. "But..." She quickly got out her phone and opened her text from last night. She found Stella's number and sent her a hasty text asking if Snowball was chipped.

A few minutes later her phone chimed with a text.

Yes. Everything okay?

She's missing.

Oh, no! I'll keep an eye out at the shelter in case anyone comes by. Please update me or let me know if you need me to help search.

Stella was sweet, but she didn't have it in her to allow someone else to see her failure. Cisco was enough.

"Let's go walk the street. Maybe she's somewhere nearby," Cisco insisted and took Marisol's hand. Without his guidance, she didn't believe she'd be able to make it out of her home alone.

"I left the window open..." she muttered softly as soon as the elevator doors closed. "And now she's gone. I'm so stupid."

"You aren't stupid," Cisco said, his words almost a growl. "This was an accident. It could have happened to anyone."

It could have, but it happened to *her*. Which made it feel even worse.

When the elevator doors opened again, Cisco led her out and straight to the doorman. She followed him blindly, her body on autopilot. "Have you seen a white cat recently?"

The young man thought for a moment before shaking his head. "Can't say I have. I'm sorry, sir."

"Will someone let Marisol Roberts know if a white cat is found?"

"She's wearing a pink collar," Marisol added.

The man nodded. "Of course. I'll let the front lobby people know. I hope you find your cat, miss."

"We will." There was no room for argument in Cisco's words. She was glad one of them felt confident.

"Let's start this way." Cisco gestured to the left, heading toward the majority of the downtown restaurants. "Maybe she smelled something."

Marisol lived in the middle of the city. It wasn't a residential neighborhood where few cars passed and no restaurants lined the streets. No, her house was by a major highway with tons of people coming and going at all times of the day. Images of Snowball walking into the middle of the road and a car not seeing her filled Marisol's mind. As quickly as they came, she pushed them away. She couldn't think like that. It would only drive her crazy.

Cisco's warm hand squeezed hers. He was the only thing keeping her grounded at the moment. "We will find her," he promised. "We'll start this way and go from here."

Marisol nodded, offering no resistance as she let herself be dragged along. Every step felt like a monumental effort, as if gravity itself was working against her. Moving on her own felt impossible, a chore she wasn't willing to take on right now.

Cisco's voice rang out as he called for Snowball, his tone laced with concern. Marisol knew she should help, should at least try. Wandering aimlessly like a ghost wasn't doing any good. But her body refused to cooperate, weighed down by exhaustion and by emotion. Her mind screamed at her to move, to push through it, but all she could do was stand there, trapped in the disconnect between thought and action.

They combed the streets, calling Snowball's name into the night. They stopped at restaurants, questioning staff, and checked with shop owners, hoping someone had spotted a fluffy white cat wandering by. They searched back alleys, peering behind dumpsters and under parked cars, their footsteps echoing in the dimly lit spaces. Everywhere they looked, cats prowled the city—strays of all colors darting in and out of sight—but none of them were Snowball.

With each hour that passed, Marisol felt her hope wither, crumbling piece by piece until all that remained was a dull, aching void in her chest.

"We will find her, Marisol. I promise," Cisco said, his voice steady but not as certain as before. It was the tenth time he'd reassured her, maybe more, but this time... this time, she heard the hesitation. The exhaustion. The creeping doubt that neither of them wanted to acknowledge. Hours of searching had worn him down, just as they had her.

And yet, he still pushed ahead, with Marisol following behind him, calling out for a cat who stole her heart.

THEY FAILED.

Cisco walked with her back to her house in silence. Even he looked at a loss for what to do now. She almost felt the need to reassure him, but she just didn't have it in her. She saw from the corner of her eye the way he constantly checked on her, opening his mouth to say something, but then immediately closing it.

There wasn't anything to say.

"You should go home." Marisol's voice was barely above a whisper. "Thank you for your help today. I'm sorry you had to miss work for this." She actually didn't know if he worked today, or if he had plans, but if he did, Marisol had ruined them.

"I didn't have work today. I'm not going home." He slowed his pace to match hers.

"There's nothing else you can do."

"I'm not going home," he repeated. His firm tone told her there was no budging with him.

They fell back into silence as they walked the final block to her condo. Cisco's hand stayed on her back. It was a small gesture, but it brought her comfort. When they approached the front door, the young man who was working earlier was no longer there. He was replaced with the nighttime doorman, an older man with salt-and-pepper hair. Mr. Barnes, she believed his name was. He had been working here longer than Marisol had lived here.

"Good evening, Miss Roberts. You have a visitor," Mr. Barnes said, opening the door.

Marisol's brow furrowed. "A visitor? I'm not expecting anyone."

"Marisol!" a familiar voice exclaimed when she walked in. Both her and Cisco's heads swiveled to the side just as Stella rushed over with a brown box carrier in her arms.

"I have been trying to call you for the last hour! The front desk man said you weren't in," Stella said.

Marisol instantly searched her body for her phone. It was snug in her pocket, and she pulled it out, trying to light up the screen. *Dead. Of course.*

"I'm sorry. I guess it died."

"Apparently," she huffed, though not angrily. "I've been trying to call you to tell you I have Snowball!"

"What?!" Marisol nearly leaped out of her skin. That was when she took a better look at the brown box Stella was carrying. White fur flashed through the holes of the box, and an angry meow sounded from inside.

Without thinking, she dropped to her knees and scooped Snowball out of the box. Snowball jumped into Marisol's arms, looking perfectly fine except for a spot of dirt on her tail. She instantly began to purr, snuggling into her chest.

"Stella, you found her!" she cried.

"Not me, but a nice woman brought her in. Poor woman had some scratches on her. Anyway, she said she didn't know where to take her but thought her owner might be looking for her. I immediately drove here. I kinda had to look up your information to get your address. Not exactly ethical, but I figured you'd forgive me." She shrugged.

Marisol wasn't a hugger. But emotions took over, and she threw her free arm around Stella. "Thank you," she whispered.

"Oh." Stella chuckled and hugged her back. "You're welcome. I'm just glad Snowball is back where she belongs. She was not happy with me holding her."

"Thank you so much," Cisco's deep, masculine voice sounded from behind her.

She felt Stella tense before looking at Cisco. Marisol felt her sudden intake of breath before Stella whispered, "Your man is hot."

She pulled back with a shaky laugh. "Yeah, he is. Stella, I seriously can't thank you enough. Can I pay you? Buy you dinner?" Something. She needed to do something to show her appreciation.

Stella apparently didn't believe so because she shook her

head in protest. "I'm just glad Snowball has been found safe. Being a first-time pet owner can be hard, but I know you'll figure it out. It's clear how much you love her."

"I do. I really do." This grumpy little cat had dug her claws deep into her heart and hadn't let go.

"I better get going. You two enjoy your night. I'll see you on Tuesday." Stella offered them one last smile before heading out.

Marisol felt a hand on her back, and she looked up to Cisco's warm smile. "Let's get you and Snowball back home." He reached down to take the empty box, and, as if working on autopilot, Marisol started to walk toward the elevator.

The events of the day had finally caught up to her. The stress. The horrible thoughts of her inadequacy. The constant feeling of being a letdown...it was all too much. A person could only beat themselves up so much before it took its toll.

Cisco was murmuring something to Snowball about her "adventure" in the city during their elevator ride up. She was barely listening, trying everything to keep herself together.

When the elevator opened again to her floor, she made a beeline for her door. The moment her hand wrapped around the knob, opening it, was the moment her body stopped fighting.

"Everyone is home, safe and sound," Cisco said, walking in.

But Marisol wasn't listening. She made it all the way to her couch before falling down with Snowball still in her arms. She felt her body cave in, pulling Snowball tighter to her chest.

And when the first tear fell, she couldn't stop the sob that racked her body.

CHAPTER 20

Cisco

Marisol had been stressed all morning and rightfully so. Snowball was missing, and even though she had only had the cat for a short time, they already shared a strong connection. Most of the day, she followed him, numb, completely devoid of emotion. Her eyes told him she was nearing her breaking point.

And now they hit it.

Snowball wiggled out of Marisol's lap and trotted off to her bedroom. Her cries got louder as she dropped her head into her hands.

His body gravitated toward hers, lowering himself on the couch next to her. "Princesa." He pulled her closer.

She whimpered but didn't argue. "Don't call me that. I'm not a princess," she murmured weakly.

Cisco elected to ignore her. "Snowball is home and safe. It's not your fault she got out."

"It is, though. I left the window open," she replied miserably.

"But not with the intent of Snowball getting out. She's safely back where she belongs," he assured.

"I can't take care of her. I can't keep her safe."

"Of course you can—"

Marisol pulled out of his grip and jumped to her feet. "Just stop!" she screamed, giving him pause. "You don't understand what you are talking about. You don't get it!"

"Then make me get it!" Cisco was on his feet, closing the distance between them. "What don't I understand?"

His heart broke at her pained expression. She was wearing her heart on her sleeve, and it was crumbling right in front of them. Her cries were no longer those of anger, but of deep-rooted sorrow. He knew this darkness. Hell, he had been in that darkness and fought his way out. He wasn't completely free of it, but he held the reins now.

"I'm not a good person—"

"Bullshit." His anger flared, but he tamped it down the best he could. Not anger at her, but anger that she couldn't see she *was* a good person.

"It's not!" she cried, her voice rising, edged with desperation. She was spiraling, sinking fast as the darkness threatened to consume her. But he was there. Steady, unwavering for her. He would catch her, hold on tight, refusing to let go, no matter how many times she tried to shove him away.

"Why aren't you a good person, Marisol? Huh? Tell me." Cisco reached out for her, expecting her to pull away. She looked like a frightened caged animal, ready to bolt. When his hand gently wrapped around her wrist, she jerked back.

And came undone.

"Because I can't take care of anyone! I was meant to take care of her, but I didn't. I would rather look away and ignore it because it's easier for me," Marisol shouted.

He had a feeling they were no longer talking about Snowball. This went deeper. Snowball was just the final straw.

"Who couldn't you take care of?" he asked.

Marisol was already pacing, no longer looking in his direction. She was lost in her own head, fighting her invisible demons.

"I constantly let my sister go up against my mother alone. I should have been the one to protect her. To stand up for her! It was my job as her older sister to be there for her. But I wasn't. I chose cruelty because I didn't want to face the things she was going through with our mom. It was easier being the favorite, molding myself into the person Mom wanted me to be. No matter how much I hated it.

"So, you see why I shouldn't have ever brought home an innocent animal that relies on me. I can't take care of people because I'm fucking selfish and entitled. I'm a horrible person, Cisco. You need to get out before you get tangled up with me. You should go." The last words were barely more than a whisper, but he heard them as if they were shouted.

He didn't know she had a sister or that her relationship with her mother was troubled. But hearing it now, something inside him just clicked. His understanding of Marisol—the way she acted, spoke, constantly looked uncomfortable in her own joy—it all made sense now. She didn't think she was deserving of those things.

She was wrong.

Wordlessly, Cisco took her hand and pulled her out of the living room. "Where are we going?" she asked, confused, but didn't fight him.

Cisco didn't answer. He brought her into the bathroom and flipped on the light. As expected, her bathroom was pristine. No dirty clothes or wet towels cluttered the floor. It smelled of lavender, and a small candle burned brightly in the corner. Unlike the rest of the house, this room seemed untouched by the hurricane of emotions from this morning.

"Here." Cisco brought her in front of the mirror, tilting her chin up with his finger so she was looking at herself in the reflection.

Marisol's usual perfectly styled hair had been hastily thrown into a bun with strands sticking up everywhere. Her sweats were too big, and her shirt had a coffee stain on it. It was far from her normal put-together look.

And yet she had never been more beautiful. Puffy eyes, runny nose and all. She was gorgeous.

"What am I supposed to be looking at?" she asked, biting her bottom lip. Her eyes darted around the room, probably wondering when he'd let her leave. But he wasn't going to let her leave until she realized how hard she was being on herself and acknowledged how hard she was working on becoming better.

"The woman in the mirror," he came up behind her and rested his hands on her shoulders, "this is the woman you're mad at. The woman you claim is an idiot and not worthy of good things because of the mistakes of her past."

"I'm not a good person," Marisol said, voice raspy from crying.

"Because you lost Snowball? Because you couldn't protect your sister?" Cisco prompted.

Marisol nodded, her bottom lip trembling. "Because I'm selfish. I only think about myself. I hurt the people I love, and I don't even know how to show them I care. I let my mother shape me into someone I barely recognize, and the worst part? I can't even bring myself to hate her for it. I don't blame her. I let it happen. I went along with it willingly."

"You were a child. A child who wanted her mother's love and could only get it by pleasing her."

"That's what Alice said." She chuckled humorlessly. "But if that's true, why was I awful to my sister as an adult too? You know she was dating Archie before me? Yeah. I stole her boyfriend—"

"Honestly, she should probably thank you for that." That earned him an elbow to the gut. "Right, sorry. Go on."

"I made her come to our engagement party—knowing it was going to hurt her—because my mother told me to. I could have fought harder. Could have done something different. But I took the easy way out. It doesn't matter how many times I say sorry. It's not going to fix my past mistakes."

"No, it won't," Cisco agreed gently. "But it has changed your future."

Marisol scoffed, but Cisco pressed a gentle kiss to her cheek. It effectively silenced her.

"This woman"—Cisco pointed at Marisol's reflection in the mirror—"is a beautiful, kind person who knows when to ask for help. Who has been actively working on her own shit and demons with therapy. Are you perfect? Hell no, but none of us are, Marisol. We've all made shitty choices and mistakes."

He knew damn well how one simple mistake could cause an avalanche of bad shit. It was hard to get out of it when everything else seemed to be spiraling out of control. It was easier just to give in until it wasn't, and you were drowning in all your decisions. Thoughts of his own past plagued him, but now was not the time to bring it up. This was about Marisol.

Silent tears rolled down Marisol's face, eyes wide as she looked at him through the mirror. She looked like a lost child, desperately seeking guidance.

"You aren't a bad person, Princesa. You're a person. You've

made mistakes. And now you are taking the steps you need to change that. That takes a lot of dedication and self-reflection. And you know what? Not many people can say they are putting in the work to change."

"I want to change," she whispered. "I want to be a good big sister like Lola deserves."

"Don't just do it for Lola. You can change for you. It's okay to want to be more or better than what you are." Cisco gently rubbed his hands up and down her arms. They were cool to the touch and full of goosebumps.

"You know what I see when I look at you?" he asked.

"Hmm?" she asked but flinched like she was afraid of the answer.

"A strong, capable woman. A woman who wants to experience life and make meaningful connections. A woman who seeks out the help of others to make that a reality. One that I'm thankful for giving me the time of day."

Cisco reached out and wiped away a few more tears that stubbornly rolled down her cheek. Marisol turned in his embrace, flinging her arms around his neck and nuzzling her head against his chest.

"Thank you," she whispered, "for everything."

"My pleasure, Princesa." If she called again tomorrow, and they had to go through it all over again, he would. As long as he was with her.

Marisol was taking up residence in his heart, making him feel things he hadn't felt in a long time...or ever. It was strong and new, and he wanted to see how it would develop. For the first time in his life, work wasn't the most important thing to him anymore.

Cisco's arms went around her waist and pulled her close.

She fit perfectly against him, as if she were always meant to be there.

"Cisco?"

"Yes, Princesa?"

"Will you stay the night with me?"

He had never answered yes to something so quickly.

CHAPTER 21

Marisol

No one outside her family had ever spent the night at her house. Even then, it was only Lola and her husband, Javi. It wasn't as if she was opposed to company; she simply didn't have people worth inviting over. Never had a girls' night where all her friends would eat way too much, drink far too much wine, and watch sappy romance movies. She definitely never had a man she was interested in staying the night.

Until now.

Her heart pounded so hard, it felt like it might burst from her chest. A whirlwind of nerves and excitement tangled inside her, each battling for dominance. She twisted her hands together, the motion a subconscious attempt to release the anxious energy coiling within her. Lost in her thoughts, she barely registered the movement until a pair of large, warm hands gently enveloped hers. Startled, she looked up.

Cisco—had he always been this close?—stared back at her. He brought her clasped hands to his lips and kissed her gently. "You look beautiful."

His words were enough to pop the bubble of anxiety looming over her. A laugh burst free from her lips, slightly too high in pitch. "I just cried all over you. My eyes are puffy, and my makeup is fucked. I know I'm the furthest thing from beautiful, but you're sweet for saying that."

"It's the truth." He lifted his hand to tuck a strand of hair behind her ear. "You've never been more beautiful to me."

Years from now, someone, somewhere, would ask her about the moment she knew she had found her person. And her answer wouldn't be a huge, grand gesture of love, or a romantic stroll through a park.

No, it would be the story of a bathroom, a lost cat, and far too many tears. And, of course, the man who had supported her all throughout the day, never once complaining.

This feeling was sudden and new. Powerful and fragile. She kept it close to her heart, not ready to dip her toes into the vast ocean of this emotion until she was certain he'd join her.

But she did kiss him.

Her body gravitated toward him, pulled along by an invisible string. They met in the middle, a clash of tongue and teeth. Cisco backed her up until Marisol's ass hit the counter. Hooking his hands behind her thighs, he lifted her up onto it.

Cisco moved between her legs, and she had no choice but to open for him until she straddled his hips. Heat rushed to her core, and the lacy underwear she wore pulled tight in the center, creating friction. It was hot and felt so damn good, but it wasn't enough.

She needed more.

Needed him.

Without thinking, her hands ran under his shirt, feeling the hardness of his muscles. This man was sin incarnate, detailing each of her wildest fantasies. But even in her wildest fantasies, the men had never looked this good.

Cisco broke the kiss, causing Marisol to whimper embarrassingly. "Do you want my shirt off, Princesa?"

The heat in her eyes told her he wanted less clothing between them. That a swarm of emotion burned brightly inside him, but he was still checking on her. Making sure this was what she wanted. The normal doubt that plagued her mind when making decisions wasn't there.

"I want it," she said with certainty.

In one easy movement, he had his shirt off, tossing it to the ground. All of his tattoos were on display, stealing the breath from her lips. Not a single part of his torso was free of tattoos. A few decorated his hips then disappeared into his jeans. She wanted nothing more than to see where those went.

Sex had never been something she desired.

She definitely didn't understand the thrill of it because Archie had left her less than satisfied on many occasions. She had thought she was the problem because it took a lot for her to climax. After all, Archie never seemed to have a problem orgasming. The only enjoyment she had gotten from it was when it was all over.

He certainly never soaked her panties like Cisco was currently doing.

"You want these off too, Princesa?" Cisco's husky voice made her snap her attention up from his groin. She refused to be ashamed at staring at him like she wanted to eat him for dessert. Because, quite frankly, that was exactly what she wanted. He fingered the waistband of his jeans, toying with her.

In response, she took off her shirt, exposing her black bra. It wasn't one of her sexiest or frilliest bras, but it did make her boobs look great and perky, so she couldn't complain. Now it was his time to stare at her, lust in his expression. This was what it felt like to be desired...and it was a damn good feeling.

"Off," she said, speaking with a new, growing confidence. "I want them off."

Cisco never tore his eyes from hers. He undid his belt and then the button on his jeans. He took his sweet time pulling down his zipper, but it was worth it in the end. He dropped his jeans and stepped out of them. He wore only black silk boxers, and they did little to hide the erection he sported.

"Wow," she murmured.

"A lot of tattoos, I know." He chuckled.

Right. She was definitely talking about the tattoos decorating both of his legs, all the way up to his hips, and not the large cock he was hiding in those small boxers.

"Your turn, Princesa." Cisco approached her, reaching for the waistband of her joggers. He waited, giving her time to put a stop to it if she wanted. But she didn't want to stop. If she stopped now, her body would never forgive her.

She lifted her ass off the counter the best she could, and Cisco discarded her pants next to his shirt. His gaze went down to her very obviously wet panties, and a sly grin crossed his face. It shouldn't be hot, but it only served to turn her on more.

"Cisco?"

"Hmm?" he asked, clearly distracted. His hands went to her back, fingering the clasps of her bra.

"I...I mean...it's just that—" She took a deep breath, knowing she probably sounded like an inexperienced fool. She definitely felt like one.

Cisco waited on her patiently, not unhooking her bra yet, but also not removing his hands either.

"I just don't want you to get upset if you can't...uh, make

me finish. It's me and not you," she assured quickly as his brows drew together.

This was it. He was going to say he wasn't interested in a girl he couldn't get to climax. She was aware it was an ego thing, and the last thing she wanted to do was hurt him.

She braced herself for the worst...but it never came.

Instead, she felt tension leave her chest as her clasp came undone.

"If you haven't finished, it's not you. It's because your partners are shit and don't know their way around a pussy."

Well...okay then. She supposed that settled that.

The straps of her bra slid down her arms, and cold air hit her nipples. They hardened to painful points. Cisco's thumb gently caressed her, sending jolts of pleasure straight to her core.

"These men don't know how to handle a princess when they have one. But I do," he said before dropping and kneeling on the floor of her bathroom between her spread legs.

Oh shit, this was happening.

Marisol didn't have time to be self-conscious because Cisco leaned forward, the top of his nose scraping across her wetness. "Fucking perfect," he groaned as he inhaled. "I think this pretty pussy needs my attention. Don't you agree?"

Yes. Yes. And fuck yes, she thought but could only manage a simple, shaky nod.

It was all Cisco needed though.

Without another word, he yanked off her panties, letting them pool on the ground. It hardly seemed fair that he still had on his boxers while she was completely exposed to him in every single way. But it was incredibly sexy.

Cisco pushed her legs farther apart, placing his large hand on her stomach and gently easing her down until her back hit the mirror. She was on full display for him, completely at his mercy. Yet she still couldn't help but feel she held all the power. Like, if she wanted it all to stop, he would, without question or anger.

But stopping was the last thing on her mind.

The first sweep of his tongue caught her off guard, and she shivered. "You taste so sweet, Princesa. So fucking sweet."

Marisol didn't have a chance to reply before his tongue lapped at her again, pushing through her folds to taste her cream. When he pulled back, she saw her arousal glistening on his lips.

"This pussy is mine tonight," he purred.

Tonight and every night if he wanted it, but she didn't have the nerve to say. "More," she said instead. "Please, Cisco."

"Gladly." He smirked and buried his head between her thighs again. This time, he ate her out in earnest, licking at her. His tongue found her clit, teasing the sensitive bundle of nerves, and she shivered.

"Oh, god..." she gasped as if she were in church and Cisco was the Holy Spirit working his way through her. Except this felt so much better and didn't leave her feeling guilty.

It left her wanton.

She reached down, running her hand through his hair and arching into him. This was not how she pictured the night going, her getting eaten out on her bathroom counter, but it was the best possible ending to an extremely tumultuous night.

Marisol's body jolted as two fingers brushed against her folds, finding their way inside her. Her body clenched around them, needing to be filled more but taking what she was given. Her legs shook as Cisco sucked her clit back into his mouth.

Molten heat coiled low in her belly, and waves of pleasure pushed her closer and closer to the edge. She had put up with bad sex for too long. If she knew getting eaten out felt like this, she would have dumped Archie way before they got married.

Cisco was right. It wasn't her that was the problem. It had never been her.

"Cisco..." Her voice quivered, muscles tensing. Cisco did not relent. If anything, it spurred him on even more.

She rode his face, chasing her pleasure. When she found it, her orgasm hit her hard, ripping through her body. Her breathy moans turned sultry and lasted longer. Cisco kept licking and fucking his fingers inside her until she went limp in his arms. Even then, he didn't pull back for another few minutes.

So this was what it felt like to be satisfied by a man. She truly had been missing out for so long.

When he stood, his boxers were gone. She hadn't even seen him do that, but she couldn't concentrate on much at the moment...except for the hard cock bobbing between them.

It put the men of her fantasies to shame.

A small white bead pooled at his tip. She wanted to lean forward and lick it off, needing to taste him like he tasted her. Before she could do just that, Cisco picked her up and threw her over his shoulder. She shrieked as he patted her ass.

"I need you in bed now, Princesa. You wouldn't happen to have condoms, would you?'

"I'm on birth control," she said automatically, heat rushing to her cheeks. "But I can get condoms. There's a pharmacy downstairs and—"

"Nah, I don't want to stop. I'm STI-free, and you're the only woman I plan on having sex with."

She shouldn't feel butterflies over something so simple, yet there they were, fluttering in her stomach. It felt an awful lot like commitment, something that should have sent her into a panic. She braced herself for the familiar fear of being tied to someone, of losing her freedom. But it never came. Instead, a different fear settled deep inside her—the fear of losing him.

"Just me?" she breathed, her voice barely above a whisper as he effortlessly tossed her onto the bed.

"Only you. There is and won't be anyone else. You're mine for as long as you'll have me," he said gruffly.

You're mine.

For as long as she wanted.

It felt so fucking amazing to be wanted and chosen for her and not what her family could offer.

"I want to feel you," she said, looking down between his legs. She would definitely feel the stretch of his cock, but she needed that. She also needed to see him lose himself when he slipped inside of her.

"You're so fucking beautiful," he groaned, gripping her firmly as he pulled her to the edge of the bed. With deliberate ease, he spread her legs wide, his gaze roaming over her with unrestrained desire. Once again, she was laid bare before him, and the intensity of his attention sent a thrill through her. She basked in it, preening under his hungry stare. The way he looked at her, as if she were the only thing that mattered, filled her with a confidence she had never known before.

The first brush of his cock against her pussy had her shivering. The tip of his head pushed between her folds, teasing her. Then, in one fluid motion, he pushed inside of her, and they moaned in unison.

Marisol felt the burn of his cock stretching her. It wasn't unpleasant, especially when he reached between them and stroked his thumb against her clit. "Relax for me, Princesa."

She hadn't even realized her body had tensed. Probably because it had been so long for anything other than her vibrator to be inside her. And her vibrator was much smaller than Cisco's cock. Her body was still on edge from him devouring her pussy, but she craved more. Getting one taste of an orgasm wasn't enough and never would be again.

Cisco Ramos ruined her, and she was loving every second of it.

"So fucking perfect," Cisco panted, and his hips began to thrust into her. Immediately, her legs wrapped around his torso, pulling him close and forcing him deeper inside.

Too damn good.

Her pussy responded in kind, tightening around him until it drew out a deep, throaty moan from Cisco. It only spurred him on, as if he wanted to claim every inch of her pussy, making sure everyone knew it was his. Because it was. She'd gladly let him fuck her whenever the need arose because she craved him just as much. Cisco awoke something within her that had lain dormant for so long. She'd never had a chance to explore her sexual side like this.

Marisol ground wildly against him. He whispered a curse under his breath, and before she could register what happened, Cisco pulled out and flipped her onto her stomach. She struggled to situate herself on all fours, but before she could get her bearings, he pushed in from behind her.

This new position felt filthy in the best way, leaving her completely exposed. He was deeper than ever before, and the stretch was intense, almost overwhelming, yet she craved every inch of him. His strong hands gripped her hips, controlling the rhythm, guiding her movements to match his. Each thrust sent a shockwave through her, and the sound of their bodies colliding filled the room with raw, unfiltered pleasure.

"Baby..." Marisol moaned, her voice trembling as she

arched her back, pressing herself against him, desperate for more.

"I want you to play with that pretty clit, Princesa. Can you do that for me?" he asked breathlessly, clearly not far from his own orgasm.

"Yes." She dropped lower, moving a hand between her soaked thighs. Her body jerked with each thrust, but she managed to rub circles around her aching clit, creating the friction she needed. Between him and her own hand, she knew she wouldn't last long.

"Good girl," Cisco purred when she obeyed.

And fuck, did she have a praise kink? Because hearing Cisco call her a good girl flooded her pussy. She liked it. She liked it *a lot.*

Her orgasm came fast out of nowhere, ripping through her body. She screamed out, her moans muffled by the sheets. Hot liquid filled her as Cisco held on to her hips like a lifeline. Him filling her up felt like the final stage in his claiming of her. His sticky seed dripped down her thighs, but she was too far gone to care.

No longer having the strength to hold herself up, Marisol dropped her hands from between her legs and fell onto the mattress. Behind her, Cisco pulled out with a groan. She expected him to fall into bed next to her, but he didn't. Instead, she heard a cabinet opening, and then a light flickered on and off.

Something soft soon touched her leg, causing her to jolt. "It's just me, Princesa. Let me clean you."

She should feel mortified having him clean his cum out of her, but she was too fucking satisfied and tired to care. It felt nice to be pampered; it wasn't something she had ever experienced with sex before.

Soon, the bed dipped beside her, and Cisco's warm body pulled Marisol into his arms. She turned to face him and nuzzled into the crook of his neck. "Stay," she said again, even though he already agreed earlier.

"I'm not leaving you," he said.

She wondered if that meant he wasn't leaving her now, or he wasn't leaving her ever.

She didn't have the chance to think over it long because sleep soon claimed her, pulling her under.

CHAPTER 22

Cisco

Something heavy plopped down on his chest followed by a fluffy tail hitting his face. Cisco groaned. Despite his better judgment, he forced his eyelids to open and was immediately blessed with the view of Snowball's butt. *Lovely.*

Not exactly the sight he wanted to see after a night of passionate sex with the woman he was falling for.

Curled up next to him was a very naked Marisol, covered only by a thin sheet. She was cuddled into his side, her head resting on his shoulder. Her hair was sprawled out across the pillow and his face, but he had no complaints.

She was fucking beautiful.

Visions of last night replayed in his mind. His head between her legs, tasting heaven. The moans she made as she writhed underneath his touch. How he felt when he was inside her. It was all perfect.

And he wanted more.

Cisco turned his body, much to Snowball's protest. The cat meowed angrily at him before prancing out of the room. Probably for the best. He didn't need Snowball seeing the things he was about to do to her mother.

Cisco pressed his lips to Marisol's shoulder, pulling her closer. The sheet slid down, exposing the expanse of brown skin he wanted to lick from head to toe. She smelled so fucking good, like fruit and candy. One taste wasn't enough. No, he was addicted now.

"Cisco?" she murmured in her sleep, a sultry, throaty morning voice.

His cock hardened at the sound of his name.

"Morning, Princesa," he purred, leaving a line of soft kisses from her shoulder up to her jaw. A soft moan escaped her lips, fueling his desires. Fuck, her moans of pleasure were music to his ears.

She settled on top of him, their bodies pressed together. His hard length throbbed against her belly as she wiggled on top of him, creating friction. He groaned, and Marisol giggled. "Someone's awake."

There was no denying it.

"Awake and hungry," he murmured.

Marisol placed her hands on his chest, lifting herself up. It gave him the perfect view of her tits and hard nipples. God, she was perfect. He wanted to bury his head between her chest and suffocate himself. Seemed like a good way to go.

"I can order us breakfast," she offered and tried to move off the bed.

She didn't get far before his arms wound around her waist and pulled her back. "Stay."

The beautiful smile she gave him was enough to lose his damn breath. "Well, if you're hungry, I need to order something."

"I'm not hungry for food," he said, licking his lips.

Marisol tilted her head to the side, one brow arched in curiosity. Then, realization dawned, and she gasped, her full lips forming a perfect "O." A rosy flush spread across her cheeks, the sight of her flustered expression impossibly endearing.

"Oh. I see. What are you hungry for?" she asked coyly, biting her bottom lip.

She already knew the answer, but he decided to humor her anyway. "You."

Heat flashed in her eyes, a hunger that matched his own. She leaned forward, her lips brushing against his ear. Every hair on his body stood up on end. "I'm right here, Cisco. Come take me," she murmured.

"Sit on my face, Princesa," he said. "And give me my breakfast."

Marisol's confidence wavered as her body tensed. "Sit on your face? Wouldn't that...uhm, like hurt? Could you breathe?"

"Breathing is overrated." If she only knew, moments ago, he had been prepared to drown himself in her tits.

"Cisco, I don't want to hurt you—"

He reached up, cradling her head in his hands before pulling her down to him. His lips met hers in a fiery, passionate kiss. His tongue flicked out, forcing her open for him. She obeyed willingly, allowing him to explore her mouth. Morning breath be damned, she was still the best thing he had ever tasted.

He pulled back after a moment, and she gasped, chest heaving. "Let's make one thing very clear, Princesa. When I say sit on my face, I need you to sit on my fucking face and let me eat."

She took in another shuddering breath but this time didn't

argue. She nodded once and pushed herself up until she was straddling his waist. He motioned her forward with a crook of his finger. She was slow to listen but cautiously began to scoot up his body. She stopped just shy of his face. Her pretty pussy was close but still unattainable.

"More. Hands on the headboard," he encouraged but didn't push. She needed to be the one to make the decision. Even if that left him turned on and waiting.

"If you die, it's not my fault," she said at last, moving up the last few inches until she was finally straddling his head.

"It's very much your fault, but I consent." He smiled wickedly, his hands coming to grip her thigh. He could see her arousal glistening between her legs. The first lick of his tongue had them both moaning out in ecstasy.

He dug his fingers into her thighs, pulling her down so she was no longer hovering over him but fully seated on his face, just like he wanted. Marisol gasped, grinding down on him. "Cisco..." she whimpered.

Dragging his tongue up the seam of her pussy lips, he found her clit, sucking the bundle of nerves into his mouth. "Ride me," he growled, voice muffled.

But he knew she heard because she lifted her ass slightly, grinding herself back down on his face.

He had died and gone to heaven.

"Cisco...baby." The moan left Marisol's lips. Something about her calling him baby drove him fucking crazy. He liked it. Liked it too damn much. It was something he wanted to hear days, weeks...hell, *years* from now. It would never get old. Waking up next to her, pulling her onto his face, and indulging in his own personal paradise.

Already, Marisol's thighs shook. He knew she was still sore from last night, which made him far cockier than he deserved.

He brought his hands up to grip her ass, squeezing. Her bounces became more frenzied, and he helped guide her movements.

"Fucking perfect," he breathed into her pussy, not knowing if Marisol heard him, or if she was too close to the edge to pay any attention to him. The thought of her using him to take her own pleasure was fucking hot. He'd be her toy if she wanted.

A few moments later, Marisol clenched around his head and came on his tongue with a needy moan. His face and chest were wet with her desire, as if leaving her scent on him to deter others.

He was a claimed man.

He was *her* man.

They hadn't said it in so many words, but they didn't need to. He knew where he stood.

Marisol was slow to move off him, her chest still heaving. He expected to see her blushing, but he only saw a sense of immense satisfaction on her face. Good. Confidence looked great on her.

Marisol took one look at him and laughed. "I think we need to shower."

"We're showering together," he said.

There was no protest on her end. She slid off the bed, her glorious naked body on full display for him. Part of him wondered if he'd be able to tattoo her again, wanting to add to her story. And it would be him to tattoo her again because no other man would ever get the pleasure.

Marisol was *his* canvas. *His* muse.

"It would save us water if we showered together. Better for the Earth," Marisol mused.

Cisco nodded in agreement, suddenly the spokesperson for the Go Green movement. "Much better for Earth."

"Just make sure to keep your hands to yourself, Cisco." She winked at him and disappeared into the bathroom.

He did not, in fact, keep his hands to himself. Or his mouth. Or his cock. Granted, he never promised her anything, and after he had her up against the shower wall moaning his name, he figured he'd be forgiven.

When they finally managed to pry themselves out of the shower, Marisol got out first, handing him a hot-pink towel. He raised a brow as he took it, but she just shrugged. "I like pink," was all she said as she changed into a silk robe. Pink, of course.

Cisco tied the towel around his waist, hoping he'd be able to find his clothes thrown throughout the room. He wished he planned better and brought clothes to change into, but he hadn't expected to stay the night.

"I need to feed Snowball!" Marisol called from her bedroom. "I'm putting your clothes in the washer too."

So, he'd stay in a pink towel for longer. There were worse ways to spend his morning. The only thing he could do was fix his hair, using a flowery-smelling mousse he found on Marisol's counter to style it. It wasn't perfect, but he had spent long enough in the bathroom.

Cisco found Snowball first once he entered the kitchen. She was licking up her food, happy as can be with no remorse at having her owner panicked about her whereabouts yesterday. He was just happy they found her, not knowing how he'd support Marisol if they didn't.

Marisol leaned over the counter, reading something on her phone with a frown. She didn't look happy at whatever stole her attention. "Are you okay?" He felt silly for asking the question, because it was obvious she wasn't.

Marisol's head snapped up, startled by his voice. Indecision colored her features, and he wondered if she was going to tell him what was on her mind or downplay it. He hoped for the former because, after last night, they were well past the latter. Or so he hoped.

After a moment of silence, Marisol sighed and dropped her phone. "It's my mom."

Instantly his interest was piqued. "What about her?"

"She's reminding me that she wants me over for dinner." She quickly pushed herself off the counter. "But I'm just going to say I'm busy—"

"We should go."

"What?" Marisol paused, looking at him like he just sprouted another head and not like he suggested attending a family dinner.

"Why not? We can go together," he suggested, his tone gentle but unwavering.

Cisco didn't know every detail about her relationship with her mother, but he knew enough just from things Marisol did or said. It was deeply strained, fractured in a way that might never be repaired. He wasn't sure if fixing it was even possible, and he certainly didn't want to be the one to push Marisol into something she wasn't ready for. Still, he believed she deserved the chance to show her parents just how much she thrived without them.

Besides, at some point, he'd have to meet them. Sooner or later, he would come face to face with the people who had shaped Marisol, for better or worse. And, truthfully, he wanted to understand her more—to uncover the unspoken pieces of her past that made her the woman she was today.

"I don't know. My mom is...intense. She's not going to like..." Marisol gestured to his tattoos.

Cisco raised a brow. "Do you like them?"

"Of course I do."

"Good. I'm not dating your mom, Princesa. I don't give a damn about what she thinks of my tattoos. People are always going to have their opinions on them. We can't help that."

"I know, but you don't know my mother. She's a lot, and I don't want her saying something that is going to fuck up what we have."

Ah, so there was the problem. Marisol feared he'd run away after seeing how controlling her mother was. He was used to being stared at and judged. It no longer bothered him like it once did. Her mother had no real ammunition against him, other than his looks. She had no way of knowing about his past —nobody did. He wasn't worried about it.

Marisol crossed the kitchen and stopped in front of him. She wrapped her arms around his neck as Cisco snaked an arm around her waist and pulled her closer.

"You ashamed of me, Princesa?"

"Not even a little." She leaned up to kiss him gently.

Cisco let his lips linger a moment longer before pulling back. "Then we'll go. And afterwards, we can come back here, and I can bury my head between your thighs again."

The reddish tint to her cheeks was adorable. He liked how bashful she could be about sex, but then also ride his face like her life depended on it.

"Surely you are going to grow tired of that." She tucked a loose strand of hair behind her ear.

"Maybe when I'm dead, but even then, I doubt it."

Her laugh filled his chest with warmth. He loved hearing it. Loved seeing her smile. She didn't do it often enough, and each time he was able to make her let her guard down, he counted that as a win.

"Fine," she conceded. "We can go. Just don't say I didn't warn you."

"I promise not to hold it against you." He winked and leaned down to kiss her one last time. He couldn't foresee dinner with her parents going badly.

And even if it did, he planned to be by her side through it, even if that meant rearranging some appointments at work. Tiny would have her work cut out for her, juggling his schedule, but he needed to be with Marisol this weekend. Even if that meant he'd be working a few extra hours, his girl was worth it.

Marisol

Was it possible for someone to die from having her heart pound out of her chest? Because at the rate her heart thumped anxiously inside her, she was certain it was trying to separate itself from her body. But it didn't get really bad until they reached the entrance to her parents' property.

Intimidating iron gates with red brick walls surrounded the entire estate. The house sat back another half mile from the entrance, nestled behind the sparse forest area. A black box with a number pad sat right outside the gate. Cisco's car came to a rolling stop. She was too busy pulling down her blue dress, making sure it covered the tattoo on her thigh, to notice they'd arrived.

"Passcode?"

His words took a moment to register in her overactive mind. Her leg began to bounce, and she swore the space around her was caging her in, becoming smaller and smaller by the moment. Her heart was thudding so loud, it was the only thing she could concentrate on. Pounding over and over and over—

"Princesa." A gentle hand went to her bouncing leg, stalling her movements. She blinked once, the fog in her mind slowly clearing as she looked up to stare into Cisco's warm brown eyes. They grounded her in a way nothing else could.

"It's going to be okay," he said, his voice soothing something deep inside her. She might not quite believe him, but she wanted to believe everything would be okay. "It's just one dinner. We eat their food, and I take you home to Snowball."

"Right, okay." She breathed in once before giving him the four-digit passcode. Cisco was quick to type it in. The gates squeaked as they opened, in desperate need of WD-40. The driveway to their house was full of twists and turns, until finally the grand Mediterranean-style villa came into view.

Cisco let out a whistle as he parked behind an older pickup truck. It belonged to Javi, so at least she knew her sister was already here. Maybe seeing her grandchildren would mellow her mom. Not likely, but there was a little hope.

"They're *rich* rich," Cisco said with admiration in his voice. "Damn, Princesa. Did you grow up here?"

Marisol shook her head. "No, they only moved into this house a few years ago. Though my childhood home looked similar. It's my mother's favorite architectural design."

There were no subtleties about the house. No expense was spared when you ran a thriving winery business. The interior of the house only proved that. When Marisol led Cisco inside, they entered the grand foyer with a soaring ceiling. A massive window at the top bathed the room in natural light. The curved staircase to their left led up to the guest bedrooms and her father's office.

Marisol hesitated slightly, gathering the last of her courage, before taking Cisco's hand. His warmth felt good, providing her with the strength and security she needed to take the first step down the hall. She heard high-pitched giggles coming from the outside family room, an enclosed outdoor area her parents enjoyed entertaining in. It was located next to their outdoor kitchen, overlooking the beautiful landscape of their backyard. Just last year her parents had finished their pool, complete with a hot tub. Her father said he had wanted a pool for a long time, but Marisol knew he wasn't the best swimmer and built the pool for his grandchildren.

Just as she suspected, when she opened the door to the outside living room, her niece and nephew were getting ready to swim, taking advantage of the last hour of sunlight. Javi struggled with Fabian, trying to put the floats around his chunky arms. Lola rubbed sunscreen into Camilia's back. Both Javi and Lola were in swimwear.

Marisol was surprised that Lola decided to wear a two-piece. Not because her sister didn't look absolutely stunning in a two-piece, but rather because she liked to keep her body covered up when around their mother. The absolutely unhinged and completely awful things their mother had said to them, but more specifically Lola, over the past few years would leave them both in therapy for the rest of their lives.

Her father turned from his position at the grill when he heard the door shut behind them. His face lit up, and Marisol couldn't help but smile. For as strained as her relationship with her mother was, her relationship with her father—though not thriving—was still pretty good.

"My girls are here." He wiped his hands off on the cloth next to his grill before coming over and giving Marisol a hug. He smelled of charcoal and fire. "And who is this? He looks familiar." He pulled back to look over Cisco.

All eyes were on them now. She felt the curious stare of her sister and brother-in-law. "Dad, this is Cisco. My—" Her brain went blank. Her...what? "Friend" wasn't right. Friends didn't give each other amazing orgasms or eat them out first thing in the morning. But was "boyfriend" the right word? They hadn't talked about labels, but she knew her feelings for him were stronger than any other man she had in her life before. She certainly couldn't address him as "lover." That term seemed dated, and anything involving the L word needed a private conversation that wasn't in front of parents.

Luckily, she didn't have to look like a complete fool for long. Cisco offered her father his hand. "I'm the boyfriend. I believe we met at your store not too long ago."

Her father pondered this before realization dawned. "Ah, yes. The young man interested in the spot next door. How's that going?" Leave it to her father to always find a way to talk about business.

Cisco, luckily, didn't seem to mind. "Should be squared away soon. Looks like we're going to be neighbors."

"You don't say? How exciting. What is it you plan on opening? Should I be nervous about competition?" Her father laughed good-naturedly, but Marisol still squirmed uncomfortably.

"Daddy..." she warned.

"Unless you also plan on opening up a tattoo parlor within your store, I think we're good." Cisco chuckled, falling into an easy conversation with her father, almost as if they were picking up from the last time they spoke.

"Tía!" Camilia grinned and ran over to Marisol, throwing her arms out for a hug.

No one could be upset or stressed when Camilia came running for a hug. She crouched down to meet her niece, and soon a chubby toddler came running up from behind his sister to join the hug. "Tía! I two!" It had been his go-to phrase since his birthday a few weeks ago.

"Are you going to go swimming with us? Mamá Lola said you weren't, but I told her I was going to ask you anyway."

"Your mommy is right. I need to stay back and watch all of your cool tricks," Marisol said, hoping it would satisfy them.

Camilia contemplated this and finally nodded. "Okay. Someone needs to take pictures." She skipped back over to her father. Fabian was on her heels, always following his big sister around. It was cute. Camilia was a great big sister, making her look like a natural. She took her brother's hand, explaining why he needed to be careful in the pool.

She couldn't stop her heart from lurching. That was what a big sister should be. Someone who protected their younger sibling. Something she had never done for Lola.

Her sister whispered something to Javi, who nodded. He caught Marisol's eye and offered her an amused smile before leading the kids to the pool. Lola made a beeline for Marisol, taking her hand. "We're getting drinks. Be right back!" she called and pulled Marisol inside. She had only a second to look back at Cisco, but he was still talking with her father. It looked friendly.

She hoped it was.

As soon as the door closed, Lola spun on her. "Who's that?"

"I thought we were getting drinks." Marisol walked past her sister to the wine fridge.

"You're stalling," Lola argued.

She was. But she had good reason to stall. Her relationship was still so new with Cisco. She didn't want to ruin anything by opening her mouth and saying something wrong.

Lola wasn't having it. "You have a boyfriend?"

"It's news to me too." She shrugged, grabbing a sweet wine. "Drink?"

"No, Javi and I are trying for baby number three. Our last one."

Marisol's eyes widened. "What? Really?" Her sister had never mentioned wanting a third baby. Though that was not news she would have shared with her in the first place. She would have told her friends, which made Marisol oddly jealous. It was her own damn fault though.

"Yes. Now back to you. Where did you meet him?"

Marisol knew she wouldn't be leaving this room until she satisfied her sister's curiosity. Apart from Alice, she hadn't told anyone about Cisco. Normal siblings talked about this shit, didn't they? Maybe it would be good to tell Lola. Especially since she wanted Lola to share important parts of her life with her. Marisol had to be willing to do the same. At the very least, it could offer her some perspective.

With her mind made up, she poured herself a glass of wine. The first of many, she was sure. "I met him when getting my tattoo, actually."

"Really? He was there getting one too?"

"Uh, no. He was the artist. And the owner."

Lola's eyes grew comically wide before she burst out in laughter. "Oh my god, Marisol. I didn't know I was sending you on your first date when I booked the appointment."

Marisol's cheeks flamed. "Me either."

"I didn't know you were into the tattooed guys. Reminds me a bit of Javi. Should I be nervous?" Lola raised a brow.

All color drained from Marisol's face as she adamantly shook her head. "No! Of course not. I would never—I mean, I know I did, but I wouldn't—"

"Geez, Mar, I'm kidding. I'm over the whole Archie thing. Does this mean Archie is out of the picture finally?"

"I wish," she sighed, her heart rate going back to normal. "Still waiting for him to sign the papers."

"Are you serious? That fucker is—"

"Girls." Both Lola and Marisol jumped at the new voice. Neither one of them heard their mother come in, but there she stood, all five feet of her. She was dressed to the nines, like she always was. Even just sitting outside was an event to her. The black and white dress she wore was surely new since Marisol had never seen it before. She paired her outfit with matching pearl earrings and a necklace.

"You're taking an awfully long time here. I figured you got lost." She tried to peer around Lola to see Marisol, disapproval coloring her features.

"We were just coming out. Weren't we?" Lola grabbed water off the table. She offered their mother a tight smile and headed back outside. Back to safety.

Trying to make the same clean escape, Marisol grabbed her wine glass and followed her sister. Right before she could make it to the door, her mother reached out to touch her arm. "You didn't tell me you were bringing a guest," she said, her voice deceptively friendly. Marisol had heard it many times before, though, and knew the anger lurking underneath.

"Yeah, sorry. It was a last-minute decision. He was at the house—"

"He was at your home?"

Fuck. She said too much. Marisol shrugged, which only irritated her mother more. She knew how she felt about nonverbal responses. "Yeah."

"I see." She pursed her lips together in a tight line. "He's...

different from the men I usually see you with. Quite different from Archie."

That was the point. She never wanted to date an Archie again. She had her fill of those types of men. "He treats me well." Better than well, but her mother didn't need to know more.

Marisol thought that was the end of the conversation, but her mother couldn't let it go. "You're still married, though, aren't you, dear?"

"Technically," she gritted out.

"I see." More judgment. More anxious nerves coiling low in her belly. "Not ideal, would you say? People talk about these kinds of things. Reputation is everything, dear. Archie's. Yours. Our family's."

This was why she didn't want to be here. She knew her mother would have a problem and start to make Marisol doubt all of her decisions. She hated how easily her mother could stir up doubt within her. The familiar need to make her mother happy and give in was strong, but she had worked so hard to make strides for herself. She refused to let her mother set her back.

"No one's reputation is at stake here. This is a family dinner, one you invited me to—"

"Yes, just you," her mother interrupted.

"Well, it's not just me anymore, Mom. It's Cisco too. I know you thought Archie was the man I should marry...that we should simply work out our problems, but we can't. I don't love him, nor do I want him as a husband. I'm happy, Mom. Can't you just be happy for me?"

Luciana's lips pursed into a tight line, nostrils flaring with quiet anger. Marisol knew what she was going to say before she spoke. "I'm so disappointed in you, Marisol. Whether you like it or not, you are still a married woman and must behave like one."

A mixture of anger and shame rose inside her, but before she could respond, her dad stuck his head inside the door. "Camilia is calling for you two. You better get out here before she comes and gets you."

Marisol was saved for now, which was good. She feared she'd say something to her mother she'd regret later. But she still had the entire dinner ahead of them to survive.

"THEY DON'T MAKE 'em like this at the steakhouse," Travis said, placing the steaks down on the glass table, opting to eat out by the pool rather than use their formal dining room in the house. "Cooked to perfection. Anything above medium rare is a crime."

Their father always gave the same speech every time he made steaks. Marisol met her sister's eye, and they shared a silent laugh.

Amongst the plate of steaks was one grilled chicken for their mother. Luciana avoided most red meats like the plague, so she always made sure chicken was available. For the longest time, Marisol had followed in her footsteps, but a person could only eat so much poultry before the very thought of it made her sick. Usually, her mother would make a comment about Marisol's food choice, but keeping silent told Marisol just how upset her mother was about Cisco being here. It made her blood run cold.

There were also hot dogs for the kids, since steak didn't impress them. Javi was getting their plates ready, adding extra ketchup for Fabian while Lola scooped fruit onto Camilia's plate.

Without prompting, Cisco made her plate, picking out the steak and mixing up a Caesar salad to pair with it. He placed it down in front of her, kissing her temple when he was done. In front of her whole family, like it was the most natural thing in the world. Marisol rarely, if ever, showed any displays of affection with past partners, but her feelings for Cisco needed to be expressed in the open. Even if that meant her family were witnesses.

Her mother's cold gaze bore into her, but Marisol did her best to ignore her as she cut into her steak. Her mom was a ticking time bomb, and she'd have to deal with the explosion eventually, but not until she absolutely had to.

Conversations around the table flowed easily, mostly led by her father. He asked Javi about his contracting jobs. Marisol didn't quite understand how it worked, but apparently he took a big job for some fancy hotel. By the looks of it, Lola seemed incredibly proud of him.

And Lola's bookstore was flourishing. She had officially hired two new people to help around the store and promoted another one to manager. This allowed her to take some much-needed time off to spend with her family. And now that they were trying for a third child—which she didn't share at the table—it would give her peace of mind, knowing her shop was in good hands.

Javi updated her father about his sister, Ofelia, and Ofelia's baseball player husband, Maverick. Although their children, Arturo and Violeta, weren't technically Travis's grandchildren, her father always treated them as if they were. Currently, they were traveling with Maverick for his season but promised to catch up with everyone over dinner soon.

Eventually, the conversation circled around to Marisol and Cisco. At first, the answers were innocent enough for her father. He wanted to know what was going on in her life, so Marisol divulged a little information about how she adopted a cat named Snowball and that she would probably start volunteering at the shelter. Her dad asked about the shelter a bit, excited that Marisol found a "positive" way to spend her time.

After leaving the winery business, Marisol had been lost. She was fortunate enough to not have to worry about money because her father took care of her, and she had a good amount of money saved away in an account she had since birth. It wasn't the money he was worried about though. It was her loneliness.

Then, the conversation took a shift when her mother spoke up. "So, how did the two of you meet?" She eyed Cisco like he was the leftover trash she forgot to take out. If Cisco noticed, he didn't show it. His face remained calm, even smiling at times.

Her own composure was quite different. Despite the nice Californian breeze, Marisol felt hot all over. Her face flushed, and she couldn't stop her leg from bouncing, a tell-tale sign she was nervous.

"How we met?" she repeated the question, earning another glare from her mother. She couldn't tell them how they met because then she'd have to divulge that she got a tattoo, and Cisco was the one who gave it to her. Her mother would absolutely explode if she heard that.

"We met at therapy," Cisco said before Marisol could come up with a lie. "Marisol was leaving a session, and mine was just starting. I thought she was beautiful, and, well, here we are."

Not technically a lie, she realized. They did run into each

other at therapy. It just wasn't what she thought of when thinking about their first meeting.

"I see," Luciana said. "It's just a shock to me." She laughed, expecting the rest of the table to join in, but no one did. Still, it didn't deter her. "Marisol is still married, you know. That's why I'm confused."

"Luciana," her father chastised.

"What? Can I not be protective over my daughter?" she asked, feigning innocence.

Marisol wanted the earth to open up and swallow her whole. A warm hand settled on her thigh. She looked down to see Cisco gently squeezing her. The small touch provided more comfort than it should, and she relaxed slightly.

Oblivious to the discomfort around the room, her mother continued to speak. "You said you own a tattoo shop? Does that require schooling?"

"I graduated from Cornell University. Helped me start my shops." He took a sip of wine and made an appreciative sound. "Is this yours?"

Her father's face brightened. "It is. Our bestseller. What do you think?"

"Pretty damn good. I might be a frequent customer at your store once it opens. Dangerous to have me so close." They laughed, but Marisol watched her mother tense.

"Close? What do you mean close?"

"Cisco here is going to be our neighbor. Another shop is opening up by the store," her father said, taking a big bite out of his steak. Some of the juices ran down his cheek, staining the front of his shirt.

Her mother's disapproval only grew. "Our clientele doesn't match those who frequent tattoo shops. The last thing we need are thugs hanging outside our doors. No offense to you, of course," she said to Cisco, even though she definitely meant that to be insulting.

"Mother," Marisol hissed, trying and failing to keep her voice level. She wasn't used to standing up to her mother, and it scared her shitless. "Would you let it go? The only thing you are accomplishing right now is creating an awkward dinner. Cisco is my boyfriend—"

"Oh, there is no need to be throwing out titles, Marisol," her mother interrupted. "This is all so sudden, and you aren't even divorced yet. Why throw someone else into the mix? Archie is doing his best to go about this civilly, and from what I understand, you have done nothing but drag your feet. Honestly, dear, I just worry about you. You're not acting yourself. Maybe your therapy isn't working as well as you think it is. That's why I stopped going to mine. I found it didn't help me. You may want to consider doing the same."

Her earlier bravado slowly deflated. Her mother wasn't even trying to listen to her or hide the fact that her preference was firmly in Archie's favor. It was never about her happiness, only the image she wanted to uphold. More surprisingly, her mother's revelation that she quit therapy was just another slap in the face that Luciana never really cared to mend the broken relationships she had with her daughters.

Stubborn tears stung her eyes, but she refused to let them fall. She heard her father and Lola whisper something to her mother, but she couldn't make out what they were saying. She couldn't hear anything but her own insecurities pounding in her skull.

"Did you know Archie harasses her?" Cisco's voice cut above everyone else, even within her mind, and the whole table quieted, all looking at them. His jaw clenched as he stared down her mother, not wavering under her penetrating glare.

"He's the one dragging his feet about the divorce. He uses it to control her because he knows he has no power without her. But despite that, Marisol still thrives. She can still laugh and create the life she wants. If you cared enough to know anything about your daughter, you'd see just how wonderful she truly is, but how terrified she is to upset you. Maybe if you cared about your daughter and not some image you want to convey to god-knows-who, you'd realize just how much you are missing out."

Silence followed.

Her mother opened and closed her mouth. A fish struggling out of water. Her cheeks flamed red with both anger and embarrassment.

"This is oddly familiar," Javi muttered under his breath, earning a light smack from Lola, who tried to hide her smile from her husband.

"Luciana, you do this every time," her father's patronizing voice boomed around the table.

But Marisol's eyes were fixed on the man beside her. The man who saw through the bullshit her mother spread. The man who defended her, even if that meant her family hated him for it. But how her family felt about him didn't matter. Probably never did. He only cared about how Marisol saw him.

At that moment, she knew.

Knew Cisco would defend her from her family. Save her from herself, if she needed that.

Knew the feelings inside of her were strong. Stronger than anything else in her life.

Because Cisco was hers. And she loved the man. It fucking terrified her, but she had let fear hold her back for too long. She refused to lose a chance at happiness.

While the table argued, Marisol jumped out of her chair.

All eyes turned to her once again, but this time she didn't care. "I need a few minutes."

"Honey, please." Her dad tried to reach for her, but she moved out of his grasp.

"I need a few minutes," she repeated, voice stronger than before. Her father hesitated but nodded. She didn't even acknowledge her mother.

Before anyone could say anything else, she grabbed Cisco's hand and pulled him out of his chair. He eyed her suspiciously but didn't argue when she led him into the house and straight to the bathroom.

CHAPTER 24

Cisco

Cisco knew very little of her family. As far as he knew, Marisol and her father had a pretty decent relationship. She blamed herself harshly for the treatment of her sister, so their relationship was rocky, though it appeared both women were trying.

Then there was her mother. Cisco didn't make it a habit of judging women, but she was a vile person with too much time on her hands. She knew exactly what to say to get under someone's skin and play it off as concern. Cisco was tired of it and hadn't even been around her for more than two hours. He didn't know how Marisol put up with a lifetime of that bullshit.

When his girl stood, saying she needed a moment to compose herself, he was all too happy to follow her out. When the door shut behind him, Cisco couldn't hold back any longer. "Your mother is a viper. I couldn't sit back and let her talk to you that way. Fuck, Princesa, I'm sorry for suggesting we come. I didn't realize it would be that bad."

Marisol didn't respond, and he grew wary. Did he say something wrong?

She pulled him down a hall and into a guest bathroom the size of a small bedroom. Everything in this damn house was big and screamed money. No...not money. Abundance. Too much.

"Marisol, are you upset?" he asked, his worry skyrocketing.

Marisol grabbed the band around her wrist and pulled back her hair, securing it with the black tie. "No one has ever stood up for me like that," she said at last. "No one has put me first before my family. No one has made me feel wanted like you have, Cisco."

He was rendered speechless. And then she dropped to her knees, and he understood the reason for the bathroom privacy all too well. His cock hardened, seeing this magnificent, beautiful woman on her knees for him.

Honestly, what he did was bare minimum. She deserved so much more than him simply standing up for her. It made him wonder what type of men she dated in the past. If they were all like Archie, he had a good idea of her past relationships.

"I need to show you how much I appreciate what you did." Her voice grew sultry, going straight to his cock. She didn't need to do this, but who was he to tell her no? Marisol made quick work of his zipper, pulling it down. His cock strained against his boxers, but she expertly pulled him free of his confines.

Her hand wrapped around his cock, pretty red nails digging into his skin. Cisco groaned, reaching down to fist her ponytail. She looked up at him, dark eyes full of lust.

He licked his lips and nodded. "Go on then, Princesa. Show me your appreciation."

Marisol's tongue flicked out, teasing his tip. She moved her hand to the base of his cock, dragging her fingers down his length. He groaned, using one hand to brace himself on the wall behind her. The muscles in his back tensed as her warm, wet mouth took him down her throat. He wasn't small by any means, but she worked him down her throat like the fucking goddess she was.

She was going to be the death of him.

"Fuck, Marisol," he groaned, tugging on her hair. Her tongue teased his tip, swirling around to lap at the precum already forming. He felt like a damn teenager getting blown for the first time. He was going to finish embarrassingly fast if he didn't get his body under control.

Marisol pulled back to suck on his tip. Her hand moved along his shaft, squeezing him perfectly. Not as good as her sweet pussy pulsing around him, but still incredible. He tugged on her hair, drawing a long moan from her. He wanted nothing more than to feel between her thighs and see if she was wet for him. If sucking his cock got her going too.

"Marisol..." he warned as she deep-throated him a second time, making soft gagging noises when he thrust his hips forward. He did it again and again, taking her mouth at a rapid pace. She kept up, though, eagerly taking his thrusts. It was messy and perfect. *She* was perfect. And he never wanted to lose her. That he was certain of.

He moaned her name again, the only warning he was close. Luckily, she understood and eagerly sucked on his tip. It was too much. His hips faltered, and he came with a grunt, wishing they didn't have to be quiet. Even though he suspected her family was still outside, he didn't need someone walking by and hearing them.

Marisol groaned, swallowing him down. She pulled away from his cock with a loud pop, licking her lips. The damn woman pulled back with a smirk, a teasing gleam in her eyes.

She stood up like she didn't just give him amazing head and dusted off her clothes. "I'm going to tell my parents we are leaving."

"Yeah, okay," he said breathlessly.

"Will you come with me?"

Honestly, if she asked him to put on a clown costume and follow her mom around on a tricycle, he would. Whatever the fuck she wanted. He nodded once and situated himself, covering up once again. He didn't think walking out with his cock on full display would be appropriate.

Marisol opened the door, leading him back out of the house. He got the perfect view of her shapely ass as she walked, doing little to settle the need growing inside him. The tense conversation around the table ceased the moment Marisol appeared. Her father and Lola had the sense to look apologetic at her for Luciana's behavior, but her mother's haughty attitude didn't waver. If looks could kill, Cisco would be a dead man.

"Thank you for dinner, Daddy," Marisol said, her voice strong. Pride surged through him because he knew how difficult this was for her.

"You don't need to leave now, Mar. We'd love to have you stay," Travis said.

"Thanks, Daddy. But I think it's best if we go." Marisol reached for Cisco's hand, intertwining their fingers together. "I'm sorry we had to cut things short."

Travis cast a disappointed look toward his wife, shaking his head. Luciana sighed. "Really, Marisol. Don't be upset. You know I love you, and I'm just trying to understand the dynamic between you and the...young man you brought home with you."

"Mom, you need to say sorry and move on," Lola came to

her defense. "I thought you said you were working on this in therapy."

"We were," she assured. "But like I said, I wasn't seeing a difference. Anyway, we would love for you to stay. We don't see much of you these days." Luciana pouted, and Cisco had to try very hard not to roll his eyes at her obvious attempt to guilt-trip her daughter.

Luckily, Marisol saw through her mother's antics. She probably knew them better than anyone. "I would rather go home. I have to take care of Snowball—"

"Who is Snowball?" Luciana interrupted.

"My cat."

"You have a cat?"

Clearly, she hadn't been paying any attention to her daughter when she spoke about Snowball and volunteering. Marisol ignored her and looked over at her sister. "I'll call you later, okay?"

Lola nodded, offering her a timid smile. "Okay. Marisol?"

"Yeah?"

"I'm proud of you."

Marisol stiffened, and her eyes glazed over. Cisco wondered if she had ever heard those words before. Judging by her reaction, he didn't think so. He made a mental note to tell her that more.

"Thank you," she whispered.

Before they left, Marisol went around to hug her niece and nephew and her father. She hated that Camilia and Fabian had to witness the earlier drama, but hopefully it didn't scar them too badly. Travis got up to walk them to the door.

From the doorway, Cisco started his car, and Marisol headed out. Before he got too far, a hand clamped down around his shoulder. He tilted his head back to see Travis watching his daughter walk away.

"Do you care about my daughter, son?" he asked, not looking at him. His attention stayed on his daughter.

Cisco did. A lot. Maybe he even loved her, but he couldn't tell her father that before he told Marisol. "I do. She means a lot to me," he said instead.

Travis nodded. "You seem like a good man. Just please..." He broke off in a sigh. "Don't hurt her. And let her know she can be herself, not what her mother wants her to be, and I will still love her just the same."

"That seems like something you should tell her," Cisco said. "It would mean more coming from you than me."

"I know...and I have. But I think she needs someone else to love her as she is and not what her mother wants her to be." Travis tore his gaze away from Marisol and took in Cisco. "She's happy with you. I can tell."

"I'm happy with her." Those words weren't adequate enough for how he felt, but they'd have to do for now.

"Good. Keep making her happy." That was the last thing Travis said to him before dropping his hand from his shoulder. Without another word, Cisco went to join Marisol in the car.

CHAPTER 25

Cisco

For the next few days, Cisco stayed with Marisol. After their less-than-stellar dinner with her family, he felt as if he understood Marisol better and the reasons why she was who she was. It didn't make him feel any less for her. If anything, his affection for her only grew until he could no longer deny he loved her.

He loved Marisol.

It was an all-consuming feeling he felt deep within his bones. It was also different from anything he had ever experienced. The need to have her right next to him and protect her was strong. Yet he couldn't find the words to tell her yet, only because she was still dealing with the fallout from their dinner.

She needed time to process, and he'd give her that. However long she needed.

"I have another therapy appointment this morning," Marisol said during breakfast. Cisco wasn't much of a cook, but he could make a simple omelet. She had opted for only veggies, while he filled his with bacon.

"Do you want me to take you?" he asked through bites.

Marisol chuckled and leaned over, rubbing her thumb along his chin. "Dropped some eggs there." She let her thumb linger before falling back. She tucked a stray lock of hair behind her ear and shook her head. "No, but thank you. I just wanted to speak with Alice before I meet with Stella and the other volunteers tomorrow evening."

"Oh, that's right. You excited?"

She shrugs. "Kinda. A little nervous. But Stella is really nice. I just hope she doesn't think I'm incapable after the whole Snowball situation."

"She won't," Cisco insisted. "Because she also saw how distraught you were over losing Snowball. She knows it was an accident."

That earned him a timid smile. "Thank you."

Cisco winked at her and then finished up his breakfast. He had to get to work soon and knew he'd probably need to go home tonight. He needed to do laundry and run a few errands. Since spending the past few days with Marisol, he had neglected many items on his to-do list. He needed a few days to get his affairs in order.

Once Marisol finished eating, Cisco took their plates to the sink and washed them off. "Call me after your meeting tomorrow. I want to hear how it goes." He rounded the island to place a soft kiss on her forehead.

Marisol preened underneath him, wrapping her arms around his neck and pulling him back down for a proper kiss. Her lips against his always got him going, and if he didn't have clients today, he'd drag her pretty ass back to her bedroom and make her scream his name twice before he left.

He was so tempted.

Then Marisol broke the kiss, a flush to her cheeks. "I'll talk to you later."

"Later. I want to hear your voice before I fall asleep tonight." Cisco untangled himself from her, still smelling her candied scent as he walked out the door.

"Tiny, my favorite teenager. What's my schedule looking like today?" Cisco asked as he walked through the doors of Golden City Tattoo. Before leaving Marisol, he had snuck a glance and saw he had clients, but not any specifics. Tiny was manning the front desk, sipping on one of her gross iced coffees she liked so much. It was mostly sugar, and Tiny had the biggest sweet tooth of anyone he knew.

"If you had other favorite teenagers, I would be worried." She narrowed her dark eyes on him. "And you have a bit of free time this morning, but then you have two clients, both slotted for four hours. All artists are in and fully booked today."

Cisco liked longer sessions. That usually meant bigger pieces, and he could get creative with it. "My station ready?"

"Duh. Did I start yesterday?" She rolled her eyes. "Also ordered new gloves. I realized they sent me the wrong size last time. I'll take that raise whenever you want to give it to me."

Cisco laughed, coming up next to her and rubbing her head. She hated that and immediately hit his hands away. "What if I buy you lunch? We even?"

"I have your credit card. You were going to buy me lunch anyway. Throw in money for the new Willows record, and I'll call it even," she countered.

"You drive a hard bargain, but I guess I can do that." In truth, Cisco spoiled the hell out of Tiny. He liked to. He had no siblings of his own, and Tiny was the closest thing he had to an annoying little sister.

Cisco's phone began to buzz in his pocket. He reached for it, seeing it was Ernesto. He had been expecting a call from him for the last few days. "Gotta take this, prima. Come get me when my first client is here."

Tiny saluted him as he went into the back toward his office. Once the door was shut, he answered the call. "Ernesto. You better be calling me with good news," he joked.

There was silence on the other end of his phone. Cisco thought that was odd because Ernesto was usually speaking the moment he answered his call. "Ernesto?"

There was a cough on the other end before Ernesto's voice filled his ear. "Hey, man. You got a minute?"

Even if he didn't, he did now. The dejection in Ernesto's tone had him on edge. He took a seat at his desk, putting the phone on speaker and setting it down. "Yeah. What's up?"

"I got a call back from the agent on the San Francisco property," he said.

He had been waiting to hear back for weeks to see where they were in the process. He finished all his necessary paperwork; all they needed was to formally accept the offer. "Okay, so is it done? Place mine yet?"

"That's the thing, man, they pulled out. Rejected."

Cisco heard the words, but his brain couldn't seem to process them. It made no sense. He offered above asking price and was prepared to be competitive. "Why? What the hell happened?"

"They got wind of your record, man. I'm sorry. I don't know how that happened."

The blood in his veins went cold as his whole body tensed. He didn't talk about the incident often. In fact, he made sure it was buried from his record. No one should have had access to it, unless they combed the entire internet or happened across his file.

The incident in question happened in college, and it wasn't his fault. But that didn't matter because it nearly fucked up his entire life. He spent months...if not years, trying to rebuild himself. Obviously, he was able to, but it took so fucking long.

"How?" he gritted out.

"I told you, I don't know—"

"Even if they found out, why the fuck is it a reason to pull out? That shouldn't matter," Cisco interrupted.

"Normally it wouldn't," Ernesto agreed, speaking quickly, as if afraid Cisco would cut him off again. "But this district is full of elitists."

"What the hell do you mean by that?" Cisco tried to keep his voice at a normal level, even if his anger continued to spike the longer this conversation went on. He knew Ernesto was just the messenger and shouldn't be the one to get his ire, but unfortunately he was.

"The place is a tourist's wet dream. It brings in a lot of revenue for a lot of people with money. The seller feels that your background could...diminish the reputation of the district."

"What the actual fuck, Ernesto? How does that make any sense? It's a fucking tattoo shop."

"I don't know! It doesn't," he quickly agreed, "but I can't change his mind, man. All I can say is you might want to get with your lawyer and ask him how these records were leaked. In the meantime, I'll keep working with the agent. Let them know it's a misunderstanding. And listen, there are other spots we can look at too. I can have five other locations in your email in the next hour."

It wasn't even about the location anymore, though Cisco

had desperately wanted that building. The foot traffic and clientele would have been amazing, but he could work with other places. What angered him the most was how someone unburied his past. Shit he hadn't thought about in years.

"I'll call you later. If you learn anything, call me back." Cisco didn't give Ernesto a chance to reply before he hung up and searched for his lawyer's number. These days, Elias mostly dealt with his business matters, but he had once been an integral part of getting Cisco's name cleared.

Elias answered on the second ring. "Mr. Ramos. How can I help you today?"

"Elias, tell me how I just lost a property for my next shop because they found my records?"

"Shouldn't be possible. Tell me what happened." Keys clicked on the other end, no doubt Elias searching something on his computer.

Cisco told him about his conversation with Ernesto. Elias didn't interrupt him, just typed away. It took him a few moments to respond. "I'll need to look into this. I'm not seeing anything on my end. Listen, give me a few days to sort this out, and I'll call you when I have an answer."

It wasn't exactly what he wanted to hear, but he supposed it was better than nothing. "Is there anything I can do in the meantime?"

"Nothing for you to do. Let me take care of this. Try not to worry about it." Cisco was glad Elias wasn't here to see him roll his eyes. Yeah, if only it were that simple: just to not worry about it. It would be the only thing on his mind.

"Yeah, fine. Get back to me when you can," he said, sighing.

"Have a good day, Mr. Ramos. I'll call you when I know more," Elias promised, and the line went dead.

Cisco dropped his head into his hands, feeling drained. His day hadn't even started yet, but he was already over it. He eyed his phone, half tempted to call Marisol. He could explain everything to her and have another person tell him it would be okay. But he also didn't want her to worry, especially after the disastrous dinner at her parents' they were still recovering from. She had enough on her plate. No, he could handle this on his own.

A knock came from the door, and a second later, Tiny stuck her head in. She eyed him once and furrowed her brow. "What's wrong?"

"Nothing," he lied. "What's going on?"

It was clear Tiny didn't believe him, but she didn't push him either. That was why he loved his cousin. She knew when to push and when to back off. "Your first appointment is here. Want me to bring him back?"

And just like that, he needed to get back to the real world. Just because his world was imploding didn't mean time stopped until the problem was fixed. He nodded once. "Yeah, I'm ready."

Tattooing would at least let him escape. And later he would call Marisol, and things would get better. He trusted Elias to handle the problem. It was a waiting game now.

CHAPTER 26

Marisol

After her session with Alice the day before, where she told her all about her mother's behavior at dinner, Marisol was apprehensive to attend another—even if this dinner was supposed to be casual among friends. Alice assured her this would be different, and Marisol would have a great time if she allowed herself to.

She tried to remember that as she exited her car, mentally preparing herself to go inside the restaurant. They were going to meet somewhere Marisol had never heard of, but, according to her quick research, they sold decent subs and salads. There was absolutely nothing to be nervous about, and yet she couldn't help but think about everything that could go wrong. She could say something dumb or not connect with another volunteer. God forbid she accidentally said something that offended another person.

Those thoughts spiraled through her mind as she made her way to the hostess stand. The young Black teenager smiled at her. "Welcome to Soup's House. Party of one?"

"No, uh, I'm actually supposed to be meeting a group here. I'm not sure if they arrived yet," she admitted.

"Do you know who the reservation would be under?"

"I think Stella?" She actually didn't know. Normally, she would have this information, but it was a testament to how nervous she was.

The hostess clicked on her computer and then nodded. "Your party is here. They are in our private room. Follow me." She smiled and led Marisol through the restaurant. It wasn't prime dinnertime yet, but already the tables were full of couples and families. The industrial feeling of the restaurant made the atmosphere relaxed yet professional. The hostess stopped once they reached two gray sliding doors. She knocked first before opening them.

"Another member of your party is here!" she called and then looked back at Marisol. "Enjoy your meal."

Four unfamiliar faces and Stella turned in her direction. Stella beamed, jumping up from her spot. "Marisol! I'm so happy you could make it!" She crossed the room and threw her arms around her.

Startled, Marisol awkwardly hugged her back. If Stella noticed her hesitation, she didn't seem to mind.

"Let me introduce you to everyone," Stella said, pulling back. "These two in the striped shirts are Paul and Antonio."

One of the men waved. "I'm Antonio. Paul is my partner, who decided to match me today."

Paul gasped, lightly shoving his partner. "Don't believe him. I got dressed first, and he said he wanted to match. Not me."

"His words were 'that's too gay even for me.'" Antonio rolled his eyes. "Men, am I right?"

The nerves she felt a moment ago slowly disappeared.

Antonio and Paul were the type of people who could get along with everyone, a trait she envied. "It's nice to meet you." She smiled.

"The guy with green-and-black hair who looks like he just rolled out of bed is my husband, Blaine. And the cute pink fairy-looking woman is Izzy," Stella finished.

Blaine reminded her of a lead singer from an early 2000s rock band. He had the grunge look down, with his navy-blue shirt and ripped jeans. His messy hair swooped across his forehead, obscuring his left eye from view. He reminded her of Cisco a little bit, mostly because Blaine was also covered in tattoos. He nodded in her direction. "Nice to meet the woman who was able to tame Snowball."

"Oh my god, that was you?" a sweet, melodic voice asked. Izzy turned to smile at her, and Marisol understood the fairy description. Izzy looked like she just stepped out of a fairy tale with her frilly pink dress. Her heart-shaped face and button nose only added to the effect. "It's so good to meet you. How's Snowball doing?"

"Really good. She has definitely made herself at home," Marisol said, deciding to leave out Snowball's escape fiasco.

"Come sit by me." Stella led Marisol to an empty seat. On the table were a few appetizers. Spinach artichoke dip, finger sandwiches, and a large serving bowl of Caesar salad. "Feel free to eat anything. We like to get a bunch of appetizers and share."

"Some of us share." Antonio smirked, staring pointedly at his partner. "And some of us inhale like a human vacuum."

"And I'll do it again," Paul said, unabashed.

"Honestly, it's a little impressive how quickly you can make a basket of chips disappear," Izzy chimed in.

Paul grinned, reminding her of a black-haired Ryan Reynolds. "It's my specialty."

The banter between them was easy and lighthearted. Marisol could tell they were more than just people who volunteered at the same shelter, but friends too. None of them made her feel like the third wheel in an already established friendship. In fact, she was the shiny new toy everyone wanted to know more about.

"So, what do you do for a living, Marisol?" Paul asked.

This was always an awkward question because she didn't have a job. People often looked down on her when she said that, though, thinking she lived off Daddy's money. And while that was mostly true, Marisol had been saving her own money since childhood, learning how to invest from her father. Even without her father's money—which she often told him he didn't have to supply her, but he refused—she could still live her comfortable lifestyle.

"Well, I used to work at the family business. We run a winery," she said. "But I recently stepped back. I'll help my dad occasionally. Sometimes I'll help my sister out at her bookstore, but...that's about it," she finished lamely. She didn't have much of a social life...at least until she met Cisco. She enjoyed her life, but it did sound boring when she spoke about it to others.

But apparently not to this group. "Nice." Blaine grinned. "I want to be a stay-at-home trophy husband, but Stella says I'm not pretty enough."

"That's not true." Stella rolled her eyes but laughed. The two of them looked like a cute goth couple you'd find in a Tim Burton movie. "You are plenty pretty enough, but if anyone is going to be a stay-at-home spouse, it's going to be me. Then I could spend all my day with cats and dogs. I prefer them over people...except for you all."

"Nice save, Ella." Blaine laughed.

"Please tell me you aren't grossly in love," Izzy said to Marisol. "I can't be the only one here that's single."

Just thinking about Cisco had her smiling, and that didn't go unnoticed.

"Oh, she definitely has a boyfriend—"

"Antonio!" Paul interrupted his partner. "Don't assume her sexuality."

"Oh, right, sorry. I hate when people do that to me," he said sheepishly.

"No, it's okay. I, uhm, do have a boyfriend. It's new though. His name is Cisco," Marisol said.

"No fucking way." Blaine slapped the table, causing the dishes to rattle. Marisol jumped, startled by the outbursts and worried she might have said something wrong until he said, "Cisco the tattoo guy? The one who owns Golden City Tattoos? He's damn good. I'm a little in love with him too."

"Oh! That's why he looked familiar!" Stella exclaimed. "When I"—she paused, offering Marisol an apologetic smile— "ran into him at your place, I swore he looked familiar." Marisol was glad she didn't expand on why Stella ran into him, since it was the night she lost Snowball.

Marisol only smiled as they continued to chat. She sipped on the water a waiter brought for her, shoveling some salad onto her plate. It was nice being out like this where there were no expectations. She didn't have to be anyone other than herself.

Eventually, the conversation died down, and Stella took that as an opportunity to dive into the reason why they were all here. "So, let's talk about fundraising."

"Yes, please. And can we all agree that inviting the local marching band is a bad idea? The number of traumatized pets I had to soothe last year still haunts me." Izzy shivered.

"No, we want to do something big to get the community involved. Our shelter needs the funds, especially if we want to raise money for the expansion," Paul said.

Marisol cocked her head to the side. "Expansion?"

Stella nodded. "Yeah, the shelter is at capacity. We are a proud no-kill shelter, but we also can't keep taking pets in because there's no room. We have the land though to add extra kennel rooms."

"Yeah, but the only problem is that we're working with no money to put this fundraiser on. We just have us," Blaine sighed as he pushed around a crouton on his plate. "I can't paint faces another year in a row. I made that little girl cry, and I've never recovered."

"It was a truly awful pony," Paul said sympathetically.

"It was a bear!"

"Yikes." Paul made a face before taking a sip of his water.

She pulled out a small pink notebook and pen from her purse and opened it to a new page. She titled the top "Shelter Fundraiser" and looked up, surprised to see five sets of eyes all looking at her. Never liking being the center of attention, she squirmed uncomfortably in her seat.

"Sorry, I just work best when I write things down," Marisol said to the table.

She expected looks of contempt, a response from years of disapproval, but that never came. If anything, everyone around the table scooted in closer, intrigued. Clearly she had the spotlight now.

"I've planned a few events for my family and their friends," she said modestly. "I would love to plan this one. With all of your help, of course. I don't want to overstep. But maybe if you could tell me things you'd love to see at a fundraiser."

"Keep in mind, we have no money. Hence the need for a fundraiser," Izzy added.

But Marisol shook her head. One perk of having the last name Roberts was that people were eager to fulfill requests in hopes that strengthened their relationship with her family. "Let's just say I know people."

"You are officially the coolest person. If I were straight, I'd kiss you. With your consent, of course," Antonio said, causing Marisol to laugh and Paul to smack his chest.

"Agreed. Minus the kissing part. You seriously are the coolest right now. I'm so glad we connected." Stella reached for her arm and gently squeezed it.

Her touch felt...nice. Like a friend. Like maybe, after thirty years, she might have found a real, genuine friend group.

Everyone at the table listed things they wanted to see, ranging from dunk tanks, to face painting by a real artist, to food trucks. Marisol made a note of each suggestion. She couldn't deliver on everything, but she already had ideas of contacts she could call.

"Do we have a date for this?" Marisol asked.

Stella bit her lip. "Ideally? A month from now."

So, short notice. But she had worked under more limited time constraints in the past. It wasn't impossible, but rather a challenge she liked to take on.

"That's doable." She heard the sighs of relief around the table as she made note of the date. Marisol looked over everything, knowing she had her work cut out for her. "I'm going to get started on this. I want to keep you all as informed as possible, so is there a good way to do that?"

Izzy nodded, her long, honey-colored hair bouncing in her enthusiasm. "We will add you to the group chat. Just be warned, it can get crazy."

"I think I can handle that." Marisol grinned. Izzy handed her the phone, and she quickly typed in her number before handing it back. Izzy added her into the group chat.

"Everyone text her who you are so she can save the numbers," Stella said.

"Oh, good idea. I hate getting thrown into group chats and having random-ass numbers texting me. Like who am I talking to? Marco from HR or the cutie from Cubicle 23," Antonio said.

"I'm the cutie from Cubicle 23," Paul said proudly.

All their texts came in at once, and Marisol half expected her phone to power off, never having seen this much engagement before. She saved their numbers and had to agree with Antonio. It was nice knowing who you were texting and not just seeing a random number.

"And with that, our monthly meeting has concluded. Same place next month?" Stella asked.

"Well, we probably want to meet a few more times between now and the fundraiser. So, let's just check our calendars and wait for Marisol to give us updates?" Blaine suggested.

The table murmured their agreement and stood up. Marisol quickly got out her purse, grabbing a twenty. Before she could leave it on the table, Stella stopped her. "Blaine's dad owns the restaurant. He feeds us for free. Oh! He might be a good person to ask about the fundraiser. Maybe he'll want a booth to sell food at. Blaine and I will talk to him."

Shoving her wallet back in her purse, she got up and followed everyone outside. She found out quickly that she was amongst a hugging group because everyone hugged her goodbye and told her it was nice to meet her.

"I'll text you soon, Marisol. Thanks again for your help. I can't tell you how much we appreciate it," Stella said. Blaine started to lead her to the car but shot a smile over his shoulder, which she returned.

Marisol's mouth hurt from smiling as she walked back to her car. Making friends as an adult was hard, and especially when it had never been her strong suit. But she thought maybe she just earned herself five new friends.

It was a pretty damn good feeling.

CHAPTER 27

Marisol

Baby.

Damn, I like when you call me that.
Whatever it is you want, yes.

Did you send me these flowers?

There should have been chocolates too.

*Sends picture of half-eaten box of
chocolate*

Ah, perfect. Save me one.

I won't.

Why did you send these? I love them,
obvs.

> Because I'm proud of you. I want to spoil
> my girlfriend. Insert a thousand other
> reasons.

> Okay, I'll save you one chocolate. 

M arisol smiled at her phone and looked back up at the beautiful floral arrangement on her kitchen island. It had all her favorite flowers: marigolds, roses, and angel's breath. She didn't think she'd ever told Cisco her favorite flowers, but she had these throughout the house. If he cared enough to pay attention—which he did—it wouldn't be hard to figure it out.

That was the thing about Cisco, though: he genuinely cared about every aspect of her life.

Last night, after leaving the restaurant where she met up with the other volunteers, she had instantly gotten into her car and called Cisco. She told him everything and didn't stop to breathe once. She didn't even think she allowed him to get a word in.

Even when Marisol pulled up to her home, she stayed in her car for another hour just talking to him. Cisco had seemed a little distracted, but when she asked about it, he just said he was tired but so excited for her. Since she had no reason not to take him at his word, she believed him.

He hadn't been able to come over last night, which made her feel strangely lonely in her own home. Sure, she had Snowball, who was a great cuddle partner, but she still missed the hard, warm presence of Cisco next to her. Was this what being in love felt like? She felt so out of her element but wasn't scared like she normally was when big life changes came at her. This time she was excited to see what the future held, as long as Cisco was in it.

Her mother be damned.

Marisol was still admiring her flowers when her phone rang again. She half expected to see Cisco calling her, but was surprised to see her dad's name and picture come across her phone. She hesitated, hand hovering over the phone. Should she answer?

The last time she spoke to her father was at the family dinner a few days ago. It wasn't her father's fault...but he also didn't try very hard to stop it. He had called once since then. She hadn't answered, but ignoring him a second time? It would only be a matter of time before he came knocking down her door.

She couldn't put this off anymore.

With a sigh of resignation, Marisol answered the phone. After all, it wasn't her father she was upset with.

"Hi, Daddy."

"Marisol!" her father's voice boomed in her ear. She could hear a lot of noise in the background and knew she was on speaker.

"Are you driving?" she asked.

"Yeah, but don't worry. I have you hands-free," he said, like that made her feel better. Her father couldn't multitask most of the time. "I wanted to check in with you. I haven't heard from you since our dinner."

"Yeah, well, I've been busy," she said.

"With your volunteering?" he asked.

It took Marisol a moment to remember that she mentioned it at dinner, but she didn't think her parents thought much about it or remembered. Her father always found ways to surprise her though.

"Yeah, I mean, kind of. I had a meeting with the other volunteers yesterday. It went really well."

"Excellent!" her father said, as if she just told him she aced a test she was worried about. "Whatever you need, let me know. I want to help out any organization my girls are interested in. Lola has me donating to libraries in her district. I got a few cards from the kids. Can't read most of them, but it's cute."

"I'm actually glad you brought this up." Since she had appointed herself as the event planner for the fundraiser, having her father's support would help. It wouldn't hinder her process, but it would definitely make it a lot easier.

"I'm helping create a fundraiser for the animal shelter. I have a few contacts I'm going to reach out to in hopes they want to help sponsor the event. I was wondering if you wanted to have a booth at the fundraiser selling your wines? A percentage of those proceeds could go back to the shelter," she asked, feeling like one of his business partners.

"That's a good idea, sweetheart. All proceeds will go to the shelter. Make note of that, okay? I'm very proud of you, Marisol. This is good work you're doing."

Marisol smiled bashfully, even though her father couldn't see her. Twice today she had two very important men in her life say they were proud of her. It was a damn good feeling, giving her a high. For once, she felt like she was doing something good. Something that wasn't just for herself, but others.

"Thanks, Daddy. I'm really enjoying it. If you have any other recommendations of people I should reach out to, please let me know."

"I will," he promised, then he paused. All she heard was the sound of his turn signal. After a moment, he said, "I actually called to invite you to the soft launch party for our new store. I hope you and that young man of yours will come. I've already spoken to Mom. She feels badly for how she acted and wants to see you there."

It took everything in her power not to scoff. It was a cold day in hell when her mother apologized. She didn't doubt that her mother would want to see her there, but she greatly doubted she wanted Cisco with her.

"I know it's a lot to ask, but I really want my girls there," her father said. There was a soft cadence to his voice she hadn't heard before. Like he was holding back his fear, possibly thinking she would refuse him.

Honestly, she had half a mind to do just that. Mostly to avoid any awkward encounter between her mother and Cisco. But this was her father. She had always been close to her father and supported him in his endeavors. She didn't want to miss out on this major milestone for him, simply because she feared her mother. Alice said she needed to find a way to still be part of her family without letting her mother dictate her position.

"Okay," she said at last. There was a sigh of relief on the other end of the phone. "I can't promise Cisco will come, but I'll be there. When is it?"

"I'll send over the invitation. I can't wait to see you, sweetheart. It might be a good time to ask around about your fundraiser, too. But listen, I've made it to my appointment. I need to go, but I'll get that information to you. Love you, and I'll see you soon."

"Love you too, Daddy. Bye," she said as the line went dead.

Clicking through her phone once again, she found Cisco's name and typed out a message.

> So…how do you feel about another family party?

CHAPTER 28

Cisco

Work was slow. On top of that, there were two cancellations. Cisco had a pretty aggressive cancellation policy to persuade clients to reschedule. Of course there were special circumstances, but both clients had no excuses. According to Tiny, they were short in their responses and didn't offer her an explanation.

The two clients weren't random either. They had been long-time clients. One was a successful businessman, and the other played football professionally. For them to cancel and not reschedule their appointments was odd. He couldn't help but feel like it had something to do with the reason he was passed up for the building he wanted for his next shop. Perhaps that was just his anxiety talking.

However, there wasn't much he could do. His lawyer and realtor were working on it. He just had to wait, which was something he hated doing.

He was distracted most of the day, doing his best to push his worries to the side and give his other two clients who hadn't cancelled his full attention. He also didn't want his dark mood to trickle down into his conversations with Marisol.

His girl was on a high after her meeting with the other volunteers yesterday. It was rare to hear such excitement in her voice as she spoke, and he wanted her to keep that feeling a little longer. Which was why he didn't need to bother Marisol with this news. He'd share that dark history later. If his lawyer was as good as his high price point deemed, then this should all be settled in the next few days.

He hoped.

The last message he got from Marisol, though, had him scratching his head in confusion. Another family party? Last one didn't go great—minus their moment in the bathroom. He couldn't ask her more about it because his last client of the day arrived, and he needed to devote the next four and a half hours to the chest piece that snaked around his neck down to his pecs.

After that grueling session and arrangements for a follow-up in a month, Cisco and Tiny were the last two left and closed up the shop. Normally, Cisco was teasing and joking around with Tiny as they closed down, but today he was too deep into his own mind. He couldn't even appreciate the music Tiny put on as they cleaned.

"What's wrong with you?" she asked as soon as they got in his car. He had promised her parents he'd drop her off after work.

"Nothing is wrong with me," he said, his grip on the steering wheel tightening. Cisco then made a reckless turn onto the busy interstate, earning himself a shriek from Tiny and honks from the pissed-off driver of the car behind him.

"Could you maybe not try and kill me just because you're

pissed about something?" Tiny gasped, gripping her seatbelt like it was her only lifeline.

Seeing her this scared made him ease his grip. He silently cursed himself for his impulsive driving. It was one thing if he was alone, quite another when he was in the car with his cousin.

"Fuck, T, I'm sorry. I just have a lot on my mind," he apologized.

"Clearly. You've been a zombie all day. Did you and Marisol break up?"

"What? No." He shook his head adamantly. He could see why she would think that, but if that were the case, he would be much worse. "No, Marisol and I are fine. It's...remember that property I checked out to open the next shop?"

"Yeah, the one in that bougie-ass neighborhood?" she asked.

"Yeah, that one. We should have been closing on it this week, but Ernesto called me and said they pulled out."

"What?" Tiny's confusion matched his own when he first heard the news. "Why? That doesn't make any sense."

"Yeah, well, apparently they dug into my past and found shit that was supposed to be buried. *Is* buried. I don't know how they got that information, but they did, and they didn't want someone like that to be in the area."

"What the fuck? That's not fair. First off, you were proven innocent in those charges. It should have never even been a thing."

"But it was," Cisco said, turning into her neighborhood. "I have people working on this. It should be fine soon. If you see or hear anything, you'll tell me, right?"

"Duh." She grabbed her bag from the back seat. "Try not to kill yourself in the process though. It'll get figured out."

Cisco wanted to have her attitude about it, but his nerves were shot. Still, he nodded and leaned over to hug her. "Need me to order you lunch tomorrow?"

"And my friend Tori too? She's coming over to hang out tomorrow. Pizza will be great." Tiny unbuckled and got out of the car. Before shutting the door, she offered him one last wave before heading inside.

Cisco waited until she was safely inside her house before pulling out. For now, he was going to try and have Tiny's attitude about this. He needed something to distract him, so he quickly found Marisol's name in his phone and called her. The ringing came through his car speakers.

A few seconds later, Marisol's sultry voice filled his car. His body immediately responded to her. "Hey, baby. How was work?"

Fuck, he really liked being called "baby." He didn't think he was one to like pet names for him, but clearly he was a fool. "Princesa, it's much better now. Do you have any chocolate left for me?"

"Only one. The others were very delicious. Thank you again." He could hear the smile in her voice.

"You're very welcome. You deserved them." He paused before asking, "So, want to explain your text from earlier?"

Marisol groaned. "My dad called. We chatted, and he apologized again for the family dinner. He agreed to be a sponsor for the fundraiser, though. Said all proceeds can go to the shelter."

Cisco was impressed by that. "Count me in too. I can offer an array of small tattoos. All proceeds can go to the shelter as well. I'll hand out flyers for the shop too. We both win."

"Really? Thank you, baby. I'm writing you down right

now." Papers crinkled on the other end as Marisol took notes before speaking again. "We also talked about the opening of his new store. He, uh, actually invited us to a celebration party at his store. He hoped we'd both be there."

Cisco liked Marisol's father. He was a good man who truly valued his daughters. Her mother, on the other hand, was a different story. She prioritized image and status over their well-being. It wasn't that she didn't love them, but the way she expressed it often felt hollow, more like a transaction than genuine affection.

"Will it just be us there?"

"No, not for something like this. I'm sure my father will invite friends and employees from the winery. I don't think it will be as bad. For sure easier to miss my mom."

Cisco nodded even though she couldn't see him. "Do you want to go?"

"I mean...I want to support my dad. I want to be there for him, but you don't have to go—"

"I'll go," he said. "If you want to go, then I'm going too. If you want me there."

"Of course I want you there. I just want you to have the opportunity to say no. I seriously wouldn't blame you," she assured.

Cisco planned on being in Marisol's life for a long time. That meant her family was also part of the package. He wouldn't let a small woman scare him away from her daughter.

"I'll go," he said again, with more conviction this time. "We can celebrate your dad."

"Really? Thank you. This means a lot to me," Marisol said.

"Enough to have me come over and eat that last piece of chocolate?"

"Come over, and you can have more than chocolate," Marisol said, a purr in her voice.

He had never driven faster.

CHAPTER 29

Marisol

Tonight's event was cocktail attire, giving Marisol the perfect excuse to wear the new outfit she bought last week. The tight-fitting crop top was a mustard color with ruffles on one side. The matching skirt hugged her curves perfectly, giving her the illusion of a bigger ass. It showed off a decent amount of leg, due to the high slit on the side, but still covered her tattoo as long as she was careful. To complete the look, she wore simple black high heels.

Her hair and makeup were another matter. Marisol loved styling her hair. She found it relaxing to accentuate her already wavy hair with fuller and dramatic waves. Her makeup was light...for her. She decided on a bronzy eye look today paired with a nude lipstick.

Two hours later, she was finally finished. Cisco had left her bedroom long ago, and she heard the sounds of the TV from the living room. After grabbing her black clutch, she headed out to where Cisco was watching highlights from some baseball game.

"I'm ready and—oh." Marisol halted, eyes going wide. She

was pretty sure her mouth was open as she stared at the man lounging like a sex god on her couch. He wore black slacks that hugged his muscular thighs nicely. The black button-up he wore was not one she'd seen before, and she had definitely never seen that maroon jacket. Cisco left the top few buttons of his shirt undone, showing off more of his tattoos that snaked up and around his neck.

Suddenly, she no longer wanted to go to the party. And was her home getting hot? Because her body was definitely hot. A cocky grin spread across Cisco's lips, and damn if that didn't make her wet.

She needed to sit down. Preferably on his face. Most definitely his face.

"Like what you see, Princesa?" He pushed off the couch and stalked toward her. "Because I definitely like what I see." His voice, like velvet, made her knees weak. And then his arm encircled her waist, pulling her close to his hard chest. He took her in hungrily, heated gaze going straight to her core.

Really not a great time to get turned on when they were about to go see her parents. Clearly, her body didn't care, not when her boyfriend looked this damn good. Honestly, it was a travesty she couldn't chain him to her bed and never let him leave. Though...he might be into bondage. Which made the thought even hotter.

"We're going to be late." Her voice sounded breathy to her own ears. Still, she didn't pull away.

Instead of answering, Cisco leaned down, and her breath caught in her throat. Then he kissed her. Part of her thought of her lipstick and how she'd definitely have to reapply it now, but then her horniness kicked in, and she kissed him back.

She had never been one to believe in the whole "spark" thing people claimed to experience when they kissed the person they loved. Marisol was no prude. She'd kissed plenty of men, but none of them felt like this. None of them made her knees weak and her panties soaked.

None of them were Cisco.

The first brush of his tongue had Marisol melting. A soft moan left her lips as she parted for him, eagerly letting him take control. One of his hands tangled in her hair, cradling the back of her head, while the other rested on her cheek. It was both sweet and possessive. A familiar, overwhelming emotion overcame her. The same emotion she felt each time she was around Cisco, only now it was stronger.

She loved him. She knew that without a doubt. It was one of the only things she was certain about in her life, while everything else was up in the air. She needed to tell him, and she would. Soon.

Cisco pulled away from her too soon, leaving Marisol whimpering. She stuck her bottom lip out, grabbing hold of his lapels to pull him back. His deep, manly laugh did little to squash her lust.

"We need to go, Princesa. Let's get to the car."

"But—"

"Car. Now," he said with a teasing smile on his face.

"Fine." She wasn't happy about it, but she led him out of her home and to the elevator. She waited until Cisco got in behind her to press G1 for garage, level one. On the way down, he kept his hand on the small of her back, but that was the only touch he gave her. Despite knowing he made the right call, her body felt betrayed, wanting even.

Cisco's car was the first one she saw once they stepped out of the elevator. He moved past her to open the car door for her. As soon as Marisol was in, he shut the door and got in on the driver's side.

"Do you need the address?" she asked him.

"Nah, I know where it's at." There was a slight strain to his voice that she couldn't quite decipher.

Before she could ask him about it, Cisco turned on the radio and backed the car up. His hand moved to rest on the exposed skin of her thigh. The warmth of his hand instantly calmed her spiked nerves. Not over seeing her father, but the potential of her mother being there and acting...well, like her mother.

"What are you thinking about over there?" Cisco's voice cut through the fog in her head. The hand on her thigh moved up, almost indecently so.

"Just about tonight. Nervous," she admitted.

Again, his hand moved. This time under her skirt to finger the lace of her panties. Of their own accord, her legs spread slightly. As much as she could in her fitted skirt.

"Nervous?" he hummed, like it was a foreign concept to him. "How about I help calm your nerves?"

"How?" her breathy response came.

Instead of answering, Cisco's hand slipped between her thighs and rubbed her through her panties. If this was his method of settling her nerves, she had to admit she was a fan. A big fan.

"Cisco." She spoke his name like a warning. But a warning for what, exactly? "You're driving," she finished lamely.

"Very astute, Princesa," he teased her. This time his finger slipped under her panties and rubbed the seam of her pussy. "But I'm very good at multitasking."

"What if you crash?" She seriously needed to shut up because she didn't want him to stop. If they crashed, they crashed. But she needed to feel *something* after she saw him wearing that suit.

"I won't crash." His finger found her clit, rubbing slow, teasing circles. Soft whimpers filled the car. "Mmm, Princesa, your moans are better than any of my music."

A part of her felt embarrassed, but another part didn't care. She ground down on his finger, not caring if that made her look needy. She *was* needy. "More," she whispered.

"What was that? I don't think I heard you properly."

Now he was toying with her. That cocky grin told her he could hear her; he just wanted to hear her ask again. "Cisco, more," she said louder.

"Ah, that's what I thought you said." He chuckled as one finger plunged into her wet heat. It wasn't his cock, which she would definitely get later tonight, but it worked for now.

The finger on her clit moved faster. The car rolled to a stop at the traffic light, and Cisco leaned over to kiss her neck. "You're going to come on my fingers before we get there, Princesa." It wasn't up for debate. His words were final, and she had no problem following orders.

The light turned green, and Cisco moved back to the wheel. His fingers remained inside her, teasing and fucking her slowly. It was delicious and dirty, something she had never done before.

Each bump on the road and turn had Cisco going deeper inside her. She moaned and clenched around the second finger he added. While she writhed in pleasure, Cisco kept his eyes on the road, not acting differently than any other car ride. The only indication he was as affected as her was the impressive bulge growing in his pants and the white knuckles around the wheel.

A mile marker indicated they were close to their exit. Cisco must have noticed this at the same time because he was no longer playing with her. No, he was fucking her. His finger slid in and out of her with ease as wetness pooled between her thighs.

"Cisco…" she moaned, his name filling the car. Marisol's hand flung out to grab hold of the door handle, trying to ground herself.

Her clit was so sensitive, and it only took one more touch to have her seeing stars. Her orgasm came on quickly, overtaking her body. She shuddered, moaning and arching her back off her seat.

"So beautiful," Cisco panted, his voice full of lust. He removed his fingers from inside her and put them in his mouth, never once breaking eye contact with her. It was dirty and sexy. She found herself squeezing her legs, her body heating even though she just found her release.

This man was perfect and all hers.

Marisol really wished she had an emergency pair of panties in her purse, but she hadn't planned on Cisco fingering her the entire thirty-minute drive to her father's store. The last thing she needed was to be talking to one of her father's friends with her desire-soaked panties on. But it was also kind of hot, so she wondered what that said about her.

Cisco was still smirking when he found a parking spot in a nearby garage. "You ready to go, Princesa, or do you need a minute?"

Oh, she definitely needed a lot of minutes, but if she did what she really wanted to do, they'd never go into the store or get through this party. The quicker they showed up and made their presence known, the faster she could get him home and do all the naughty things she wanted to do with him.

"Why would I need a minute?" she asked, feigning innocence. His laugh followed her as they exited the car.

The sun was just starting to set, and a light breeze brought a certain chill in the air. Nightlife was just beginning here with groups of people roaming the streets, going in and out of buildings. Bars, restaurants, and shopping kept most people entertained, but live music from a grassy park area also gathered a crowd.

Her father's store was located in the heart of it all. He was nestled between a steakhouse and a building for sale. "Hey," she pointed to the for-sale sign, "aren't you purchasing that property for your tattoo shop?" She remembered him walking out of the building with another man, just as she and her father were leaving the shop.

Next to her, Cisco tensed. She glanced at him, noticing his set jaw and the way his eyes narrowed at the store. Did she miss something?

"I'm not sure they'll take my offer," he said briskly, not offering any more explanation.

"Oh, I'm sorry. Did they say why?" she asked.

This time she didn't miss the red flush starting at his neck and going up to his cheeks. His lips were pursed in a thin line, and he shrugged. "Not really."

She had a feeling that wasn't the total truth, but she didn't push him on it. Clearly, it wasn't something he wanted to talk about, and she respected that decision. But she hoped he'd open up to her when he was ready. Which clearly wasn't now.

"Marisol! Cisco!" Her father's boisterous voice stole her attention from Cisco.

Travis Roberts wore his favorite beige suit that reminded her of Big Daddy from *The Princess and the Frog*. Complete with the beer—or in his case, wine—gut. Travis excused himself from greeting the guests at the front door and met them on the sidewalk. Marisol hugged him, and despite the tension within their family, she was happy she could come out and support him.

"Congratulations, Daddy. I'm proud of you," Marisol said.

"That means a lot to me, sweetheart. I'm so happy you and Cisco could come out tonight." Travis pulled away and reached to shake Cisco's hand. Cisco's weird mood from earlier was gone, and he greeted her father with a smile.

"Thank you for inviting us. You chose a great location for your shop," he complimented.

"Fought tooth and nail for this property. Expecting great things from it, especially if you're going to be my neighbor now." He clapped him on the back.

Marisol watched as Cisco tensed. Clearly, her father didn't notice and didn't see the sign on the shop next door. She was certainly not going to bring it up.

"Come on in, you two. Sample the wines and eat the food. Your sister and Javi are here. I know they'll be happy to see you. Sadly, they left the kids with Javi's father for the night," her father sighed, looking genuinely sad.

Marisol couldn't help but laugh. "Well, of course they did. This is for wine. Do you really want to have two kids running around?"

"If those kids are my grandbabies, I do!" he said petulantly.

Marisol rolled her eyes. "I'm sure you can see them later. But for now, enjoy your night." Then, as an afterthought, she asked, "Where's Mom?"

"Oh, she's inside talking to friends. She knows to be on her best behavior for the night."

She somehow really doubted that but nodded all the same. She reached back for Cisco's hand again, leading him through the building. The back wall of the shop was made of stone with shelves to display different wines. There were a few high tables with barrels as the base. Food and glasses of wine and sparkling water sat atop those. She loved the rustic feeling of the store and was happy her dad went with the design.

Many of the people here she recognized, either from previous events she attended or those who worked at the winery. She didn't see her mother amongst everyone but figured she stepped out to go to the bathroom or fix her hair. Lola and Javi were speaking to two women. One had their arm over the shorter one, and they were all laughing at something Javi said.

The two women were some of Lola's best friends, Mona and Mattea. It once made Marisol extremely jealous of her sister for having such close friends, and it still did at times, but mostly she was happy. Happy because her sister deserved people in her corner when she couldn't be there. But also happy because Marisol might have found her own group.

Lola must have sensed her staring, because her sister soon glanced up and offered Marisol a small smile. She returned it with a wave. Lola leaned over to whisper something to Javi. He nodded once, and she broke away from the group, walking toward her sister. "I didn't think you'd be here," she said in greeting, offering Marisol a hug.

Hugging anyone besides her father, niece, and nephew was still new to her, but she returned it. There had been a lot of hugging in the last few weeks. "I came because it's Dad. Plus, Mom's attention is usually off me at things like this."

Lola pulled back and greeted Cisco. "Javi and I aren't staying long. I suggest you two make an early departure as well."

"Trust me, I plan on it." She just needed to be around enough to let her face be seen, and then they could go.

"You can come join us if you don't want to mingle," Lola said.

As tempting as that offer was, she knew her father would appreciate her making her rounds. "Later. There are a few people I want to say hi to."

"Well, you know where we'll be," Lola said before turning and walking back toward her husband and best friends.

Marisol exhaled loudly, already feeling overwhelmed by the number of people here. Cisco gently rubbed her shoulders. "Should I get us some wine? I feel like we need wine."

Despite her nerves, Marisol laughed. "Yes please. And maybe some of those finger sandwiches?"

"On it. Stay here, Princesa." Cisco kissed her cheek, then she no longer felt his warm body on her back. It didn't occur to her until now how much of a calming presence he was to her. Without him, she felt exposed. Had these events always been like this?

Finding an unoccupied table, Marisol wandered over to it, putting her clutch down. Part of her wished she had reached out to Stella and invited her, but she didn't know if that would be weird. After all, they barely knew each other, but she liked hanging out with her. Was that enough to be considered a friend? Why was adulting so damn hard?

"Marisol," a familiar voice came from behind her.

The hair on the back of her neck rose, and her smile instantly vanished. As if in slow motion, she turned, listening to the rapid beating of her own heart. When she saw who stood in front of her, every horrid memory of him came rushing back. Because standing only a few feet in front of her was Archie.

CHAPTER 30

Marisol

"What are you doing here?" Marisol scanned the room, trying to catch the person who set her up. Surely this couldn't be real. There would be no other reason for Archie to be here if someone wasn't playing a cruel joke on her. But no one was paying them any mind. She couldn't even see Cisco or Lola, and she hated the vulnerability that came from being alone with Archie.

Archie was handsome, if you were into pompous privileged men. He was an intimidating presence with his freshly pressed suit tailored to his body. Piercing blue eyes held so much judgment for all they came into contact with. And perfectly tousled hair, appearing effortless, when Marisol knew it took him a good thirty minutes to achieve the style.

She didn't know how she ever stomached being around this man, let alone sharing a bed with him.

Annoyingly, Archie raised a perfectly sculpted brow. "Is that any way to greet your husband?"

"Ex-husband," she supplied automatically.

"Well, not technically. On paper, we are still very much married." He smirked, his smug voice grating on her last nerves. He had a way of getting under her skin, making her lose all concepts of rational thought. Archie didn't love her. He simply wanted to control her and use her influential name for his own nefarious means.

It wasn't lost on Marisol that he didn't answer her question. "Why are you here, Archie? Who invited you?" It couldn't be her father because he knew how uncomfortable Marisol was around Archie. Was it her mother? She was conniving and undermining, but would she really stoop this low? Yes, yes, she would. Because Luciana wanted just as much control over Marisol as Archie did.

"I'm here to celebrate your father's opening." Archie gestured around the room at all the other guests. "I should be here for this. I'm still part of the family."

"But you're not!" she snapped.

An elderly couple near them peered over anxiously at the feuding pair. Marisol knew she needed to keep her temper in check, no matter how easy it would be to give in to the anger growing inside her. She needed to not make a scene. A lesson she learned from her mother long ago.

She did her best to push down the bitter taste of her anger and forced herself to speak with a softer tone. "It's wildly inappropriate for you to be here, Archie. You are not family, whether you sign those papers or not. Honestly, it's pathetic that you don't know when you aren't wanted."

A red flush creeped up the back of Archie's pale skin, and he tensed his jaw. "Pathetic?" he asked, a menacing cadence to his voice. "You want to know what's pathetic, Marisol? You—"

Archie trailed off, his attention moving behind her. Marisol felt the warmth of another person before an arm went around her waist, pulling her back into a sturdy chest. The familiar smell of mint and cedarwood filled her senses, and she instantly relaxed.

Cisco. He was here.

"Do you want to finish that sentence?" His deep voice was meant to be intimidating, and judging by the way Archie tensed and took a step back, it was effective. But to her? It went straight to her clit, igniting her body. This man coming to her defense was definitely a new kink she'd discovered.

Archie cleared his throat, looking uncomfortable. "So, you brought your new...friend."

"Boyfriend," Cisco corrected. "She brought her new boyfriend."

Despite his obvious discomfort, Archie pointedly looked over Cisco, forming his own judgments. "Boyfriend? Marisol couldn't possibly have a boyfriend because she's a married woman. Besides, you're not the type she usually goes for. Marisol likes them rich; she likes a man who fits in with present company. She doesn't work, after all. Someone has to provide for her lavish lifestyle."

For a moment, Marisol was stunned. A silent gasp left her lips at the audacity Archie believed himself entitled to. Not once did she ever ask Archie to buy her anything. Not once did she ever use him for his money. If anything, it was the other way around. She was fortunate enough to have a rich family, but also learned how to invest and save her money. She wasn't a helpless, clueless woman who spent money senselessly.

It was insulting to even insinuate that.

She wasn't the only one who thought that either. Cisco's anger was palpable, radiating off him in waves. She was nervous and wasn't even the object of his anger. "You know nothing about her," he snarled. "But doesn't surprise me when it comes from an entitled idiot who leeches off those he surrounds himself with."

Archie's eyes narrowed, cheeks flushing even redder. He wore his emotions on his sleeve, having no semblance of a poker face. "I would be careful if I were you," he threatened.

"What is going on over here?" a familiar voice came from behind Archie. All heads swiveled toward Luciana.

Marisol hadn't seen her mother until now. She was in a midnight-black dress that went to the floor. The bodice cinched her waist, showing off her figure. In her hand was a glass of white wine. Luciana didn't look shocked to see Archie here, making alarm bells go off within Marisol.

"Mom, did you know Archie would be coming?"

"Of course I did. I invited him," she said evenly, as if not remembering—or caring—that Marisol was no longer with Archie. It was like the final dagger in her back, reminding her that her mother would never respect her decisions or boundaries.

"Why would you do that?" she asked incredulously. She shouldn't have been amazed that her mother would pull a stunt like this, and it definitely shouldn't hurt as much as it did, but Marisol couldn't help but feel betrayed. For so long, she believed her mother did these things because she showed her love differently than others. But now Marisol was starting to realize that her mother didn't love her at all. Maybe she never had.

But her mother still did not get it. There was no spark of remorse in her expression. "Archie has been a big help to the winery. It wouldn't be right to celebrate this immense accomplishment without him here."

"I can't believe this." Maybe she was the fool. A fool for believing her mother would behave any differently. Well, if this was how her mother conducted herself, she didn't want to deal with it tonight.

Turning toward Cisco, she met his gaze. "I want to go home."

"Oh, don't be like that, Marisol," her mother said from behind her. She didn't have to see her to know that Luciana was rolling her eyes. "Honestly, you show up with a man like *that* and expect all of us to just be okay with it?"

Marisol never considered herself a reactionary person, but you wouldn't be able to tell at that moment. She spun around, wanting nothing more than to punch Archie in his stupid, handsome face, mostly because she couldn't punch her mother. But she ignored him as she looked at the thinly veiled anger in her mother's expression.

"What do you mean by *that* man? You mean the man who cherishes me like I'm the most important thing in his life? The man who has seen me at my lowest and stayed with me just to see me smile again? Do you mean the man I love?"

The words left her mouth so easily. She had never been surer about anything in her life. She loved Cisco, and she didn't understand why her mother couldn't just be happy for her. The mother who always claimed to love her but would never allow her to make her own decisions. Well, Cisco was the best thing to have ever happened to her, and she refused to let her mother ruin this.

"You don't love him—" her mother started, but Marisol was quick to interrupt.

"I do!" she said, causing a scene. Let everyone witness Archie's and her mother's true colors. She didn't care that people were staring. It wouldn't have been an issue at all if her mother didn't insist on inviting Archie.

Luciana glanced at the growing crowd, gripping her wine glass anxiously before turning her attention back to Marisol. A moment later, her eyes widened in horror. "Marisol! What is on your leg?"

Marisol looked down to see her tattoo peeking out from under her dress. Her anger had distracted her, and she hadn't noticed her dress moving. Great. Another fucking thing her mother could hate her for. Except Marisol couldn't bring herself to care. "It's a fucking tattoo, Mom. You may not have noticed, but my boyfriend is a tattoo artist. I'll proudly wear his work because, once again, I love him."

"You cannot love a felon, Marisol!" her mother's voice rang around them.

All other noise died away as Marisol's brain slowly processed her words.

Felon? That was laughable. "Just because he has tattoos doesn't make him a felon. God, Mom, do you even hear yourself?"

"Princesa—" Cisco reached for her arm, but Luciana smacked his hand away.

"Don't touch my daughter, you convict!" Luciana shrieked, playing the role of the worried mother. She only did this when it suited her.

"You don't understand what you are saying." Cisco frowned. His body tensed, and he looked like a statue, unmoving.

Marisol paused, not understanding what was happening. She had never regretted coming to an event more than this.

"It's pathetic to make up lies simply because you don't like someone. Let's go, Cisco." She grabbed his hand to pull him away.

"It's true," Archie said before she had a chance to escape. "Ask your boyfriend about his time in college. The people he hung out with and associated with."

Marisol was prepared to blow it off. She *wanted* to blow it off and leave, no longer wanting to listen to any more slander. But when she looked at Cisco's face, something made her pause. He looked...angry, sure, but there was something else there. Was it panic? Dread? A combination of the two?

"Cisco?" Marisol's voice was gentle, barely above a whisper, but he heard her all the same. He met her gaze. "What are they talking about?"

She made up her mind that it didn't matter. If what they were saying was true, and Cisco had some sort of illegal past he didn't tell her about, she didn't care. She knew the man he was today, and that was all that mattered. Did she wish he had told her beforehand? Sure, but it didn't mean she wanted to learn about it this way.

"I'll tell you about it when we get home," he said, pressing his lips into a thin line. She knew he was barely containing his anger, so the best thing to do for both of them would be to get out of there.

Except Archie couldn't read the damn room.

"Your boyfriend was arrested for selling illegal substances. His involvement was discovered when one of his clients was found unresponsive. Police found copious amounts of cocaine in his car," Archie said with all the smugness a man who thought they one-upped another could muster.

"How the hell do you even know that?" She wasn't going to believe Archie simply because he said something. She knew this man was a liar and would say anything if it would advance his own career or status.

"It pays to know people in high places. Especially cops." Archie laughed.

But it didn't last long.

The next second, Cisco moved from behind her, cocked back his arm, and slammed his fist into Archie's nose with a sickening crack.

Then the room exploded into chaos.

CHAPTER 31

Cisco

His past was being brought to light, pulled from the deepest crevices he long ago buried. That moment in his life had nearly ruined him, and all because he had been in the wrong place at the wrong time. The cops took one look at him, pegged him for a druggie, and falsely accused him of something he had no part in.

There's no *innocent until proven guilty* for brown men in the justice system. It is always a fight for innocence when people in power see you as guilty. At that time, his family didn't have money to afford fancy lawyers. He was appointed one who didn't seem particularly interested in him or his case.

If it weren't for his entire family scraping together every last penny to afford a semi-decent lawyer, he'd be left rotting in prison. It was because of this lawyer that Cisco had a solid alibi with various witnesses. He had been at the library that night, working on a group project. The true perpetrator was his roommate, a guy named Matthias, who sold drugs around campus for extra money. He was paranoid the cops were onto him and would blame him for the student's overdose, so he planted all his supplies in Cisco's car.

Matthias was a wealthy white kid, son to a wealthy white family. Last he heard of the case, Matthias only received a pretty steep fine and community service.

Even years after the trial, Cisco faced backlash from it. Always having to explain what happened and how he hadn't been involved. Nothing he said mattered though; people already made their minds up when they heard about his situation. He had missed out on many jobs. So, the moment he started to make money as an artist, he put in effort to wipe everything from that part of his life completely away. And it had worked.

Until Archie.

It all made sense now. The denied building. The cancelled clients. It was all Archie's pathetic attempt to isolate Marisol and have her all to himself. Anger like he had never experienced before coursed through his body. It was one thing for someone to try and fuck up his life, but another thing entirely for a person to try to control Marisol's as well.

Marisol, the woman who loved him. And the woman he loved more than anything.

His body acted of its own accord. He cocked his fist back before his mind could process the fallout this would cause. The moment his fist collided with Archie's nose, Cisco had to admit he felt a lot better. Archie lost his balance, his arms pinwheeling before he fell down on his ass.

Someone screamed. Maybe multiple people.

"Call the fucking police!" Archie hissed, getting back up. His expression could have obliterated Cisco on the spot. The deep-seated hatred in his eyes made Archie look crazed. That was only cemented when Archie lunged for him.

"Cisco!" Marisol screamed.

He didn't have time to acknowledge her though because Archie came at him swinging. It was clear the man had never been in a fight in his entire life because his swings were wild and unhinged. Still, one managed to connect with Cisco's jaw. It didn't hurt as much as it pissed him off even more.

But Archie wasn't stopping, and Cisco wasn't just going to stand there and let the man throw punches at him. No, fuck that shit. Someone needed to put this spoiled dick in his place, and Cisco was just pissed enough to do that. All his inhibitions went out the window seeing his smug face. He'd regret this later, but he didn't have the ability to do so now.

Cisco wailed on him again, hitting the bastard in his stomach. Archie keeled over, gasping for breath. It was the distraction he needed to tackle him to the floor before Archie could come for him again.

"What the hell is going on here?!" a loud voice boomed behind him. It sounded like Travis, but he couldn't be certain. The room was bathed in blue and red lights, and he didn't hear the cops until it was too late.

Someone grabbed his arms, pulling him back. Cisco's body was in fight-or-flight mode, and he tried to jerk out of the grasp until he saw another person charging for him. A man in uniform.

A fucking cop.

He remembered vaguely Archie had called out for someone to call the police, but he hadn't expected someone to make the call, much less them getting here so quickly. The second officer stopped before he reached Cisco and leaned down to help Archie up.

His murderous expression did little to ease Cisco's nerves that this would end in any other way than him being booked.

He pointed a finger at Cisco and yelled, "I'm fucking pressing charges. Get him out of here now!"

"No!" Marisol cried.

At that moment, Cisco's heart broke. Not for himself, but for his girl. He knew how hard it was for her to be around her mother, especially when her mother was disappointed in her. Now Marisol would have to deal with this.

Cisco didn't regret punching Archie. The bastard deserved it. But he did regret the look of pure terror and confusion written across Marisol's face.

He hated being the one to have caused that.

"What is going on?!" Travis yelled again, his pale face flushed red. "I demand answers!"

Luciana hurried to her husband's side, tears in her eyes. Cisco wasn't convinced they weren't for show though. There seemed to be a wicked delight aimed at him when Luciana looked his way. "Cisco attacked Archie. I told you, honey, he isn't any good for our daughter! He's embarrassed us in front of our friends and family on your special day. We can't allow this."

"That's not the whole story, and you know it," Marisol cried. Instead of running toward her mother, she ran to Cisco. The second cop tried to grab for her, but Marisol easily avoided his grasp.

"I'm so sorry, Cisco. I'm so, so sorry. I'll fix this. I promise," she said, tears streaming down her face. He had only ever seen her cry this hard once before, when Snowball ran away. It had pained him then, and it pained him even more now, knowing he was the reason for it.

"Don't worry about me, Princesa." But even as he said it, he knew it was stupid. If the roles were reversed, he'd be nothing but worried about his girl. "I'll be fine."

"This is all my fault—"

"Absolutely not." Cisco's voice came out firmer than he meant it to. When he spoke again, he tried to be gentler. "Don't for one second blame yourself for this. Archie had it coming, and I would do it again. I'll be fine."

The cop holding him cuffed him, reading his Miranda rights, but Cisco was barely paying attention to any of it. His gaze was locked on Marisol's. Her devastation was palpable, and he wanted to yell at someone to comfort her since he couldn't be the one to do it.

Luckily, someone did come up. Lola wrapped her arms around Marisol, murmuring something into her ear. Marisol didn't appear to be listening. She was crying too hard to take anything else in. He wanted to reassure her one more time before dealing with the shit he was about to go through, but he didn't get the time.

The officer turned him around and pushed him forward. Every eye in the room was on him. He saw the judgment being passed on him, and as much as he wanted to say it didn't affect him, it fucking cut him deep. Each penetrating gaze made him question his own worth. Maybe he was the monster these people tried to make him out to be. But if being the monster meant punching bastards like Archie for a woman he loved, then he'd be her monster.

Their eyes followed him outside, where the cop opened the door to the back of the squad car and pushed him in. The last thing he saw before being driven away was Marisol's broken face before he couldn't make out her features anymore.

CHAPTER 32
Marisol

She couldn't watch Cisco being escorted away, knowing this whole thing was her fault. It didn't matter that Cisco didn't blame her. Marisol blamed herself. She should know better. Her mother had never hidden her true colors, so she had been a fool to think this could have gone any other way. Granted, she had not expected Cisco to get arrested, but she had a bad feeling about this party since this morning.

She should have listened to her own intuition. It was a mistake she didn't plan on making again.

Contrary to popular belief, Marisol didn't like being the center of attention. Every eye in the room was on her. Their stares of judgment and contempt made her stomach churn. She had to remind herself that they didn't matter. Their opinions were irrelevant to her life.

"Marisol," Lola whispered from next to her. She barely registered her sister's arms around her. It didn't bring any comfort. The only comfort she wanted right now was on his way to get booked. "We should go. Javi will take us to the police station—"

If there was more her sister said, Marisol ignored it. Her attention zeroed in on the man who had caused all of this and the woman comforting him. It sickened her to see her mother reassuring Archie, but it also served to cement the fact that this woman would never be the mom she so desperately craved.

That realization fucking hurt. But it had been a long time coming.

Right now, Marisol channeled all of her anger at Archie. She had half a mind to punch him herself, but she wanted to say her piece, once and for all. She approached the man. Something in her expression must have given him pause because he tensed.

"Marisol, do you now see the type of person you willingly brought to your father's opening party?" His voice was nasal from the obvious broken nose he was sporting. She hoped it hurt when it was set back in place.

"Archie, shut the fuck up," Marisol seethed. Shocked gasps from the guests around the room didn't deter her, though she was pleased to see Lola smirking from the corner of her eye. She at least had one person in this room on her side.

"Marisol! What has gotten into you?" her mother sputtered. Her cheeks flushed with embarrassment, eyes darting around the room, probably surveying all the people she'd need to do damage control with.

But Marisol no longer cared. She'd deal with her mother soon. One evil at a time.

For the first time ever when Marisol glared at Archie, he looked uncomfortable. Scared, even. Good. He should be.

Marisol poked him hard in the chest, emphasizing who she was talking about. "You have been nothing but a menace since coming into our lives. Newsflash, Archie, I never loved you and never will. This pathetic attempt to keep me tied to you ends today."

"I don't—"

"I'm not finished talking!" Marisol interrupted. She had never seen Archie look so flabbergasted, his mouth slightly ajar. "Whatever this weird relationship you and my mother have to try to keep me married to you, it ends today. You will sign the papers, or I will go after everything you are worth. Trust me, you won't survive that."

This was something she should have done a long time ago. For too long, she had allowed this man to string her along, and for what? To put off the disappointment and fight she knew would come from her mother? She couldn't live like this anymore.

"I'm done accepting shit I don't want just because it makes it easier on everyone else," Marisol continued. "Our marriage should have never happened. I risked my relationship with my sister just to marry a man who is as interesting as unseasoned chicken and thinks three minutes in bed is a long time."

Marisol didn't mean to say the last part, but she didn't regret it. Especially when Lola nearly doubled over in laughter. Her mother, on the other hand, looked ready to smite her where she stood. It was finally time to address the woman who had been at the center of her problems for as long as she could remember.

"And you," Marisol said, rounding on her mother. "You're done controlling me. I'm done trying to earn your love and being terrified of messing up. You're my mother! You should just love me. I shouldn't have to earn it or make myself into something I'm not. But all you care about is our image and how others perceive us. Well, look around, Mother." Marisol gestured around the room at the curious eyes. It was like watching a train wreck; you just couldn't look away.

"Your worst fear is people seeing us as less than perfect. Reality check, Mother, we are far from perfect. Never have been. And if your friendships depend upon perfection, those aren't true friendships. I can't keep feeding into your delusions. I'm so damn tired trying to be the perfect daughter and feeling like the lowest person in the world."

Luciana looked around the room nervously, a tight smile on her face as if she were trying to reassure everyone—again only caring about what others thought of her. "Marisol, honey, I understand this is difficult, but let's talk about this in private."

"You don't understand, Mom. There's no more discussing it. I'm done. I love you, but I'm so damn tired of trying to earn your love. I deserve better. As of right now, I don't have a place for you in my life."

The words hurt. Hurt a lot. But there was also a certain freedom in them. Her mother's watery eyes almost made her fold and take back everything she just said, but she didn't think she'd have the strength to cut her mother off twice. No, she had to remain firm in her resolve.

"And Archie," she said, glaring at him again. The bastard looked ready to bolt, and she hoped he did after this. "If I don't have the divorce papers signed and to my lawyer by the end of this week, I will end you."

With that dramatic—but very real—declaration, Marisol turned on her heels and stormed for the door. Lola reached for her, but she was barely hanging on by a thread. The only reason she wasn't a sobbing mess was due to the adrenaline coursing through her veins. She feared if she stopped and let herself process everything that just transpired, she'd be useless in helping Cisco out.

"Marisol, honey, wait!" her father's loud voice rose above all else. His words slowed her down.

She was tempted to turn around and let him take care of everything, but a small part of her also blamed him for allowing this to go on for as long as it did. He had to have seen the way her mother treated their daughters. He would intervene at times, but it wasn't enough.

"Congratulations, Daddy. Sorry for how it turned out," she said instead.

"Please, Marisol. Wait."

But she didn't wait. She pushed past the lingering guests at the front door. With Cisco's keys in her purse, she tracked down his car. A few times, she heard her name being called, but she could have also been imagining it. Regardless, no one stopped her from getting into the car and completely breaking down.

It was like the dam broke.

She couldn't control her tears any more than she could control the growing ache in her heart. If there was ever a moment she wished she could do over, it would be to never have attended this party. That way, the man she loved wouldn't be on his way to jail. What the hell did Marisol even do? She had never been in a situation like this before. She was crying so hard, she could barely hold her phone to search for the closest jail.

She was far too distracted and her vision too blurry with tears to notice two figures approaching her car. When the driver's side door opened, she screamed, throwing her phone at the person. She heard someone curse, but didn't hear her phone hit the ground. They must have caught it.

"Out, Marisol. You can't drive."

That voice was familiar...

"Javi?" she sobbed. It took another moment for her vision to focus on the man in front of her, but, sure enough, her brother-in-law stood there with his hand out and a grave expression on his face as he looked her over.

"Marisol, please let Javi drive. I'll sit in the back with you." Her sister popped up behind her husband.

"I can't..." she hiccupped. She was probably a snotty mess, but, honestly, Marisol didn't have it in her to care. "Cisco...he needs me. I have to—"

"I know. Javi will take us there. But you need to get out. Please, Marisol." This time her sister leaned down. If she didn't know better, Marisol would have sworn she saw tears in her sister's eyes as well. She didn't understand why, though.

Slowly, she nodded. Her body shook as Lola helped her out of the driver's seat and into the back. True to her word, Lola got in next to her, holding Marisol close. She had a fleeting thought that she was the big sister and shouldn't have her little sister comfort her or see her like this, but it was too late. The tears wouldn't stop coming.

The driver's door shut once Javi got in. "Know where to go?" she heard Lola ask.

"I got it, Preciosa. Buckle up. I'll get us there soon," he said.

Marisol didn't know how Javi knew where to go, but she was glad he did. It gave her time to turn off her brain and self-loathe some more in her sister's arms. Lola, to her credit, didn't seem to care that Marisol was getting her shirt wet with her tears and messy with makeup smudges. As a mother, she was probably used to having weird stains on her clothes.

It felt like forever, but in actuality was probably only fifteen minutes before they reached the county jail. Javi parked right out front, but they were one of the only cars in the parking lot.

"Cisco is here?" Marisol asked.

"He should be." Javi turned off the car.

Marisol wasted no time getting out of the car. "We're coming with you!" Lola said as Marisol took off in a jog. There was no use in arguing with her sister. Besides, it felt better to not be alone.

Marisol took the stairs to the front entrance two at a time before bursting through the doors with Lola and Javi not far behind. The small blond man behind a plexiglass wall looked up. He seemed put off by being forced to do his job. "Can I help you?" he asked, looking at the three of them with mild curiosity.

She was sure they were a sight to see. All dressed up, but then she had makeup running and tear streaks down her cheeks. Marisol approached him, desperate for answers. "Do you have Francisco Ramos here?"

The cop sighed and turned to his ancient-looking computer, typing something in. Marisol tapped her fingers against the metal ledge outside his desk. The cop was taking his sweet time, nearly making her combust with anxiety.

"Francisco Ramos, you say?" he asked.

Doing everything in her power not to strangle this man, Marisol said, "Yes." She hoped it didn't come out as a hiss.

"He's being processed. It's going to be a while, miss. My advice? Come back in the morning. If he can be released, it'll be then," he said, oblivious to Marisol's mounting anger.

Leave and let Cisco stay a night here? What if he thought she left him here and didn't want to help him? The betrayal of having stuck up for her, only for her not to come and bail him out.

"Please," she begged. "I can't leave here without him. It was all a misunderstanding."

"Be that as it may, miss, you can't leave with him," the cop said, showing little empathy. "Like I said, come back in the morning, and if he can be released, he'll be released. Can't change the system."

"But—"

"Marisol," Lola's gentle voice came from behind her. Her hand rested on Marisol's shoulder. "We'll come back first thing in the morning. I promise."

Marisol whirled around, panic-stricken and on the verge of breaking down once again. "I can't leave him, Lola!"

"I know, but—"

"What if it was Javi?" Marisol desperately needed someone else to understand how she was feeling. How unfair it all was. "You wouldn't want to leave him either."

She saw the hesitation on her sister's face. "I know," Lola sighed. "It's unfair. If it were Javi, I wouldn't want to go home either. But you need to, Marisol. You need to rest so we can get here first thing in the morning. You'll be the first person he sees when he's released."

Helplessness settled deep within her. Helpless to help Cisco. Helpless to change the situation. Helpless to make it right. Her body grew tired, and all the fight went out of her. "I don't want to be alone," she whispered. Snowball was at home, but she needed another person with her.

"You won't be alone. I promise," her sister said.

Marisol wanted to believe her, simply because thinking and doing anything else was exhausting. In the end, there really wasn't any other choice but to go home, so she nodded.

"Let's go." Lola wrapped an arm around her to lead her out.

Like a ghost, Marisol followed silently. Even though her entire heart remained behind. Even in her darkest moment, she still had to keep herself together enough to contact one more person and give them the news about Cisco.

As soon as she got into the car, she called her.

CHAPTER 33

Cisco

This was familiar to him, and it didn't bring up good memories. After he was brought to the station and booked, charged with disturbing the peace and assault, the officers took him to a holding cell. The cell was poorly lit and smelled vaguely of urine, but at least he had it to himself—a small reprieve from the shitty night he'd had.

Yet, Cisco couldn't bring himself to regret it. Even knowing the outcome, he would gladly punch Archie in the face again. That dick deserved it for all the hell he put Marisol through. He was also pissed at her mother for constantly enabling Archie and putting Marisol into situations she wasn't comfortable in. His girl deserved better. The only thing he could bring himself to regret was the pain they'd caused Marisol.

She was the true victim in this. And he was locked behind these damn bars and couldn't comfort her. The look on her face when the cops put him in the squad car, right before they drove away, would forever be etched in his mind. There were very few times in his life that he felt like a failure, but this would make the top spot.

Part of him felt as if he deserved the damn cell. He didn't know how long he had been here, but he was allowed to call someone. Part of him thought of calling Marisol, but he didn't want to add any more stress to her night. So, he called his lawyer, who promised to get him out ASAP.

But clearly they had different definitions of "as soon as possible" because, according to the old analog clock on the wall, it wasn't until close to seven the following morning before an officer came to his cell. This was a different one than the two who arrested and booked him last night. This man was older, with salt-and-pepper hair. He had a friendlier face than the other two, but Cisco was still on high alert. He saw his name stitched onto his uniform: Officer Jamison.

Officer Jamison unlocked his cell door, motioning toward Cisco. "Alright, man, you're free to go."

Cisco hesitated. Surely he heard the man wrong. He was free to go? Did his lawyer finally manage to get him out? Still, he wouldn't waste an opportunity to get out of this hellhole.

Cisco stood, stretching his body. His back was killing him. He was too damn old to be in a hard jail bed and not on his memory foam mattress. Exhaustion weighed down his body, and he was ready to climb into bed and forget this whole ordeal.

But thoughts of Marisol filled his mind. He needed to reach out to her, and soon, but would she be upset with him?

Maybe she was the person coming to take him home. That thought got his ass in gear, and he walked out of the cell, ready to never see the inside of one again.

"Follow me, Mr. Ramos. All charges have been dropped,

but I need you to sign a few things before we release you to your ride."

"Dropped?" Cisco asked, cocking a brow.

Officer Jamison nodded but didn't elaborate, much to his dismay. Cisco didn't have a chance to ask him more about it before release papers were thrust into his face. Normally he was better at reading what he was signing, but he was beyond tired and more than ready to get the fuck out of here. He signed whatever was given to him.

Once done, Officer Jamison quickly scanned the paperwork before nodding and filing it away. "This way, Mr. Ramos," he said, leading him toward a large, metal door with a keypad. Officer Jamison typed in a code. There was a beep before the sound of the door unlocking. He pushed it open and stepped aside for Cisco to walk free. "Enjoy your day, Mr. Ramos."

Cisco bit back his retort that probably would have landed him back in the cell and walked out. He didn't make it even two steps before someone came hurling at him, nearly knocking him over in their rush to get to him. "I hate you so much," the voice, muffled from his clothes, said.

"Tiny?" Cisco was unable to hide his surprise. Out of everyone he thought may be there to pick him up, Tiny didn't make the list. Hell, he hadn't wanted her to know he was here.

"Marisol called me last night," Tiny answered his unasked question. "She told me what happened but said we couldn't get to you until the morning. I got a ride here, but they said I couldn't bail you out because I'm not eighteen. Which is so fucked."

Normally he would scold her in the cool cousin sort of way about her language, but he was hardly in a position to lecture her when he had just been arrested. But also, he agreed with her sentiments.

"Yeah, it's all fucked. They said they dropped the charges though. Don't know why, but I didn't question it," he said.

"I think it was because of him." Tiny pointed to someone behind him.

Today was a day of surprises because, when he looked at who Tiny was pointing to, he didn't expect to see Travis Roberts standing there looking out of place in his polo and pressed khakis. Cisco tensed, not sure if he wanted to see the man. He hadn't done anything yesterday, but that was exactly the problem. He stood passively around and let Marisol deal with her ex-husband and her mother alone.

Speaking of Marisol, his girl wasn't here. Unease stirred within him.

"Cisco," he greeted, looking far older than he'd ever looked. There were dark bags under his eyes, and his face was gaunt. His hair was in a state of disarray, and if Cisco had to guess, he'd bet he didn't get much sleep last night either.

"Travis," he said, guarded. He didn't care if he was being rude; he had no energy left for decorum. "What are you doing here?"

"I'm sure you expected to see my daughter, but I asked her to stay home so I can fix this. She didn't like that much, and probably wouldn't have agreed if it weren't for her sister, but I owe it to the both of you to make this right. Please, let's talk outside. I don't want to spend any more time here than what's necessary," he said.

Cisco shared a glance with Tiny, and she shrugged, holding his arm. She wasn't the overly affectionate type, so this whole ordeal really shook her. Sighing, he wrapped an arm around Tiny before nodding to Travis. "Fine. Let's talk."

"Thank you," he said, actually sounding grateful. Cisco motioned for him to lead the way, and Travis did, guiding them out of the station and down the stairs. The sun felt amazing on his skin, even with the slight chill in the air.

Travis walked them over to a red sports car, exactly the type of car Cisco would peg the man for owning. He leaned against the driver's door, arms crossed over his chest. "You know, I promised myself after everything that happened with Lola and Luciana, I would never let it get that bad again. But it looks like I failed my girls once more."

Cisco didn't know what Travis was talking about. He knew very little of Lola and Luciana's relationship, but if it was anything like her relationship with Marisol, he doubted it was good. And it probably hadn't been good for a long time.

"I didn't know how badly things were going with Archie," Travis admitted. "Every time I asked Marisol about it, she wouldn't say much and change the subject. Luciana said it would all work itself out, so I was inclined to believe her. I didn't know..." he trailed off, choking on his words. "I didn't know."

Tiny shifted uncomfortably as Travis's first few tears fell. It was awkward, and in a different situation, Cisco might comfort Travis. However, if this was a different situation, they wouldn't be here. Patiently, he gave Travis a moment to compose himself.

After a few minutes, Travis straightened himself up. He ran a hand through his unkempt hair and sighed. "Listen, I've made Archie drop his charges. He's going to be signing the divorce papers and cease all contact with my daughter. He's also going to make sure the slander he spread about you is resolved. I've threatened him with legal action if he approaches anyone in my family or you. That includes my wife. As for

Luciana…" Travis shook his head. For a moment, Cisco actually felt bad for him. It was evident the man loved his wife. Cisco didn't think Luciana was capable of love, though.

"I've told my wife she has to stop interfering in Marisol's life. I made her aware that she may have pushed her daughter out of her life entirely, and now she has to live with the consequence," Travis continued.

"Why are you even still with her? She sounds awful," Tiny blurted out. Teenagers gave no fucks.

"Tiny," Cisco reprimanded, but she just shrugged.

"It's a fair question." Travis didn't appear upset by the question, which was a small relief. "And I don't have a good answer for that. I love her. She is deeply flawed and has hurt our girls. I think she's lost her way, and I want to help her. Part of me knows she's capable of loving her daughters. It just happens to be very toxic. I'm not willing to give up on my family though."

"May that type of love never find me," Tiny muttered under her breath. Cisco swore she saw Travis smirk.

Travis cleared his throat. "I just wanted to deeply apologize for everything that happened last night. Please allow me to drive you home."

"I want to see Marisol," Cisco said adamantly.

"No, you don't. You smell like pee," Tiny said. "And butts. Plus, you need some sleep."

"She does have a point there, son," Travis said. "Good thing the roof in the car goes down. We can air you out a bit."

"I smell?" Cisco lifted the collar of his shirt to smell, but he wasn't getting pee or butts—whatever the hell that smelled like.

"Do bears shit in the woods? Do fish live in water? Do eggplants look like di—"

"I get it," Cisco interrupted Tiny, frowning. It got him a genuine smile from his cousin and a snort from Travis.

"Let the rich man drive us home so you can rest. I'm going to make sure you rest, or I'll steal your phone so you won't be able to talk to Marisol," she threatened.

"Damn. You're worse than the cops," he muttered. Still, a few hours of sleep would do him well. He felt like he'd keel over if he didn't get to bed. And apparently now he needed a shower.

Cisco walked to the passenger side, but Tiny scooted in the moment he opened the door. "I'm owed the front seat after what I've been through. I didn't tell my parents, so you don't have to explain this to any of the family. They think I went into the shop early."

Thank god for that, at least.

Cisco got into the back seat. He wished he had his phone on him to text Marisol, but he had left it in his car. Another thing he would have to get back. Thinking of everything he needed to do stressed him out and made him mad all over again.

"Just let me know the address, and I'll get you home," Travis said, starting his car. Tiny told him where Cisco lived, and Travis nodded, setting off toward home.

Shower. Sleep—if he could. And then Marisol.

He wouldn't truly know peace until his princesa was wrapped in his arms.

CHAPTER 34

Marisol

She hadn't moved from her bed since getting home last night. She also hadn't stopped crying. Both of these things she hated but didn't know how to change. Hell, she didn't have the energy to change. If it weren't for Lola, she would still be wearing her outfit from last night and a face full of ruined makeup. While Marisol let herself go into a dark place, Lola was there to keep her head above water.

After getting her into pajamas and making sure she washed her face and brushed her teeth, Lola led Marisol to bed. Snowball had snuggled up to her side and purred. She hadn't moved since, and Marisol appreciated the comfort her cat brought her.

She had expected Lola and Javi to leave last night. She heard them whispering in the other room, discussing what they needed to do. Lola stepped out to make a few calls, but they didn't leave. When she woke after a night of restless sleep, Javi and Lola were still there, cooking something in the kitchen.

Marisol had wanted to leave first thing in the morning but received a call from her dad. It was vague and short, but ended with him promising he would handle everything. When she tried to protest, her father wouldn't hear it. When she tried to push more, Lola had intercepted and somehow convinced Marisol it would be best to let their father handle this.

Maybe she could have pushed more, but she didn't have the energy. If her father wanted to handle it, then he'd handle it. As long as Cisco came back—hopefully not upset with her. She felt like she was the reason he was in jail. It was her family and her problems that put him in there.

Lola's soft voice filtered in from the other room. She was on the phone again, probably with their father. Marisol heard her name mentioned but couldn't make out anything else her sister said or who she was speaking to. The conversation lasted for about five minutes before Lola said goodbye.

A few moments later, there was a knock on her door. Lola peeked in, holding a steamy mug of coffee. "Good morning," she said as if testing out the waters. Seeing if Marisol would be a bitch after everything Lola had done for her. Marisol couldn't say she blamed her sister for her caution, but it still stung.

"Morning," she murmured. Her voice was hoarse from the hours she spent crying. Her head pounded, threatening to split her skull in two.

"I brought you some coffee." Lola walked to the side of her bed, placing the mug down on the nightstand. She then took a seat at the edge of the bed. "Javi is making breakfast if you're hungry."

"I'm not." Then, because she didn't want to sound ungrateful, she added, "But thank you."

"Well, it will be there when you need it." Uncertainty crossed her sister's features, almost as if she were debating what to say or do next.

Marisol understood. She hated that things were like this

between them. She wanted to fix it, but like everything else, their relationship was hanging on by a thread. After last night, she realized she didn't want that anymore. Hell, she never wanted that. She loved Lola and wanted to be the sister Lola deserved.

"I don't know if you want to talk about last night," Lola said, pulling Marisol out of her thoughts. "But I just wanted to say that I'm sorry you had to go through that. I'm sorry Cisco got caught up in it all too. Neither of you deserved that. But I am proud of you for standing your ground. I don't think I've ever seen you stand up to Mom like that."

Marisol let out a bitter laugh. She pushed herself into a sitting position, earning an annoyed meow from Snowball. The cat jumped to the empty side of the bed, making herself comfortable once again.

"I can't believe I went along with her for so long. I mean, I saw the way she treated you—fuck, I treated you the same— and yet I thought it would be different for me. But she was still trying to mold me into something she wanted. I just never fought back," Marisol said.

"Until last night," Lola replied gently. She reached across the bed to grab Marisol's hand, giving it a squeeze. It was a comfort Marisol didn't feel like she deserved.

"Yeah, and it was too late by then," Marisol muttered bitterly.

"It wasn't—"

"Lola, you know it was," she cut off her sister, staring intently at her. "I've let Mom dictate my entire life. I had multiple chances to stop it, and I never did. Call it fear or self-preservation or cowardice, but I should have stopped it long ago. Last night was years in the making, and because I waited so long to stand up to Mom, I hurt people I love."

"Cisco will understand, Marisol. I see the way he looks at you," Lola assured.

Marisol shook her head, letting her tangled curls bounce into her face. "I'm not just talking about Cisco, Lola." Of course she was worried about Cisco and what he thought of her. She didn't want to lose him. But the reality of the situation was that she had been hurting someone much longer.

"I'm a terrible sister." The words were out. With them lifted a burden she had been carrying around for years, weighing her down. They were long overdue. "I've been a terrible sister for most of our lives."

Tears stung in her eyes. But she wasn't the only one crying. Lola's eyes were wide, and tears rolled down her cheeks. "Marisol, I... Things are different now. We're different."

"It doesn't make what I did okay, and you know it!" Marisol choked out. Lola pursed her lips together, staying silent so she could continue. "I was so awful to you for so long. You deserved to have a big sister to look after you and defend you, not one who was a bitch. I want to be there for you, Lola. I want to be your friend."

"Oh, Marisol, you will never be my friend." Lola's words cut like a knife, knocking the very air from her lungs. She deserved that, but it hurt so bad.

At least it did until Lola took her other hand and pulled Marisol into her arms. "You won't ever just be my friend because you're my sister, and I love you." The tears that ran down her cheeks were not ones of sadness this time, but relief. She held her sister, maybe for the first time ever. And it was perfect.

Lola was the first to pull back, eyes red-rimmed and a beautiful smile on her lips. "You've done a lot in the past few years to actively make amends. I was angry with you for so long, but you aren't that same woman anymore. You've been an actual sister to me for far longer than you realize. You don't have to walk on eggshells around me. We deserve to have the sibling relationship we've always craved."

"I love you, Lola." Marisol's heart swelled with love and excitement for their future.

"I love you too," Lola half laughed, half sobbed.

It was Marisol's turn to take her sister into her arms and hug her. She hugged her for all the times she didn't in the past. For all the times her sister needed her, and she turned her back. Never again would that happen.

They stayed like that for a long time, taking comfort in each other's arms. This was better than the times they spent in "therapy" breaking shit. This was really what they needed.

"I don't mean to interrupt," a male voice spoke from the doorway. The sisters broke apart to see Javi with an amused grin on his face. "But, Marisol, you have a visitor."

Marisol raised a brow. For a second, she thought her mother might be here, but then she remembered her mother never visited, and Javi wouldn't have let her in. He had stood up to her a few times, and she doubted he'd shy away from a few more.

Right before she could ask, movement behind Javi caught her attention. Then, appearing behind Javi, freshly changed and well rested, was Cisco.

Without even waiting for him to say hi, Marisol launched herself out of bed and into his arms. She tripped, and her body collided into a solid wall of muscles.

Two strong arms wrapped around her waist. He smelled so good. Like home. *Her* home. After everything that transpired last night, she feared he wouldn't want to see her. And yet he was here, looking far more put together than she looked and felt.

"Preciosa, that is our cue to leave." Javi laughed from somewhere next to her. The bed creaked as her sister got up. She vaguely heard her move around the room before finally approaching her.

"We'll take your car to get home, and I'll call you later." She smiled and then looked at Cisco. "I'm glad you're here with her. You'll watch her?"

"She's safe with me," his deep, masculine voice said, enveloping her in his warmth.

Safe with me.

She vaguely heard her sister and Javi make their way to the door. The soft click of the lock had Marisol pulling back just enough to see his face. He looked at her like she was the most beautiful woman he'd ever seen, despite the fact that her hair was a mess, and she knew she had dark circles under her eyes. Cisco didn't seem bothered by that.

"Cisco, I'm so sorry. I came last night to get you, but the cop told me he couldn't release you. And then—"

"Marisol." Just one word.

It was enough to make her stop talking and bite her bottom lip. She couldn't quite tell if he was upset with her or something else. Was this the moment he would reject her? Tell her that her family was too much—*she* was too much—and that they should part ways?

But Cisco didn't say any of those things. He took her into his arms and kissed her until all she knew was him.

CHAPTER 35

Cisco

Her lips were soft against his, but the kiss was anything but. He wanted to devour her, and from the way her body molded against his, he knew she wanted the same thing. His hands roamed down to her hips, and he began to lead her backward to her bed. There were far too many clothes between them, and he wanted them off. No more barriers.

After Travis dropped him and Tiny off at his house, Tiny became a little dictator. She made sure he showered and then locked him in his room and made him sleep. Sleep didn't come easily, though. He was restless and needed to see Marisol. Despite his growing need for her, he managed to get two or three hours of sleep.

Tiny agreed to reschedule Cisco's clients and allowed him to borrow her car. He didn't even care that it was a giant piece of shit on wheels if it got him to Marisol's house, where he hoped his car would be. He thought about texting her but remembered he didn't have his phone. So, the plan was to show up and have her in his arms again.

Judging by her messy hair and red-rimmed eyes, Cisco doubted Marisol was able to get much sleep. A part of him hated that she was too worried about him to sleep, but a darker part of him was pleased. Pleased because his girl needed him as much as he needed her.

"Cisco," Marisol moaned into his lips as they reached the edge of her bed. He gently pushed her back, falling on the bed with her. Marisol let out a surprised giggle, clinging to his shoulders. "Cisco, we should talk—"

"I love you too, Princesa," he murmured into her lips. Marisol's body tensed under his as he trailed kisses down her neck. "I didn't have the chance to say it back last night, and that's my *only* regret from yesterday."

"You love me?" There was a slight hitch in her voice as he bit down on her neck, running his hand up her shirt. It was in the way, and he needed to see all of her. As if knowing what he wanted, Marisol lifted herself up so he could discard her shirt. She wasn't wearing a bra, and her brown nipples hardened under his touch.

Immediately, he pulled her back down. "If you have to ask, I haven't shown you properly. That changes now," he said right before pulling her nipple into his mouth.

Marisol let out a long, seductive moan. "But...talk..." she mumbled, clearly having trouble with her words.

"Later," he growled. After he ravished her body, they could talk until they were blue in the face, but not until then.

Marisol didn't try to argue. Instead, she tugged on his shirt until he pulled it over his head, discarding it to the floor. He wasted little time removing the rest of their clothes, until finally, her body was completely exposed to him. His hands trailed down to the tattoo on her leg, tracing his lines. "Beautiful..." he hummed.

"You did a good job." She smiled warmly.

"I wasn't talking about the tattoo, though that looks good too." He smirked as she blushed. Fuck, he loved it when she blushed for him.

His hand trailed to the apex of her thighs, feeling her wet heat. Two fingers pressed into her, and they groaned in unison at her tight channel. "Cisco..." she whimpered.

"I need you, Princesa. Fuck, I need you." There was no slow build-up, exploring her body and bringing her to the edge over and over again. Normally he was a patient man and would draw out every ounce of pleasure he could. Especially because he loved making Marisol writhe in pleasure. But today he was impatient.

Today he needed to be sheathed inside of her.

Marisol's hand snaked between them, wrapping around his shaft. He sucked in a breath as she stroked him, applying just the right amount of pressure. Her nails dug into his shaft, eliciting a hiss from him.

"I want you inside of me," Marisol said, biting her lower lip. "I need you, baby."

He didn't need any more invitation than that. Cisco moved between Marisol's legs. She opened for him beautifully. Her pussy glistened for him, but he wanted to see it dripping with his cum.

"Say you love me," he ordered. He needed to hear it again. Needed to make sure it wasn't all one big dream. He lined his cock up with her, teasing her entrance.

"I love you, Cisco."

Fucking perfection.

Without further prompting, Cisco pushed inside of her in one easy motion. Her pussy squeezed around him, sending waves of pleasure through him. Marisol's legs wrapped around his torso, drawing him inside her even more.

"Fuck, Princesa. I love you too." He leaned down to capture her lips with his. It was frenzied and messy. All tongue and teeth. Two people who couldn't get close enough to one another.

Marisol dug her heels into his lower back, rocking against him. At this rate, Cisco wasn't going to last long, but judging by the way her sweet pussy squeezed his cock, he figured she was on the cusp too.

Needing to pull her over with him, he reached down to rub her clit with the pad of his thumb. Marisol whimpered and ground into his touch. "That's it, baby," he groaned. "So fucking beautiful."

"Cisco..." The way she moaned his name had his entire body tensed. It was the last thing he needed to fall over the edge. His body spasmed as he orgasmed. Marisol wasn't far behind, clinging to him hard as if she'd lost him.

But she wouldn't. Not ever.

They stayed like that for a while. Just holding each other. He was content to stay like this the rest of the day, curled up in bed together, lazily fucking the day away. It was a tempting idea...but he knew they needed to talk. He owed her an explanation. Then he could finally put that part of his life behind him for good.

Reluctantly, he pulled off Marisol and went to get a towel to clean them both up. She looked at him intently, worry etched into her face. "Cisco?" she asked gently. "What's going on?"

He got back into bed next to her, pulling her close. He placed a soft kiss to the top of her forehead, letting his lips linger. "I never meant to keep that from you," he said after a pregnant pause.

Marisol rested her head on his chest and nodded encouragingly. His Princesa was ready to hear him out.

"It was something stupid that happened in college. I haven't thought about it in years, not since the case closed. It really fucked me up for a while, but after loads of therapy, I made peace with the past," he said.

"What happened?" Her voice was gentle, full of curiosity. There was no judgment there.

"I had a roommate in college named Matthias. Rich white kid who thought rebellion was a full-time job," he started. "We didn't talk much, ran with different crowds. He would have random people knocking at our door, asking for shit. I never paid much attention to it, but I should have because, apparently, he was selling drugs from our room.

"I guess one day a student Matthias sold to overdosed, and someone tipped him off that the cops were onto him, and he panicked. Planted all the evidence on me. When the cops came barging into our room, they barely glanced at Matthais and arrested me. It wasn't until much later that I figured out what was going on and had to defend myself. Matthias's dad lawyered him up, and they pinned the whole thing on me."

Marisol's eyes were wide. She reached for his hand, gently squeezing him. "What did you do?"

"My family pulled all their money together to get me a lawyer." He shrugged. "It took nearly a year to clear my name, and I was in jail for most of that time. Someone finally came forward and ratted out Matthias. But by that time, the damage was done, you know? People make their own judgments. Once I was able to start making money, I hired a damn good lawyer to get all of that off public record. Didn't even think about it for years after—until…"

"Until fucking Archie did what Archie does best. Stir up shit," she said. He could feel her anger over her ex-husband. It mirrored his own.

Cisco laughed humorlessly. "He stirred a lot of shit up. Somehow he was behind me losing out on the third location for the shop, and he's cost me clients."

"Archie did all of that?" Marisol shook her head. "I have to say I'm a little jealous."

Cisco furrowed his brow. "Jealous? Of what?"

"You got to punch Archie, and I didn't," she said.

Cisco barked out a laugh, shaking his head. He'd pay good money to see Marisol beat the absolute shit out of Archie. The bastard deserved it. Hell, Marisol should be entitled to it. "If we see him again, I'll hold him down and let you get some punches in."

That made Marisol beam. Her giggle was contagious, making him smile. "We better not ever see him again. Between you punching him, and me and my father threatening him, I think Archie is smart enough to get the message finally. He has to sign the divorce papers now, and then I'll be fully free."

"I won't have to be your paramour anymore?" he asked, which earned him a jab to the ribs. "Ow."

"You deserved that." She chuckled. Then Marisol sobered up, reaching out to caress the side of his face. "I just want to say I'm sorry for everything that happened. You didn't deserve any of that."

"Neither do you," he said. "And don't apologize to me. I don't blame you for anything, Princesa."

"I know. I still feel compelled to say it. Archie's fucked up a lot of things in my life. I'm not innocent either. But after everything that went down, I realized I'm so fucking tired of trying to be the perfect daughter to my mother. Trying never to disappoint her. Losing you…that would have been the worst thing to ever happen to me. I couldn't do it anymore. I couldn't…" Her words trailed off into quiet sobs.

"Shhh, Princesa, I'm so fucking proud of you." Cisco pulled her into his lap, gently rubbing her back. "You aren't losing me. Let me make that very clear. I'm so fucking proud of you for standing up for yourself. I know it was hard, but you did it."

Marisol wiped away a few tears, shaking her head. "It was a lot. Which is why I don't want to do a damn thing today."

"And we don't have to. We can stay in bed all day."

"You'll stay with me?" she asked, looking up at him. "I don't want you to go."

"And I don't want to go." He leaned down and kissed her. "Why don't we eat some of that food your brother-in-law made and watch movies in bed?"

"And you'll stay the night?"

"Try kicking me out." He smirked, which earned him a small smile. Marisol leaned back against him, and for the first time in the last twenty-four hours, he felt at peace.

CHAPTER 36

Marisol

There was a delicious ache between her thighs after a full day of sex. When they weren't cuddling or watching a movie, they were finding new ways to draw out pleasure. Naturally, Cisco excelled in every way. If she hadn't been in love before, yesterday cemented her feelings for him.

He had come clean about his past. A past he was unjustly accused of and worked his ass off to break free from. She had never had anyone betray her in the way his roommate betrayed him—though, arguably, her mother was just as bad. Still, she knew what it was like to be perceived as something you weren't. She couldn't imagine the darkness Cisco had to face. But he did face it and came out stronger on the other side. It was inspiring because it made Marisol feel she was capable of that too.

If it were up to her, she'd stay in bed all day. But earlier this morning, she got a text from Stella asking if she and the others could come over to finalize the plans for the fundraiser. After everything that happened these last few days, the pet fundraiser was the furthest thing from her mind. But it was quickly approaching, and she wanted to make it a successful event for the shelter. With so much still left to plan, she would need every spare second to pull this off.

When she told Cisco, he said he needed to go into work today to make up for the clients he had to cancel. He promised to come back after work, though, and confirmed he'd tattoo at the fundraiser. After a quick shower and breakfast, Cisco left Marisol to get her house ready for her visitors.

This would be the first time she was hosting friends at her house. It both excited her and made her want to throw up. If she had more notice, she would have hired someone to make them snacks, but all she had was a random assortment of cheeses and nuts, so that would have to do. She put out a char-cuterie board, bottled water, and wine with glasses on her coffee table in the living room.

Just in time too, because there was a loud knock at the door. Snowball, who had been playing with a stuffed mouse toy, looked up as if asking, *"Are you going to get that?"* With one final look around her house, she took a deep breath and went to answer the door.

Stella was the first person she saw, offering her a big smile. In her arms was a casserole dish with what appeared to be spinach artichoke dip. Next to her was her husband, Blaine, holding a bag of tortilla chips. "Hi! Thank you so much for letting us crash your house today," Stella said, moving to give Marisol a one-handed hug, carefully balancing the dip between them.

"I'm happy to." She surprised herself because she actually meant it. She really liked Stella and the other volunteers.

Antonio and Paul hugged her next, both carrying packages

of cookies. "This condo is insane. In a good way." Antonio looked around with wide eyes. "I need a tour ASAP."

"Careful. If he loves the house too much, he's going to move in with you," Paul whispered conspiratorially. His gaze lingered around the room, falling on Snowball, still playing with her toy. "In the meantime, I'm going to stare at your cat until she loves me."

Izzy was the last to enter. She was in another fantastical, pale-yellow dress that reminded her of a summer fairy, with her hair braided down her back. "Marisol, I'm so happy to see you again." The woman leaned in for a hug. "You have a beautiful home."

"Thank you." Marisol's cheeks hurt from smiling. If this was the price for friendship, it was one she was happy to pay. "Please come in. I have some finger foods out to graze on. Can I get you something to drink?"

"A water, beautiful. Thank you." Izzy rubbed her shoulder and made her way inside.

The others had already made themselves at home by gathering around the coffee table. Someone had found—or brought—paper plates and started to pass them out. Blaine started scooping spinach artichoke dip on everyone's plates. Paul called for Antonio, who was missing. A moment later, Antonio popped out from the hallway, holding a sequined dress he must have dug up from the bowels of Marisol's closet.

"Please tell me you didn't just break into Marisol's closet and steal her dress," Paul groaned.

"Okay, I didn't do that," Antonio said, ignoring his partner as he looked at Marisol. "This is fucking stunning. Please tell me you wore it out to a club and brought home a silver fox."

"Antonio," the others chastised in unison, doing nothing to rein Antonio in. She had a feeling Antonio did this often.

"I've never been to a club," Marisol admitted. "But I did wear it once at a mixer. Does that count? And I didn't take home a silver fox, but I was given wine."

"Wine is probably better than a man." He shrugged. "Anyway, it's gorgeous, and I think we need to go partying in it. You have a man, right?"

"She does, remember?" Stella piped up. "And he's hot."

"It's true. You should see his pictures," Blaine said.

"He has a public Facebook and Instagram, so that makes it not creepy," Stella said, earning a nod of agreement from Izzy.

"Wait, I want to see this hot boyfriend," Antonio said. "Someone show me this hot boyfriend. Paul, did you know she has a hot boyfriend?"

"Babe, how the fuck would I know she has a hot boyfriend?" Paul deadpanned. "Marisol is hot, so I guess it makes sense she has a hot boyfriend."

"Anyway," Izzy said before Antonio or anyone else could respond. "Maybe let's not talk about Marisol's hot boyfriend, and let's talk about the fundraiser coming up in a few short weeks. You know, the whole reason we are here."

Despite the chaos, Marisol found she loved it. She loved their big personalities and the fact that they genuinely seemed interested in her and her life. She made a mental note to make an effort to see them more outside the animal shelter and fundraising efforts. She took a seat in her oversized chair. Snowball immediately jumped up to rest on her lap, so she began to scratch her between her ears.

Antonio disappeared again but came out moments later to sit next to Paul. Blaine was in the other oversized chair with Stella cuddled up against him. Izzy sat on the floor, next to the fireplace, despite there being more room on the couch.

"Don't forget to get some food, Marisol," Izzy said. "The

spinach dip is the only thing Blaine knows how to make, but it's damn good."

"Oh, yeah, you have to try it," Antonio agreed. "I'll make you a plate."

Before she had the chance to answer, Antonio snatched her plate before loading it up with food and handing it back to her. She had to admit it smelled good, and her first bite confirmed it was just as good as it smelled. She didn't even like spinach much, but it was so creamy and delicious.

"So," she said between bites, "I have some vendors I'm reaching out to soon. The only thing is that they will need to set up the night before so the day of the fundraiser, they'll be ready to go."

"Not a problem," Stella said. "I can close the shelter early that day for the vendors to set up outside. At the very least, I can mark off some of the parking lot for them."

"And I can be there to direct them where they need to go as long as we have an idea," Blaine says.

Marisol nodded. She had a rough sketch of where everything could go, and it would be finalized once she got confirmation from the vendors, but Stella and the others knew the layout best. Reaching for the phone and remote, she turned the TV on and displayed her photos on the screen, opening up the sketch she made.

"Fancy," she heard Paul murmur appreciatively.

The TV showed a rough sketch of the parking lot and the shelter. Each area was mapped out and labeled. "Here's what I think I'll be able to get us," she said as a sliver of self-doubt wormed its way through her. What if it wasn't enough? What if they didn't like it? Those thoughts only threatened to silence her, so she did her best to push them aside.

"Cisco has agreed to offer a variety of tattoos. All proceeds will go to the shelter. I put him toward the back because I see his booth being popular. That way people will have to walk through everything else before they find him. Might inspire them to try other booths."

"So smart." Stella nodded. "Think he'll tattoo me?"

"I don't see why not." Marisol smiled. "He's only offering a select number of designs, though."

"Doesn't matter. I just love tattoos." She shrugged.

"We also have my dad's booth," Marisol went on. With everything that transpired, she hoped her father was still good on his word. She hadn't heard otherwise. "He's offering a variety of wines at a discounted price.

"I have a few others lined up for adults. Candles. Kitchen stuff. And a booth for personalized cups. Some pet-friendly booths too, as well as boutique pet supplies. I think they'll agree to go fifty-fifty on proceeds," Marisol said. "But let's talk about what we have set up for kids."

Surprisingly, she had many contacts for kids and knew several she could definitely count on. She met a face painter through a friend of a friend and remembered they also owned an inflatable company. She knew she could get him to agree to donate a few inflatables for the kids to play on. Marisol showed them where they were on the map, double-checking with everyone that there would be enough space.

"And, finally, I'll arrange a few food trucks. They'll agree, but I know they'll ask for a sixty-forty split. So we'd get forty percent of the proceeds, which is still not bad," she said.

Paul nodded. "That's not bad at all. Especially since we aren't paying a damn thing. Honestly, Marisol, this is pretty amazing."

"I agree with Paul. You totally killed this." Antonio reached over to pat her leg. "You're amazing." He winked.

Marisol felt her cheeks flush, touched by his words.

"It all looks amazing," Izzy agreed. "But what do you guys think about having a fenced-off area in the middle with some of our dogs out for people to view? We can offer discounted adoption fees and potentially find homes for our dogs."

"What about our cats?" Stella asked. "I guess we could do another fenced-off area. Have one of us or another volunteer man it. This would give our animals visibility," she said, thinking out loud.

"Do you think we will have room to do that, Marisol?" Blaine asked.

All eyes turned to her. A few months ago, she wouldn't have loved the pressure of people relying on her, but now she saw it as trust and a gift. That was something she could appreciate.

"We do have some room in the middle for that. I think it's smart to show off the pets people could adopt. It's the perfect opportunity," Marisol agreed. She made an X on the picture where she thought it could go. "How do you all feel about putting it here? It's pretty much dead center."

"I think that's wonderful," Stella said, her voice heavy with...emotion? When Stella met Marisol's gaze, she could see the tears filling her eyes. "Nothing like this has ever been done here before. This is going to help out the shelter so much. I—we—can't thank you enough. This is amazing."

Marisol had done a lot of crying over the last few days, and apparently that was her new normal. Her own eyes grew misty, and before she knew it, she was crying alongside Stella.

"Come here." Stella got off the chair and came over to embrace Marisol tightly.

Another set of arms wrapped around them, and Marisol

looked up to see Izzy joining in on the hug, soon followed by Antonio. "This is so cute, I could throw up." He smiled.

"And now it's ruined," Izzy said, playfully shoving Antonio off.

Stella hugged Marisol for another few seconds before finally letting her go. She wiped her eyes as she headed back over to perch on her husband's lap. "I guess we should discuss who will be willing to help guide us on setup."

"I'm in," Blaine said immediately.

"I'll most likely be working a shift, but I think Paul can help," Antonio said. Paul nodded in agreement.

"I can also help. It would be nice to have more manpower though," Izzy said, pausing. Then, as if the thought just occurred to her, she turned to Marisol. "Do you think Cisco could help? And if anyone else knows any other muscles, that will be helpful."

"I can ask." Marisol didn't know his schedule but definitely would find out.

"My sister could also help," Antonio said. "She's usually free."

"Good. I think that's all we'll need. Marisol, you'll be there to lead the setup?" Stella asked.

"Of course. I planned on being there all day," she said.

"If this is a success, which I think it will be, we will definitely ask you to do it every year." Izzy giggled. "Is it weird that I'm so excited for this?"

"Not at all! I'm pumped. It's going to be so fun." Antonio beamed. "This will be so good for the shelter, and if this goes well, we can make it an even bigger ordeal next year."

"I say we celebrate," Paul pushed himself forward on the couch to reach for the wine, "and toast to this." He began to pour glasses of wine, handing them out to everyone.

"To us, but specifically Marisol, for putting this all together," Stella said, raising her glass.

"Oh, you don't have to—"

She was immediately cut off by everyone clinking glasses and toasting. "To Marisol!" they said in unison.

It was a beautiful and humbling experience to watch friendships blossom for her. The very first friendships she cultivated herself.

She never thought she'd experience these feelings. Pride. Friendship. Love. It all made her feel like every hard decision she made over the past few years was worth it.

That *she* was worth it.

Marisol

"Marisol, you seem winded. Is everything alright?" Alice paused, her face scrunching up as she moved closer to the camera, giving Marisol a close-up of her forehead. "Are you in your car? Is this a bad time?"

"It's...fine..." Marisol said between pants. She used the back of her hand to wipe the sweat off her brow. She could only imagine how wild her windswept hair looked and how out of character her forest-green jumpsuit with a stained white top underneath were. Her disheveled appearance and gasping breath did little to quell her therapist's curiosity.

"Are you safe, Marisol?" Alice's frown only deepened, looking down her glasses at her.

"Yes, sorry, I'm fine." She silently cursed herself for never picking up running. If she did, she wouldn't be struggling for her breath right now and looking like she was running away from a serial killer.

When she finally caught her breath, Marisol balanced her phone precariously on her steering wheel. "Sorry," she said at last. "I've been working at the animal shelter to prepare for tomorrow's fundraiser and completely lost track of time. I sprinted back to my car to make this meeting."

Alice's worry washed away, easing the fine lines that started forming on her forehead. "Oh, thank goodness. You had me worried. We could have rescheduled."

Marisol didn't like missing sessions with Alice. Her therapist always grounded her and made her feel secure in her decisions. And she needed that now. She had spent the last few weeks calling vendors, finalizing plans, and setting up for tomorrow. It was all becoming very real now. To say she was freaking out would be an understatement. If she hadn't booked this session, she'd be in full freakout mode.

"I really needed to talk to you. A lot has happened over the last few weeks, and I don't think I've taken it all in," Marisol admitted, biting her lip.

Alice had been on vacation these last few weeks, so she hadn't been able to speak with her therapist about everything. She remembered a year ago when she couldn't even admit to having anxiety about something in her life and repressed the feelings. Alice had worked on pulling those thoughts out of Marisol and getting her to verbalize them. Words had power, according to Alice.

"Then let's talk. Besides this fundraiser you are putting on, what else is going on in your life?" Alice had a way of sounding genuinely interested, even though Marisol paid her to care. She had an inkling, though, that even if Alice wasn't paid, she'd still care. That was just the type of person her therapist was.

So, Marisol purged. Purged all the events that had taken place since they last spoke. She told Alice about her father's party for his new brick and mortar store. About the fight that ensued between her, her mother, and Archie, and how Cisco stood up to her and paid the price. About him being arrested and how small she felt at that moment.

Reliving one of the hardest moments of her life left her feeling both raw and strangely lighter. She only shed a few tears —it wasn't therapy without crying to your therapist, after all.

Alice didn't stop her once while she spoke. The woman simply nodded and took everything in. By the time she was done, Alice smiled at her like a mother would when proud of their child for accomplishing a hard task.

"I wish we were in my office so I could hold your hand while I said this," Alice started, causing Marisol to tense, anxiously waiting for her next words. Alice moved closer to the camera again. It was as if she was staring directly at her and not at a screen. "Marisol, I'm proud of you and the work you have done and will continue to do to better yourself."

And just like that, the tears ran down freely. She felt like the last of her walls she erected around herself finally came crashing down. The final link to her mother crumbled, truly breaking the last chain tethering Marisol down. It felt...scary. Scary but also wonderful.

"The only thing I'm still waiting on is Archie's signature on our divorce papers. Then all ties to the person I was will be completely severed. It was supposed to be two weeks ago, but my father has his lawyer working on it now," Marisol said, wiping her tears away.

"Let's not discredit the old Marisol," Alice added. Marisol opened her mouth to object, but before she could, Alice continued, "That Marisol did everything she could to survive. She may not have always made the best decisions, but she made sure she survived in a space she didn't want to be in. That same woman also loved herself enough to seek out help, and I think that takes more strength than people give credit for."

"I..." She was speechless. No one had ever talked so kindly about the woman she had been. To be fair, there wasn't much to talk about. She wasn't kind. She lashed out at those around her—mostly her sister—because she was so unhappy with herself and her relationship with her mother.

But how desperately had she wanted someone—anyone—to be proud of her? Just to say it once and actually mean it. Hearing Alice say she was proud of the person she used to be healed something inside her she didn't know needed healing.

No words were adequate to convey all she was feeling, but she settled on, "Thank you. For everything you have always done for me."

Alice just smiled. "I just listen. You've done all the work."

Alice definitely wasn't giving herself enough credit, but she knew her therapist wouldn't hear it, so she didn't press the matter. She could be thankful for her and acknowledge Alice's big impact on her life privately.

"This fundraiser of yours, it's tomorrow?" Alice asked, surprising Marisol.

"Oh, yes. Just making some final decisions on layout and logistics," Marisol said. When she left, Cisco was helping out an employee her father sent to man his booth tomorrow. Antonio was also helping since he left his shift early, but his helping included drooling over Cisco. Not that Marisol could blame him.

"Have you invited your parents?" Alice asked gently.

It was an innocent enough question, but one that held a lot of weight. Once, she would have done anything to include her mother and try to impress her, but now that stress was no longer on her shoulders.

"I invited my father and my sister with instructions to make my mom stay away," she said. It wouldn't be hard for her father to leave her mother. She wasn't a pet person, so coming to a fundraiser at a shelter—even one in the parking lot—would not be something her mother would be interested in. That, and Marisol was not ready for her mother to be in her life or any events that were important to her. She hadn't seen her since the party and had no intentions of meeting up with her to smooth things over. Maybe one day that would change, but it wasn't going to be anytime soon. Maybe not ever.

"I'm glad you included those you want to celebrate your success with. What time is it at again?" Alice asked curiously.

"It runs from ten a.m. to three p.m. Though the ending is more flexible depending on crowd size," she said.

"Well, if it's not strange for you, I would like to stop by," Alice said, shocking Marisol.

"You do? We would love to have you."

"I've been thinking about adopting a dog. I finally got my husband to agree to it. I want to take him before he changes his mind," she said with a laugh.

"Of course, then you should definitely come by. There'll be tons of pets to look at," Marisol said, happy to have Alice check out something she put together. Perhaps she just wanted to show off something she was proud of.

Glancing at the time, Marisol knew they reached the end of their session. She felt lighter than she had earlier and felt her head was clearer than it had been in weeks. She could finally hear herself think.

"Then maybe I will run into you tomorrow. But if I don't, I hope you have all the success for this event." A timer on Alice's end went off, and she quickly silenced the alarm. "That's our time. Will I see you in my office next week or do you prefer another online session?"

"Office, please. I prefer that method."

Alice let out a sigh of relief. "Me too. I'm too old for this new technology."

After teaching Alice how to log off, Marisol ended the session. Just in time, too, because the next second, Cisco peeked into the car. When he saw she was no longer on the phone, he opened the door and slid inside. "Good session, Princesa?"

Marisol tucked a stray strand of hair and nodded. "It was. Alice might drop by tomorrow. She's hoping to adopt a dog. How is setup going?"

"Done," Cisco said, surprising her.

"Done? Like all of it?" she asked, not sure if she heard him correctly.

"Like all of it." He chuckled, reaching for her hand. "Everyone else is meeting at Tino's Pizza. You up to going?"

After her busy day and eating a granola bar for lunch, she would kill for some pizza. "Yes please," she groaned.

"Good, because I said we'd go. Get that sexy ass out of the driver's seat and let me drive us," he said, reaching to squeeze her thigh.

The touch made her body warm, and she nearly forgot she was hungry...nearly. But then her stomach growled, and she remembered she was exactly two minutes away from being hangry, so she climbed out of the car, making her way to the passenger seat.

She crossed paths with Cisco in the process, and he pulled her close, leaning down to capture her lips. It was a soft, brisk kiss, but promised more for later.

"Proud of you, Princesa," Cisco said as he pulled away. "And I love you."

"I love you too." She smiled, feeling the same butterflies she always felt when she said it.

"Let's go get that congratulatory pizza and celebrate with our friends," he said.

Our friends.

She had a boyfriend, a man she loved. And now she had friends. She didn't know if this would ever stop feeling surreal, but it wasn't something she would ever take for granted.

"Let's go," she said and got into the car.

CHAPTER 38

Cisco

Cisco enlisted Tiny's help to manage the waiting list at the pet fundraiser. It was an easy sell because Tiny loved animals so much, and Cisco promised her $100 with lunch thrown in. They arrived a half hour ago to set up the station. Cisco had texted Marisol that he was here, but he had yet to see his girl. She was probably busy making sure everything was ready for today, and he didn't want to bother her if that was the case.

"So, you're only offering these designs here?" Tiny held up a laminated paper with twenty-something designs on it.

Cisco nodded, wrestling with a portable chair he bought for this reason. "Yeah. Nothing else. Those don't take much ink and will probably take me ten minutes to finish. Charge forty dollars per design."

Tiny saluted him, laying the paper down on the folding table. Their booth size wasn't huge, but it was big enough for them to work comfortably. Together, they had put up a black canopy with a fabric wall around three sides. The top of the canopy read *Golden City Tattoos* in bold golden letters. He bought it a year ago when he was asked to attend a tattoo expo as a featured artist. He had nearly forgotten about it until Tiny hauled it out of the shop this morning.

Even though the fundraiser was not set to begin for another thirty minutes, already a few people trickled in, checking out the booths setting up. The slight breeze in the air carried the smell of Cajun spices and fried funnel cakes. If he hadn't picked up breakfast sandwiches this morning, he'd be lining up outside the Cajun food truck right now. He still might later.

"Do you think they have a coffee truck?" Tiny asked.

Cisco didn't quite remember everything he blocked off yesterday from Marisol's list, but he vaguely remembered a coffee truck. "I think so. You can check before it gets busy."

Tiny pushed herself up from her chair, stretching. "Do you want anything?"

"Nah, I'm good." He barely got the words out before Tiny left. Off to get her sugary caramel latte, or whatever overly sweet concoction she drank these days. It changed every few months.

Cisco checked his phone again. Marisol still hadn't replied, but she hearted the message. She'd find him later, once everything kicked off. She was with friends, so she had people to lean on if she needed the help.

Yesterday, he didn't get to fully appreciate the event, too busy getting everything set up. It was one thing to mark off spots and an entirely different thing seeing it with the vendors in place. It was quite the production, and it was only possible because of Marisol.

She was a damn good event planner. If she ever decided to do this full-time, Cisco could imagine her being fully booked.

After much struggling, Cisco finally got his damn chair unfolded and set up properly. He was just about to bring over his tray of equipment when he heard someone clear their throat behind him. "Good morning, son."

Cisco turned in time to see a well-dressed Travis Roberts approaching his booth. He wore what Cisco would consider golfing attire, which was probably exactly where he'd be going after this event. Marisol had mentioned her father coming and not just because he had a booth here too. He was pleasantly surprised to see him alone, so at least he was honoring his daughter's wishes.

The last time he saw Travis was when he picked him up from his holding cell. It wasn't exactly how he pictured his relationship with his girlfriend's father going, but here they were. He held no ill will toward the man, even if he had been a bystander in Marisol's suffering. It was evident he loved his daughter.

"Mr. Roberts—"

"Please," he said, holding up a hand. "Call me Travis. So, this is your booth, huh? I'm sure it will gain a lot of attention."

"That's the goal." Cisco eyed Travis, unsure what provoked this visit. The man stared down at the tattoo designs on the table, tracing a few with his finger.

Travis looked up, pursing his lips. He took a moment, as if gathering his words. Cisco didn't push him, letting his curiosity simmer. Finally, Travis seemed to find the words—or courage—for what he was about to say. "I heard about the deal falling through with the building next to mine."

Out of everything Cisco expected him to say, that wasn't it. He wasn't sure how Travis would hear that information, but, frankly, he didn't care enough to know. "Oh, yeah. Sucks, but I'll find somewhere else." It more than sucked, but he'd find another location. Hopefully one that was as heavily populated as that area.

"Do you still want it?" Travis asked.

Cisco stared at Travis as if he just sprouted another head. What was this man getting at? "If that were still an option, yes." Of course he'd want that property. The location was perfect, and he'd be bringing in new clientele. He didn't give a damn if the seller was an elitist piece of shit who cared only about their image. Cisco would have enjoyed proving him wrong about "guys like him."

Travis reached for something in his pocket, pulling out a small stack of folded papers. "Well, losing the property wasn't your fault. I can't in good conscience let something my family inadvertently caused be the reason you don't receive the property for your business."

"What are you saying, Travis?" He didn't like riddles, and his brain didn't have the energy this morning to figure out what he was saying.

Instead of answering, Travis handed over the folded papers. Cisco eyed them curiously before taking them. He unfolded the papers and scanned the contents. At first he had no idea what he was looking at, but then words like "seller," "deed," and "property" all stood out to him. His name was on the document, along with the address of the property he wanted.

"Is this...?"

"It's not official," Travis said quickly. "But I took the liberty of reaching out to my agent, who got in touch with yours and the seller, and, well..." He gestured to the papers Cisco was holding. "It's yours if you want it. Just need to call your agent to get the process in motion."

"Are you serious?" Cisco found himself asking. He didn't

know how to think about Travis orchestrating all of this without his knowledge, but at the same time, he could appreciate the gesture. This property was something he wanted. And badly.

"Yes." Travis nodded. "I can't apologize enough for how things ended at my event. How you've been the only one who has made my daughter this happy. Truthfully, I owe you a lot more than this, but I hope this is a start."

It wasn't often he was rendered speechless, but this was one of those rare times. He had many thoughts rushing through his mind but couldn't find the words to vocalize everything. So, he settled on something simple. "Thank you."

Travis just smiled. "I'll leave you to it. Good luck today. I might be back around, but I can't promise I'll be getting a tattoo." He laughed.

"Well, if you do decide, I promise I won't make it hurt that bad," he teased.

Travis laughed. A full belly laugh. "Good to know, son. Good to know." And then he was gone, leaving Cisco with the documents for his future shop.

"What are those?" Tiny appeared seemingly out of nowhere with the biggest iced coffee he had ever seen. She sipped on the black straw, gesturing to the papers.

"These, prima, are what will get me that shop down in San Francisco." He beamed, the excitement for his future finally settling in.

"Oh shit, congratulations." She grinned, holding up her hand for a high-five. "I call helping with decor. You need it."

"And what's wrong with my decor?"

"Nothing, if you're a teenager rebelling against your parents for making you do homework." She shrugged. "Don't think that is the vibe we are going for. Also, there's a shit ton of people already here. You ready to go?"

He was. As ready as he could be. Still no signs of Marisol, but he sent her another quick text telling her to stop by when she got a chance. As soon as he pocketed his phone and filed away the papers Travis dropped off, his first customer arrived, an eighteen-year-old kid who wanted one of the skull designs on Cisco's list. Tiny made him sign the waiver and took his money before sending him back to Cisco's chair. Thankfully, the chair was constructed correctly and didn't crash under the guy's weight.

So, Cisco started tattooing.

The eighteen-year-old was the first of many. Thank goodness for Tiny and her ability to manage a list because he would not have been as organized or timely as she was. By the end of the first hour, he had already completed six tattoos, but the list never seemed to shorten.

"Hey, Bossman, how do you feel about me scheduling appointments for the shop? I just got asked that question," Tiny called from behind him.

"That's fine. You have my schedule?" he asked, finishing up the final touches of the moon tattoo he was doing.

Tiny scoffed, and although he couldn't see it, she probably rolled her eyes at him. Right. Dumb question. She managed his schedule and probably had it saved in multiple places.

When he finished with his client, he scooted back on his chair and went to get water from the cooler they brought. It felt good to stretch his back and stand after hunching over another person. He definitely was getting old because, in his early twenties, he could tattoo for an entire day, hunched over someone, and not feel a damn thing.

When he turned back toward his chair, he was no longer

alone with Tiny. At the table stood three people, and Marisol stood in the center. Her sister, Lola, was on one side, with her brother-in-law on the other. Her expression confused him. She was smiling, but her eyes were red-rimmed. She had clearly been crying.

Before he could ask, Marisol pushed past her brother-in-law and around the table, going straight for Cisco. He managed to move his legs, meeting her halfway until she collapsed in his arms, clinging to his shirt. She was laughing? No...crying. No...both?

"Princesa?" He rubbed her back soothingly. "What happened? Is something wrong?" He looked past her at Lola and Javi. Lola only offered him a smile as she leaned against her husband.

Her sister didn't seem concerned, so maybe that was a good thing.

"You gotta tell me what's going on before I think it's something I did," Cisco said.

This time Marisol did laugh as she pulled back just enough to look up into his eyes. "I'm sorry I didn't come here sooner. I had a phone call. And then Antonio needed help setting up the pet area."

"A phone call?" he asked, raising a brow. "What happened?"

"Oh nothing," she said coyly, a giggle leaving her lips. She was practically bouncing in his arms. "Just that I'm finally a divorced woman. Archie signed the papers!"

Today was the day when the Roberts family rendered him speechless. But it only lasted for a few seconds before he said, "Fucking finally." He cupped her face and kissed her with heat. He didn't care that Tiny or Marisol's sister and brother-in-law were watching. All that mattered was Marisol and her freedom from Archie. *Their* freedom from that bastard.

Only because he didn't need Tiny quitting on him today, he forced himself to break the kiss. The radiant smile, one free of all inhibitions, made Marisol the most gorgeous woman he had ever laid eyes on.

"Divorce looks good on you, Princesa," he hummed, earning himself a giggle.

"It really does. You look so happy, Marisol. I don't think I've ever seen you like this before," Lola said.

"Well, I have a lot to be happy for." Marisol looked straight at Cisco when she spoke.

He fucking loved this woman. More than he ever loved anyone in his life. She was divorced now, but she wouldn't be a single woman for much longer. Not if he got his way.

"You're divorced and organized an amazing fundraiser. How does it feel?" Cisco asked, aware that his next client was probably waiting somewhere nearby.

"It is going well, isn't it?" For the first time, Cisco thought he saw pride for herself shine in her eyes. "Stella has cried twice with how well things are going. She's already getting excited for next year."

"Cisco, not to hurry this along, but you're going to want to take your next client soon. The list isn't getting any shorter," Tiny said and then awkwardly waved at Marisol. "Hi. Great fundraiser. Coffee is ten out of ten."

"Thanks." Marisol laughed. "I should get going. I want to make sure everything is running smoothly, but I had to see you. I needed you to know. Plus, I missed you."

"After this, you and I are going to celebrate. I'm thinking a weekend trip. I don't care where we go as long as it's just us," Cisco said.

"Deal," Marisol said, leaning up to give him one last kiss. "I love you. I'll stop by when it's over. You'll save the last tattoo for me, yeah?"

"Princesa, I will save every tattoo for you. You're my perfect canvas." And she was. If he was lucky, then she'd be his final masterpiece.

His greatest love.

Epilogue – 2 Years Later

The pink and red flower arrangement was the only decoration in the house. Despite having the door open all day and multiple people coming in and out, Marisol could still smell the new house scent. The fresh coat of paint and new wood still lingered heavily. She wanted to bottle up this smell and make it into a candle so she always remembered this moment.

Moving into her new house with the love of her life.

As she arranged the flowers, a wistful smile was plastered on her face as a sweaty and shirtless Cisco walked in. Had there ever been a sexier sight? There was something about a sweaty man doing labor that did it for her. She wanted to lick all over his body, tasting the fruits of his labor. Perhaps that was gross, but when you had a tattooed, muscular boyfriend like Cisco, it made sense.

Cisco placed the box marked "Fragile" onto the counter next to Snowball. Their house was officially filled to the brim with boxes. Who knew they had so much shit? Her closet alone almost required an entire truck to fit into. There was no way she was going to trust her designer clothes to the moving company, so she made her brother-in-law move them with his truck.

Cisco raised a brow, catching her stare. "See something you like, Princesa?" he asked, licking his lips. Those damn lips had her drooling over him. It was extremely distracting.

"I do. Even if you smell," she teased, forcing herself not to look at the deep V of his hips. She definitely didn't need to get distracted, not when there were movers, her family, and Tiny somewhere in the house. There would be time to "break in" the home later; she just had to be patient.

"Who sent the flowers?" Cisco raised his chin, indicating the flowers Marisol was arranging.

The flowers had been delivered shortly after they got the keys and arrived at their new house. She knew the moment she laid eyes on them who sent them. There was only one person who would buy her an expensive arrangement of flowers in a crystal vase.

"My mom," she said, keeping her voice neutral. She still had very limited interaction with her mother. Most contact was through phone calls and the occasional gift in the mail. The flowers were her mother's way of congratulating Marisol on her new house—or at least that was how Marisol took it.

Cisco nodded. He still wasn't the biggest fan of her mother, and Marisol didn't blame him. She also would never force them to have a relationship. Still, Cisco was supportive of what she wanted and how much she wanted to include her mother in their lives. Marisol came to terms long ago with never inviting her mother back into her life completely because she didn't believe there was any way to mend their relationship after everything that happened.

"They're nice. Think they have a surveillance camera in them?" he asked.

Marisol snorted in a very unladylike fashion. "I wouldn't put that past her. But they are gorgeous, so I'll risk it." She smiled, finishing up arranging them before walking over to Cisco.

"I'm sweaty," he warned.

"I'm aware," Marisol hummed. That didn't stop her from wrapping her arms around him and nuzzling into his neck. He did smell, but she was learning to love his man musk. His arms wrapped around her, hugging her tightly. No matter where they were, home would always be here in his arms.

"We're moving in together," she whispered into his neck.

They had mostly been living together for the past year, but Cisco still had his own home he would occasionally stay at. But it didn't seem right to pay for two houses when they typically only stayed at hers. Cisco was the one to bring up moving in together, and at first he suggested he move into Marisol's house. But she was also ready for a new start and wanted something that would be theirs.

Six months later, they found their dream house in San Francisco, close to Cisco's new shop, leaving his Berkeley shop in the capable hands of one of his cousins. They purchased a two-story house with extra bedrooms for family. Tiny already laid claim to one since she spent a lot of time at Cisco's place. She would be going to college in San Francisco and would need a place to stay. Marisol loved the opinionated and feisty teenager, so she loved the idea of having her in the house. Plus, Tiny had bonded with Fabian and Camilia, so now she'd be able to see them more.

"About time," he said, squeezing her. Cisco leaned down

and planted a kiss to the top of her head. "This is the perfect house for us."

It was. The house was modern, complete with a pool in the backyard. Her niece and nephew fell in love with it as soon as she told them about the pool. Marisol's favorite part of the house was the massive walk-in closet. Not only one, but two, so she didn't even have to share with Cisco. Surprisingly, he had a ton of his own clothes. She had never had a partner who enjoyed fashion as much as she did.

She didn't know if this home would be their forever home. Marisol was working on living in the moment, and in the moment, this house was perfect for them. Neither of them wanted kids. Snowball was the only child they wanted to raise. And Tiny...but she didn't really count. Tiny was self-sufficient and spent most of her time in her room. They enjoyed spending their time with friends like Stella and the gang, and didn't want to give that freedom up.

Marisol was content with remaining in Cisco's arms the rest of the evening while the movers were hard at work. That was until Tiny burst into the room, holding four pizza boxes. Fabian trailed behind her, holding the box of cheesy bread. Ever since the two of them met, Fabian became obsessed and followed her around whenever he could.

"Pizza is here! Break time," Tiny called, putting the boxes on the only available counter space. Fabian lifted onto his tiptoes to place the cheesy bread on the counter, proud of himself when he managed to get it up there.

"Thank god. I was about to sneak Marisol and me away to eat." Cisco grinned. He searched the bags for paper towels.

"Rude as hell you wouldn't feed us." Tiny narrowed her eyes, flipping open one of the boxes to expose a meat lovers' pizza. Marisol's stomach took that opportunity to growl. She hadn't eaten since last night, too consumed by the move.

"Did I hear the pizza is here?" Javi walked into the room with a very pregnant Lola waddling behind him. Javi was in a similar state as Cisco, only her brother-in-law wore a tank top. The boys were doing most of the heavy lifting while Marisol and Lola were slowly unpacking. Lola had the excuse of being pregnant to work slowly, and Marisol happily took that excuse to work at her own snail's pace.

"I need sausage pizza. Baby girl is starving today," Lola groaned, moving to one of the few high chairs they had set up on the island. Pregnant lady definitely got dibs, but Marisol secured the second-to-last chair. Tiny, not wanting to miss her opportunity, took a seat in the last one.

"Are you sure you should be here any longer after this? Aren't you supposed to be on bed rest?" Marisol asked. Cisco and Javi served the sisters, placing greasy slices of pizza down in front of them on napkins.

Lola didn't answer until she took the first bite of her pizza. She groaned. "This is the best pizza I've ever put in my mouth," she said, earning a crude comment from Javi. Lola ignored him and answered Marisol. "No, my doctor said I should rest. Not that I'm on bed rest. Little miss should be here in two weeks, and we still have a lot to do. Including moving you in."

"You know you don't have to help. I know you have a thousand things to do at home," Marisol assured.

Lola shook her head, taking another bite. "Not really. We had a lot of stuff leftover from Fabian, and Javi kept a lot of Camilia's baby stuff. So we are pretty much good to go. I need to get my nesting satisfied at your new house."

"Speaking of baby, do you have a name yet?" Tiny handed

Fabian a slice of cheese pizza, who, in return, handed her his crust from the last slice, reminding Marisol of her and Cisco. Two years later and he still had not convinced her to like crust yet.

"We didn't have a name for the longest time," Javi admitted.

"But then I came up with the name!" Camilia smiled from her seat next to her father. "I said they should call her Eliza. Isn't it beautiful? Daddy said it's a nice name, and Mamá Lola cried."

Marisol raised a brow at her sister, who just shrugged. "Listen, my hormones are all over the place. I cry at everything these days. Fabian never made me this emotional," she sighed.

"He did," Javi interjected. "She just doesn't remember it. She cried all the time."

"I personally think he's lying, but whatever." Lola glowered.

Not that Marisol would ever admit this in front of her hormonal pregnant sister, but Javi was right. Lola cried all the time while pregnant with Fabian. There were days when she did nothing but cry. She was actually way less emotional this pregnancy than the last. But Marisol didn't want to die, so she wisely kept her mouth shut.

"Knock, knock!" a new voice said from the hall. All heads swiveled to see Travis Roberts walk in, carrying a bottle of his favorite wine.

"Daddy?" Marisol asked, confused. "What are you doing here?" She realized her words probably sounded rude, so she quickly said, "The house is a mess. I was going to invite you over once we got it set up."

"And miss my daughter's first day in her house? Absolutely not. There are just some things fathers can't do." He wrapped his arms around both of his girls. "Besides, Cisco invited me over."

"He did?" She glanced at Cisco. They hadn't discussed inviting her father over to help. Hell, she didn't even realize the two of them spoke.

"I did." Cisco extended his arm toward her father and shook hands. "Thank you for coming, Travis."

"And miss this? Not for the world. Camilia showed me how to take pictures on my phone. Pretty slick, huh?" Travis grinned as if he just cracked a secret code for his phone rather than a simple function.

"You should probably let me take the photos, Grandpa," Camilia suggested. She reached out her hand for his phone.

"Probably for the best. You're much better at it than me. I always get my thumbs in the photos." He reached into his pocket and handed Camilia his phone. Of course, she already knew his passcode.

Their interaction only left Marisol more confused. "What are you taking pictures of?" It seemed like everyone was in on a secret she wasn't privy to. Judging by the knowing smiles on their faces, she didn't think she was far off. "Okay, someone needs to tell me what is going on."

"I'm working on it, Princesa," Cisco said, stepping around the island. He made his way toward her, spinning her chair around so they were face to face. It wasn't often that she wasn't in the know when it came to Cisco and her family, but she was drawing a complete blank.

"What's going on?" she asked, anxiety rising in her stomach.

"Take a video, Camilia. I think that will be better," her father whispered loudly to her niece.

"You know I love you, Marisol. You have changed my life

for the better and have become my best friend. No offense, Tiny," Cisco teased.

"I'll allow it. This once," she said.

"I love you too..." Marisol said slowly. "You're scaring me, babe."

"Don't be scared," Lola whispered. When Marisol turned to look at her sister, she noticed fresh tears in her eyes. Didn't do much to alleviate the nerves growing inside her.

"She's right. No need to be scared. I'm nervous enough for the both of us," Cisco said. For the first time, she noticed the shy smile and the way he searched her face for everything she was feeling.

"I went back and forth on how to do this. Lola helped me decide it would be best to do this just in front of your family, and I had to agree. I wanted you to be surrounded by people you love." Cisco reached in his back pocket, pulling out something. It took her a moment to realize it was a little black box.

Her heart stopped.

Then he lowered himself to one knee.

Oh shit, it's happening.

Thank god she just had her nails done. Not that getting her nails done was important at this moment, but it was the only thing her mind could focus on with Cisco down on one knee in front of her. In front of her whole damn family. She never had this before. With Archie, she didn't get a proposal. It felt more like a business arrangement at dinner one night.

Cisco opened the velvet box, exposing a 14K rose gold engagement ring with a twisted band that looked like vines. It was beautiful and fantastical, exactly what she would pick for herself. Hot tears pooled in her eyes, staring down at the symbolic ring, itching to get it on her finger.

"Yes," she said.

"Princesa, I haven't even asked." Cisco beamed.

"My answer is yes," she said, not caring.

Cisco just laughed, shaking his head. "Let me do this," he said, taking her hand in his. "Marisol, I want to spend the rest of my life with you—"

"And Snowball," Marisol cut in, tears flowing freely now.

"And Snowball," he agreed. "Will you do me the honor of spending the rest of your life with me? Princesa, will you marry me?"

"Yes!" she said for the third time, throwing her arms around his neck. She vaguely heard her family clapping, but in that moment, everything faded. It was just her and Cisco. Her boyfriend. Her best friend. And now her future husband.

The man she chose for herself.

Cisco took the beautiful ring out of the box and slid it on her finger. It was the perfect size, making her wonder if he reached out to Lola about her ring size. Before she could ask, Cisco's lips were on hers, giving her the most breathtaking kiss. She gasped, her body arching toward him. Even though her brain was slow to process, her body knew what to do. She kissed him back, putting all the words she could not verbalize in that moment into the kiss. It was perfect.

He was perfect.

All too soon, the kiss broke. She was surprised to see Cisco's eyes glossy with emotion. She couldn't remember a time she had ever seen him get emotional, but it touched her deeply knowing he felt strongly about this.

"I love you," she whispered for only him to hear.

"And I love you, Princesa," Cisco said.

If someone would have asked Marisol a few years ago how she would react to getting proposed to during a move, surrounded by family who were all eating greasy pizza off napkins, she would have scoffed in their face. It would seem like the most absurd thing to happen. But now? She couldn't think of a better moment for Cisco to pop the question. This was exactly what she wanted.

The moment the two of them broke apart was when their family jumped in, offering their congratulations to the both of them. She hugged her sister as they cried together. Not only did she get the man of her dreams, but she was finally able to form a relationship with her sister. One she had wanted for so long. She had a family that loved her. A man who wanted to be with her for the rest of their lives.

It wasn't an easy road to get here. At times, it felt impossible, but she had put in the work. And now she could enjoy it with the people she loved most.

This was the ending she had always wanted.

Want More?

How will Marisol and Cisco tie the knot? Sign up for my newsletter to find out!

To stay up to date with Anastasia, make sure to subscribe to her newsletter here.

About the Author

Anastasia Dean is a pen name for Tati B. Alvarez. She lives in Austin, Texas, where she spends most days lost in her own head, creating stories. When she is not writing, you can find her vacationing at Disney World.